COLE FOR CHRISTMAS

JANET RAYE STEVENS

Happy ho-ho-holidays!

Janet Raye Stevens

GREAT BROOK PUBLISHING

COLE FOR CHRISTMAS © 2021 Janet Raye Stevens

First Print Edition: ISBN 978-1-7373103-3-4

www.janetrayestevens.com

ACKNOWLEDGMENTS

Giving birth to a book—especially my first—is a joyous event that wouldn't have been possible without the help, encouragement, and support of so many people, including my family, my best pals Ross & Jodi, my critique group: Ruth, Lauren, Sharon, Donna, and the Carols, and my Golden Heart sisters: the Rebelles, Persisters, and Omegas. Also, Tracy Brody, Christina Britton, my agent Rebecca Strauss, cover design goddess Elizabeth Turner Stokes, my editor Reina at Rickrack Books, the marvelous Melissa – The Literary Assistant, the lovely Liz Beebe, the gorgeous Gabrielle Luthy, the inimitable Fenley Grant, and the all-time fabulous Conny Cappadona.

Special shout outs to Dana Cameron who pushed me onto this sometimes bumpy but always rewarding road to publication so long ago, to Marissa Doyle and Christine Gunderson who kept me going and kept me on track, and to Suzanne Tierney and Kari Lemor, who nudged me over the finish line – I am forever grateful to you all.

For Mom, my first reader, my biggest fan, and very, very much missed

CHAPTER ONE

*K*aty Costa had a plan. Well, she had a lot of plans, most of which had crashed and burned with ridiculous frequency over the past year. But *this* plan involved only her and was too simple to fall through. Tonight, she was going to indulge in a pity party of epic proportions.

The first step toward that goal was to hit the supermarket for the four basic food groups— cookies, ice cream, chocolate, and wine. A daunting endeavor at noontime on Christmas Eve. Cars jammed the parking lot and frantic last-minute shoppers thronged the aisles. Children shrieked as an employee dressed as Santa Claus circled the store, demanding to know if they'd been good this year. The metal wheels of Katy's shopping cart wobbled. They also squeaked, a high-pitched squeal like a choir of mice that nearly drowned out "Jingle Bell Rock" hissing from the overhead speaker.

Not exactly how she'd expected to spend Christmas Eve.

If everything had gone according to plan, Katy thought she'd be spending tonight in her cozy apartment overlooking Portland, Maine's Casco Bay, with her boyfriend Ash by her side. The two of them celebrating her success in landing a promotion she'd been hoping for all year. Followed by a toast to their two-year anniversary of meeting at the Chamber of Commerce's annual holiday party. Maybe even getting a certain question popped.

Then, everything had gone sideways. The promotion had fizzled, and the job had gone to someone else. So had Ash. He'd found someone new and had dumped Katy eight months ago. To add insult to injury, she'd received notice yesterday that her apartment building was going condo and she had to move out by spring.

Ho-ho-ho.

In the space of a few months, the life plan Katy had set out after she lost her parents during high school—work hard, go to a good college, get a decent job, find a great guy, and live happily ever after—had derailed spectacularly. At twenty-seven, she had no plan and no idea where she'd be in the coming year.

But she knew where she would be tonight. Curled up on her sofa, watching the slew of holiday movies she had cued up on her TV, brooding until Santa landed his sleigh on her building's roof, or she dropped off to sleep in a sugar and carbs coma.

Despite the chaos in the store, Katy managed to quickly score the necessary ingredients for her solo holiday party, in the form of a box of reindeer-shaped cinnamon cookies, a pint of Maine Black Bear ice cream, and a packed-to-go turkey and stuffing dinner.

All she needed was the wine.

A problem, she realized when she reached the appropriate aisle. The shelves were nearly empty. Shoppers eyed the few wine bottles remaining as if they were birds of prey scouting out their next meal. Katy joined the flock. Her cart's wheels squawked an off-key tune as she moved down the aisle, scanning the slim pickings.

A large bottle of white wine on an upper shelf caught her eye. The label read *Mistletoe* in fancy cursive letters, above a picture of the kissing plant's lush green leaves and fat white berries. Not ideal, since she wouldn't be kissing anyone tonight, with or without mistletoe to egg her on, but with the wine choices limited, it would have to do.

Katy angled her shopping cart and stepped closer to the shelves. She reached up and grabbed... Not the wine bottle, but a hand. A man's hand. Connected to the long arm of a guy who'd reached for the *Mistletoe* at the same time she had.

He wore black jeans, sturdy boots, and a blue winter jacket. Roughly her age, tall, but not too tall, slim but not skinny, he had a broad nose and even broader shoulders, a strong, clean-shaven jaw, tan skin touched with red from the cold outside, dark blue eyes, and hair the color of midnight that stuck out in all directions as if in a hurry to get someplace.

The complete boy next door package. Appealing. Adorable even, if she liked that type. Or any type of guy at the moment. After what had happened with Ash, she doubted she'd be interested in any man ever again.

"You sure you want to commit to this wine?" he said. He even had an appealing voice. A little gruff, a little amused, and as comforting as a warm blanket. "Could be a big mistake."

"Mistake?" Katy realized her fingers still touched his. Her cheeks flared red hot and she snatched her hand away.

"The Mistletoe doesn't work with what you've got in there." He glanced into her shopping cart then back to her, a playful glint in his eyes. "Oh sure, it's Christmassy and all, but everyone *knows* a red wine pairs best with cinnamon cookies."

He capped off this odd bit of news with a twitch of his lips, hinting at dimples. Because of course he'd have dimples. What boy next door would be fully armored without dimples?

His smile had the desired—and charming—effect. She laughed. "Oh, really? How do *you* know that?"

He leaned closer, wrapping her in his scent, as fresh and crisp as a winter day. "They call me the wine whisperer," he said, lowering his voice, as if spilling a dangerous secret.

Katy wasn't laughing now. She felt a little breathless. And so very aware of her messy appearance. She'd helped out at the dog shelter all morning and planned to shower when she got home. She loved playing with the dogs, one of the few times she truly relaxed, but she always ended up slobbered in dog drool and smelling like a kennel.

"Oh, the wine whisperer?" she said, self-consciously smoothing her hair and taking a step back. "How does one achieve such an impressive title?"

"I dunno. Drink a lot of wine?" He shrugged. His shoulders were broad and muscular, so a shrug was a major event. "No, actually, I cook with wine a lot. My advice? For cinnamon reindeer cookies, a rich, warm cabernet will hit the spot."

"You sound like you know what you're talking about. But here's the thing. I've *never* had red wine, cabernet or otherwise."

He looked offended. Or pretended to be. "You're missing out. Cabernet is a full-bodied wine, but smooth, almost sensual. One sip of a good cab can change your life."

"That's a *lot* of pressure to put on one little sip." Was he flirting with her? More important question, was she flirting with him? It had been so long since she'd gotten her flirt on, she couldn't tell. Whatever this back and forth could be called, it felt sort of…good.

"If you don't believe me, try some for yourself," he said. "Let's see…" He scanned the paltry selection of wines, taking his time. His forehead scrunched in theatrically serious concentration. He was so ridiculous. He acted as if this were the most important decision of the year when there were maybe two dozen bottles of wine left.

"Do you think you can move this along?" she teased, making a big show of checking her nonexistent wristwatch. "The store will be closing soon. Pretty sure Santa Claus is on his way."

As if her words had conjured him, the supermarket's Santa *ho-ho-hoed* down the aisle and sidled up to them. Katy saw a kid of about seventeen under the fake white beard. Jingle bells hung from his belt, his stick-skinny legs barely filled his baggy red pants, and he had easily a dozen pillows stuffed into his velvety coat.

"Happy holidays!" Santa bellowed in a voice just past puberty. "Have you been a good girl this year?" His gaze shifted from Katy to her companion. "Have you been a good boy? Or will you be getting coal for Christmas?"

"It's *always* coal for Christmas for me," the wine whisperer said, making Katy giggle.

"You? On the naughty list?" she said. "I can't believe it."

"Sadly, it's true. I'm the *worst*." He deployed another dimpled grin. "What about you? Naughty or nice?"

He watched her closely, as if all he wanted for Christmas was her answer. Katy's cheeks burned again, roasting like chestnuts on an open flame. A mischievous voice inside her urged her to blurt out an unequivocal *naughty* and see where things went from there.

"No comment," she said instead, getting hold of herself.

"Wise woman," he said, with a hint of disappointment in his voice. He bent down and pulled out a bottle of cabernet from deep within the bottom shelf then held it up. The label read *Grinning Reindeer*, over an illustration of a deer with a goofy, gap-toothed smile.

Teen Santa gave the cabernet a thumbs up. "Excellent choice, my good fellow. That's Mrs. Claus's favorite wine." He clapped both of them on the back with white-gloved hands. "Merry Christmas, you two!" Adding a broad wink and a hearty *ho-ho-ho,* he jingled away to spread cheer elsewhere.

Katy gulped. The kid thought they were a couple. Seriously? Just because they'd been flirting and grinning at each other and bantering over completely idiotic things didn't mean... *Eep.* That was *exactly* how a couple acted. No. *Hard no* on that. Katy had vowed never to be part of a couple again and not even an appealing boy next door with killer dimples could make her break that vow. The sooner she got her wine and got out of here, the better.

"Santa's recommendation is good enough for me," she said quickly and plucked the *Grinning Reindeer* from the wine whisperer's hand. She settled the bottle into her cart. "Thanks."

"You're welcome."

He did a dorky little bow that threatened Katy's resolve. Could he stop being so adorable for one second?

"And now that we've gotten *that* settled..." He snatched the *Mistletoe* from the shelf and tucked the bottle under his arm. "I'll just take this wine for myself."

"Hey!" Katy cried, her laugh landing somewhere between indignant and amused. This guy was too much. "Wine whisperer? More like wine *stealer*. You wanted the *Mistletoe* all along, and you've been buttering me up until you got it. No wonder you're getting coal for Christmas."

"Guilty as charged, but with an explanation—" His phone buzzed, cutting him off and leaving Katy dying to know what that explanation could be. Annoyance creased his forehead as he reached into his jacket pocket for his phone. He glanced at the screen and his irritation vanished. He broke into a broad smile.

"Excuse me," he said to Katy and lifted his phone to his ear, greeting his caller with a gooey and affectionate, "Hi, there."

Katy and her shopping cart slunk away. She steered toward the checkout and got into a long line. Only one thing could make a man smile like that. Or say hello like that.

Someone special on the other end of the call.

Her cheeks flamed for a third time, but for a different reason. She should have known. The guy had no ring on his finger, but that didn't rule out a significant other. And there she'd been, getting all giggly and flirty with him, totally oblivious to what should've been obvious. Just like with Ash. Shouldn't she have known Ash had found someone else? Shouldn't she have guessed he'd been cheating on her?

The checkout line inched forward. The cash register beeped as the cashier swiped what seemed to be a thousand last-minute gifts over the price scanner. Katy passed a display of holiday stockings for dogs, filled with chew toys and squeakies and other goodies. She snagged a half dozen to bring to the shelter the next time she went to volunteer. She tossed the packages into her cart, where they landed next to the cabernet.

Her gaze shifted from the wine to the self-checkout area near the store's other exit. She spotted the wine stealer in line, smiling into his phone. She frowned. What kind of man flirted with a stranger in the supermarket? On Christmas Eve? Especially when he had someone special a phone call away.

Or...*had* he been flirting? Perhaps she'd read too much into the encounter. Could she be that lonely, still that wounded by what had happened with Ash that she'd latch onto a stranger's friendliness like that?

Katy's phone jingled and she wrestled it out of her handbag. Caller ID showed a picture of her sister Maggie on her wedding day three years ago, swaddled in so many white flounces she looked like an escapee from a marshmallow factory.

"Maggie, what's wrong?" Katy said when she heard her sister's listless voice. "You sound awful."

"I *feel* awful."

"Oh no. Don't tell me—"

"Yeah. I've been attacked by gluten. Hold on."

A panicked shuffling, followed by the sound of retching. Katy winced. Her sister had been diagnosed with Celiac Disease several years ago, and she'd been extra careful with her diet since. But every so often gluten slipped into something she ate, making poor Maggie miserable, sometimes for days.

"Sorry," Maggie said, returning several seconds later. "Jackson came home from work yesterday with some Christmas cookies his coworker swore up and down were gluten free. They were not." A pause as she cleared her throat. "I'm *really* out of it."

Katy had reached the register. Using her free hand, she moved her items from her cart to the belt. She picked up the cabernet and eyed it, tempted to abandon it on a nearby shelf with a *Take that, wine stealer* sniff of rejection. But she couldn't, for some weird reason.

"I'm sorry to hear you're sick, Mags," she said, adding the wine bottle to the rest of her purchases. "Want me to come hold your hair?"

"That's Jackson's job. Why do you think I married him?" Maggie gave a wan laugh. "I need you for something more important. I'm too sick to work, and there's a wedding tonight at Newell's."

Newell's was Newell-by-the-Sea, the seaside function facility where Maggie had been event manager since the place had opened four years ago.

"A Christmas Eve wedding?" Katy said. "Romantic, but not very practical, weather-wise." She glanced toward the store's windows. Outside, snowflakes spit from the slate-gray sky, the appetizer before today's predicted storm's main course. "If you haven't noticed, it's snowing."

"I know, but what can I do? The bride's a Christmas fanatic. She wanted Newell's because it looks like a gingerbread house. She offered to pay double my fee *and* the rental fee to let her and her fiancé book the place for tonight. You know we're closed in the winter, but if a couple wants to risk bad weather to get married on Christmas Eve, who am I to argue?" She took a deep breath, as if mustering her strength. "Anyway, it's a small wedding, only eighty people, barely enough to fill the place. With my assistant in Aruba, I figured I could handle it alone. But those Christmas cookies had other ideas."

Murmuring her sympathy, Katy paid for her purchases, picked up her cloth bag, and moved toward the exit. She knew where her sister was going with this. "And you need me to fill in for you."

Maggie sighed. "I can't leave the bride and groom high and dry. Plus, I talked Chris and Rudy into opening the place just for this wedding. If it flops because no one's there to run the show, they won't be too happy with me."

Katy doubted that. The guys who owned Newell's adored Maggie. As they should. She'd helped to turn what had once been a run-down old mansion into what was fast becoming one of coastal Maine's top functions venues.

"One problem," Katy said. "A big problem. I have no idea what to do."

"Sure you do. You've got plenty of experience. You've been helping to organize events for years."

"Yeah, meetings and presentations, product rollouts, stuff like that. Corporate events are nothing like a wedding. I have no experience in that area."

"Uh, yes you have," Maggie said. "You were maid of honor at my wedding. You ran that event like a boss. The whole thing went off without a hitch."

Katy reached the door and stepped out into the cold, heading across the sprawling parking lot to her car. Snowflakes settled on her shoulders and the wind had picked up. "Wasn't that difficult. You had your wedding planned down to the minute."

"I've got this wedding planned too. All you need to do is show up. I'll pay you, of course. *And* I'll send you my ops sheet. It has a detailed schedule for the event. You follow that and let the caterer do the rest."

Katy brightened. Her sister had said the magic word. Schedule. *Detailed* schedule. Maggie had been an event manager in training since she was a kid, scheduling play-dates and *Play-Doh* activities like a seasoned pro. After their parents had died in a car crash, she'd turned her obsession with lists and planning into a way of life. So had Katy to a lesser extent. That was how they had coped. Life had yanked the rug out from under them too many times. They'd both learned to control what they could.

"Do you *promise* everything's planned?" Katy asked. "Nothing will go wrong?"

"How could it go wrong with you on the job? Everything will be perfect." She paused and Katy feared another celiac attack coming on before Maggie said, "Except... there are a couple things you need to know."

Uh-oh. Katy squeezed her phone and braced herself.

"First, there's Blaine Dillard," Maggie said with a heavy sigh. "Blaine's the caterer contracted for the wedding. He's never worked a function at Newell's. Chris and Rudy met him at a gallery opening he catered. They say his food's amazing and recommended him for this wedding hoping he'll love our kitchen and be eager to come back."

"I've seen the kitchen, that shouldn't be a problem. Why do you sound all gloom and doom?"

"Because Blaine's a giant pain to work with. We've never met. We dealt with all the details through the phone. Not *one* of those conversations ended without us squabbling. He's sarcastic and pushy and thinks he knows everything about *everything*."

"He sounds charming. Can't wait to butt heads with Mr. Crankypants."

"Oh, but you're much nicer than me, Katy. I bet you and Blaine will get along great. Just remember to do what you can to keep him happy. I'll let him know to expect you in my place. I'm sure he'll understand."

Maggie sounded a tad doubtful on that score. She also sounded sick and miserable, so Katy hurried to finish so her sister could go crawl into bed. "Got it. Now, what's the other thing I need to know?"

Maggie paused again. "Well, I had the dickens of a time

finding people to staff this event, so—" She cut off with another retching sound, then came back with a rushed, "Christmas cookies revenge. Gotta go. Will call when I can breathe again."

Maggie abruptly ended the call. Katy winced in deep sympathy for her poor sister. Her Christmas wouldn't be very merry this year, thanks to a well-intentioned coworker's carelessness.

Tucking her phone into her coat pocket, Katy moved toward her car, wondering what was that other thing Maggie had started to warn her about. Couldn't be as bad as having to deal with a temperamental chef all day.

She glanced down at her full shopping bag, at the reindeer cookies and the wine poking out of the top. *So much for my pity party tonight.* Once again, her plans had fallen through. But Maggie needed her and there was no question she would step in to help. With their parents gone, all they had was each other, except for great-aunt Florida, who lived in Florida, to Katy's never-ending amusement.

Sisters supported each other, were there for each other, no matter what.

Only for Maggie would Katy agree to spend Christmas Eve stressing over bouquets and bridesmaids, herding guests and groomsmen, and smoothing a cranky chef's ruffled feathers.

COLE ST. ONGE swiped the *Mistletoe* wine over the price scanner, listening to his grandmother run down a long list of Christmas gifts she'd chosen for his cousins and their four million kids. He'd paid for his purchase and had neared the exit by the time she brought up her party tonight.

"So, what time should I expect you?" she asked in her sweet voice, with a dash of a French-Canadian accent.

He flinched. He'd been dreading that question. Dreading disappointing his grandmother with the news he wouldn't be at her annual Christmas Eve bash. She looked forward to it all year. So did Cole, ever since he could remember. But tonight, he had to work and miss the fun. Miss seeing his parents, his sisters, and his cousins all gathered together. Miss playing Christmas Monopoly with his nieces and nephews and letting them win.

Most of all, he'd miss seeing his grandmother in her element. Tottering around the house she'd lived in for over sixty years, wearing her sparkly Christmas sweater and yoga pants, a red bow in her platinum blonde hair, holding a whiskey and soda she never took more than a sip of, and bossing everyone around. She enjoyed the bossing around part best. At eighty-two, she figured she'd earned the right.

About the only thing Cole wouldn't miss was the question everyone would hurl at him. Now that he'd turned thirty, wasn't it time he settled down? No one would utter the dreaded *M* word—*marriage*. They knew the word still stung, almost two years after Celia had abruptly cancelled their wedding. On the day of, with the guests crowded into the pews at St. Stephen's, minutes before the organist cranked up "Here Comes the Bride."

Cole's go-to reply to his relatives' well-meaning

nagging was he didn't have the time for a relationship. Too busy working, saving money, making plans to open his own restaurant someday. The truth was more complicated. He'd gone on a few dates since Celia had dumped him, but no woman had sparked his interest enough to consider risking his heart again. He wasn't ready to let someone new into his life.

But…

When he'd touched hands with a woman in the wine aisle, the feel of her warm, soft fingers against his had been electric. Twenty-six or twenty-seven and tall, with nice curves, she had honey-blonde hair that fell over her shoulders, framing a heart-shaped face, turned-up nose, lush lips, and fair skin with a fresh glow his grandmother would call *teint éclatant*. And lively brown eyes that sparkled with intelligence and humor.

He could've said excuse me, wrestled the wine away from her and left. But something kept him there. Maybe it was those eyes or simply that she'd laughed at his dorky jokes. Pity laughter, he figured, because…*wine whisperer*? Could he have dropped any line more idiotic? But she'd laughed and he had stayed, and he'd done something he hadn't done in years.

He flirted.

"Yeah, about your party," Cole said, gearing up. He'd delayed long enough. Time to get it over with. "I can't make it tonight. There's a wedding we're catering, and I've got to work."

His grandmother *tsk-tsked* like a cricket on the hearth. "But Cole, you'll miss my cookies, your favorite treat," she said.

"Don't remind me." Her shortbread cookies were *the* best, baked with skill and love and lots of pure Canadian maple syrup. She only made them at Christmas, and everyone in the family looked forward to them all year. Knowing his relatives, they would snap up every last cookie crumb tonight and he'd miss out completely.

But he had no choice. His boss, Blaine Dillard, had contracted to cater a Christmas Eve wedding and if Cole wanted to keep his job, he had to go to work.

"Look at the bright side," he said. "Lily will be there in my place." He'd dropped off his dog with his parents this morning, where she would be petted and pampered all day, and petted and pampered some more when Mom and Dad brought her to the party tonight.

"I suppose she's welcome, but she's a poor substitute for my favorite grandson," his grandmother teased.

Cole laughed. He was her only grandson. "I'll come see you first thing tomorrow, I promise. And save me a cookie. Love you. Merry Christmas, Mémé." He said grandma in the French way, as she liked, and ended the call. He shoved his phone into his jeans pocket and stepped outside.

Snow fell over a parking lot as crowded and chaotic as the store, with people and vehicles zooming in all directions. But Cole found the woman with the brown eyes right away. She wore jeans, a pink jacket that hugged her bottom, and ankle boots that looked more stylish than snowstorm durable. The wind ruffled her long hair as she hurried across the pavement, clutching her heavy shopping bag.

Cole slowed, watching her stop to talk to a woman

leading a stubby-legged dog on a leash. Someone had outfitted the poor mutt with a jingle bell collar and a pair of antlers so tall the dog nearly toppled over. Brown Eyes put down her bag on the snowy ground and squatted to pet the pup. She scratched behind its ears, making the dog's tail wiggle wildly.

Another point in her favor—she was a dog lover, like him.

The opposite of Cole's former fiancée, Celia. One of the first things he'd done after their breakup was to adopt Lily. Could've been an in-your-face to his runaway bride. Could've been because he was lonely. Whatever the reason, the minute Lily had nudged his hand with her head at the shelter, gazing up at him with loving eyes, he'd fallen. He'd taken her home that day.

Brown Eyes stood, sending the dog and its human on their way, and continued on to a red Toyota Camry with an *Adopt, Don't Shop* ASPCA sticker on the rear bumper. A voice deep inside Cole urged him to go after her. Why? He didn't know. Maybe to apologize for stealing the wine? Because he was attracted to her? Or because he thought he'd felt something special spark between them?

Cole ordered that voice to shut up. He wasn't in the market for someone new. Besides, Brown Eyes had done a one-eighty after he'd grabbed the wine. From friendly to frosty. He hadn't been too distracted by his phone call to notice that.

Then she'd fled.

He squared his shoulders and picked up his pace, glad his grandmother's call had interrupted them. Glad he'd turned off the woman's thousand-watt smile by stealing the wine. Wine he needed for today's wedding. The beef would be a flop without it.

And *that* was the main reason not to run after her. He had work to do. Let her think him a rude jerk and go on with her life.

His phone erupted with Twisted Sister's "We're Not Gonna Take It." Blaine Dillard's ringtone. The perfect song for how Cole felt about his boss, owner of *Dillard's Catering*, and how he mentally prepped himself for any conversation with the guy.

Blaine no doubt wanted to harass him about one or another of the hundred details for this wedding Cole had already taken care of. He didn't know how he'd done it, but he'd lasted longer than any other chef Blaine had ever hired. Way longer, nearly three years.

Blaine had a Montana-sized ego he fed by insulting Cole, bullying the rest of the staff, and hitting on any woman with a beating pulse. He would've bailed long ago if Blaine didn't pay him so well. He'd been socking away every penny for the restaurant he hoped to open someday. His ill-fated attempt at marriage had slammed the brakes on that dream. After paying off wedding expenses and buying out Celia's half of their house, he'd ended up nearly broke.

He'd started to build his savings again, so he was stuck working for Blaine and taking the man's grief for the foreseeable future.

Bracing for an earful of complaints, Cole dug his phone out of his pocket. "Yeah, Blaine, what's up?" he said, all business.

"I met a girl yesterday."

How was that breaking news? Blaine met a new woman nearly every week, each more gorgeous than the last. Each equally short term. "And?" Cole prodded.

"One thing led to another and... I'm in Bennington."

Cole's temper flared as hot and fast as a grease fire. Didn't they have an event to cater in a couple hours? "Bennington? As in, Vermont?"

"Yeah, Vermont," Blaine said, as if Cole was completely dense. "I thought I could get back in time, but it's snowing like a son of a bitch and all flights here are delayed. I need you to take over tonight. Think you can manage that?"

Cole's anger took a hike, replaced by excitement. Fly this wedding solo? Take charge of the event, without his boss around to belittle him and bully everyone else? Without Blaine to hog the credit for the recipes Cole had come up with? Without the guy hitting on brides-maids when he was supposed to be helping out in the kitchen?

Yes, please.

"No problem. I got this," Cole said, biting back his glee. "You focus on yourself and what you need to do." He couldn't resist that dig. Focusing on himself was what Blaine did best.

"Yeah, cool." Blaine sniffed. "One more thing, watch out for Newell's event manager, Maggie Costa. She's sure to give you a pain in the ass. I've never met her in person, and I don't want to meet her. Talking on the phone with her was enough. She's a real control freak."

"Pretty sure they're all like that." Cole had worked with a lot of wedding planners and banquet specialists over the years. They were uptight by nature, since they had to coordinate so many moving parts to keep the event running smoothly.

Blaine snorted. "Maggie's the *worst* I've ever encountered. She acts like nobody else but her knows what they're doing."

Pot, meet kettle. And probably untrue in Maggie's case. Blaine had a way of puffing himself up at everyone else's expense. Cole would wait until he met the wedding planner before believing anything his boss said about her.

"Point taken," Cole said, anxious to end the call. "I'll watch my step."

"Good. I'll let Maggie know you're in charge tonight—" Blaine cut off with a lewd chuckle as a woman on his end of the line called his name. "Look, I've got to go. *Don't* screw this up."

A click and the line went dead. Cole stared at his phone, not quite sure what had just happened but glad it was over.

The snow that had started as flurries an hour ago came down hard and heavy by the time he reached the company van at the far end of the parking lot. He'd better get a move on before the roads got slippery.

He'd gotten up early to drop off Lily at his parents' house, then headed to Dillard Catering's home base to prep the food and supplies and load the van. Now with the wine, he had everything packed and ready to go. A quick stop at his house to shower and grab his uniform— his chef's whites, as his coat was called, and his white hat, a *toque blanc* as his grandmother would call it—and he'd be on his way.

He climbed into the van, buckled in, and steered

toward the shopping plaza's exit. He grinned. He was on his own today, for the first time in three years. This day would be a challenge, but without Blaine breathing down his neck every second, this day could also be fun.

After Celia had left him at the altar with a knife in his gut and a wounded muskrat expression on his face, Cole had hated weddings with the fire of a thousand suns.

But *this* wedding he was looking forward to.

CHAPTER TWO

*K*aty clenched her jaw as she steered her Camry up the winding, snow-coated hill toward Newell-by-the-Sea. The wind howled like an angry wolf and whipped the snow sideways across the road. Her windshield wipers *thipped* rapidly, struggling to clear the wet, sticky stuff from the glass.

She aimed a curse at Lindsay Lathrop and Todd Gaines, the happy couple who'd decided to get married in the middle of a blizzard. If not for them, she would be home right now, snuggled under a blanket on her sofa, munching on cinnamon cookies. Sipping that *Grinning Reindeer* cabernet the wine stealer had insisted she buy, to see if it was as yummy as he'd claimed or just his standard pick-up line. Moping to her heart's content.

Instead, she crept along slick roads, braving a storm that had turned ugly. A stress knot the size of a melon squeezed the back of her neck. With Maggie incapacitated, her husband Jackson had dealt with sending all the details for today's event. Katy had the battle plan for the wedding on her phone and she'd printed it out too, but a million and one worries clawed at her brain. The weather, keeping to the schedule, and especially the crabby caterer. He couldn't have been happy when he'd heard Maggie was sick and sending her sister in her place. An amateur with no experience managing weddings.

How could she possibly pull this off? She was nowhere near as good at this job as Maggie.

Not very good at her own job either, if losing that promotion said anything about it. If only she'd spoken up more, made a stronger case for herself and all she had accomplished in her four years with the company. No, she had to stop kicking herself. The position had been Casey's as soon as it had been posted. He was a stinker who knocked off early on Fridays and ate other people's yogurts out of the fridge, but he was also the CFO's son-in-law, so she never had a chance.

Probably for the best. Her job had become stifling and tedious, all spreadsheets and paper-pushing rather than meeting people and running events, which she loved. A step up the corporate ladder had only promised more of the same dull routine.

Katy peered out the windshield at the swirling snow. Perhaps the time had come to look for a new job. Definitely time to find a new place to live, since she'd just gotten notice she needed to be out of her apartment by April. Should she also…? Mr. Flirt's dimples and tousled hair flashed into her mind. So did his expression when he'd taken that call. Well, she wasn't quite sure it was time for her to move on in the romance department.

A Portland DPW truck roared by, peppering Katy's car

with salt and sand. Her Camry shimmied and shook. She squeezed the steering wheel and held on tight. *Stop stressing about your life, concentrate on the road.* She'd worry about her worries later. They'd be there, scratching at the back of her mind like a persistent cat demanding to be let in.

Finally, the pines thinned out and through the falling snow Katy saw Newell-by-the-Sea at the crest of the hill, overlooking the Atlantic Ocean.

The bride had picked the perfect venue for a Christmas wedding, an oversized gingerbread house with tall, multi-paned windows framed by black shutters, a peaked roof, scalloped eaves, and gables at the corners. The function hall addition stuck out from the south side, a long one-story structure with a chimney at the far end. The hall must've been a ballroom at one time, where the nineteenth century gentleman farmer or ship's captain who'd owned the estate had entertained.

The building's exterior was dressed up for Christmas. Snow-covered yew bushes that looked like big gumdrops dotted the front lawn, leafy green wreaths with crisp red bows hung between the windows, colorful Christmas lights twinkled along the eaves, and the roof glimmered with new-fallen snow.

Katy's spirits lifted and the knot in the back of her neck loosened a little. Now that she'd made it here in one piece, maybe the rest of the day would turn out fine.

The snowplow hadn't arrived yet and a blanket of snow covered the parking lot, making the entrance hard to find. She squinted, trying to locate it. She'd only been here for Maggie and Jackson's wedding three summers ago, when everything had been green and lush. And, as maid of honor, Katy had ridden in the limo, so she had no idea where to turn in.

A flash broke her concentration. She snapped her gaze left and saw... *A sleigh!* An honest to goodness, old-fashioned sleigh pulled by a horse as white as the snow. The bells on the horse's harness jingled merrily as the sleigh slid past and disappeared into the swirling storm.

Busy gaping at that amazing sight, she didn't notice the vehicle turning into the parking lot in front of her until too late. She yelped, jerked the steering wheel and jammed both feet on the brakes. Exactly what you're not supposed to do. Momentum and slippery roads did the rest and her car skidded straight into a boxy silver van. Her Camry kissed the vehicle with a crunch.

Katy jerked forward, then back against the seat. Her car stopped rocking and she sat a moment in shock before gingerly backing up, thankful she hadn't been moving fast enough to make the airbag deploy. Hopefully, that meant not too much damage. She shifted into *park*, left the car running, and scrambled out to inspect both vehicles and find out for sure.

Her boots sank into the wet snow as she stepped toward the van. Her body shook from delayed fear. She hugged herself, but that didn't still her trembling, or protect her from the cold. Neither did the short wool coat she'd left unbuttoned and her event manager attire underneath, white blouse, navy blue jacket and matching pencil skirt that left her lower legs exposed.

The van door opened and the driver got out, unfolding

to his full height, six feet plus. Katy gasped—the boy next door from the supermarket.

He crunched through the snow toward her, bundled up in gloves, and the winter jacket and black jeans he'd worn earlier that fit his toned legs with a sinful snugness. He wore no hat, as if daring the snow to fall on him. The snow obliged, piling onto his thick black hair.

"Well, well, if it isn't the ghost of Christmas past," she said, a little stunned and a lot flustered. From the accident, she told herself, not from seeing him. Why would she be happy to see him again? He was a flirt, a wine stealer, *and* a terrible driver. The accident had been his fault, after all. "What are you doing here?"

He had the audacity to grin, displaying those dimples to disarming effect. "I could ask you the same thing. What brings you up here in such crappy weather?"

"I'm working at a wedding here today." She tipped her head toward the building.

He put the dimples away and unpacked a scowl. An expression so fierce it nearly singed her eyebrows. "*You're* the wedding planner?"

He might as well have asked if she were the Grim Reaper, he sounded so alarmed. "I prefer the title event manager, actually—"

She cut off. Her gaze flew to the van and she saw why he'd scalded her with that look, and why he was here. Painted directly over the dent on the van's side panel were three words that drained the blood from her face.

Blaine Dillard Catering.

Oh no! Of all people to run into, literally, the volatile

chef she'd been warned to butter up at all costs. The wine stealing boy next door was Blaine Dillard.

Katy winced. Her sofa and that pity party were looking more attractive by the second.

~

COLE FROWNED, wishing he was on his way to his grandmother's right now, even though her party didn't start until seven tonight. He'd take the teasing and endless questions about his future from his relatives. Hell, he'd even take Blaine criticizing his every move over the wedding planner looking at him like that. In a flash, Maggie's expression had gone from happy to see him again to completely disappointed.

He suspected why. Maggie had talked to Blaine easily a dozen times while planning this wedding. He'd probably filled her ears with bragging tales of his own greatness with every phone call, followed by put-downs and insults directed at his underling Cole. Now Blaine had called her to say he'd be a no-show, leaving the success of the event in the shaky hands of that minion. As soon as Maggie realized who Cole was, her fears had kicked in.

And that pissed him off. He turned his irritation on her. "What a coincidence. *I'm* working this event today too," he said, like it was the last thing he wanted to do.

She gave him a wary nod and stepped closer to the van, inspecting the damage. He caught her scent. Sweet, a touch of perfume and cinnamon cookies. Worry lines crinkled her forehead.

"This isn't going to be a problem, is it?" she asked, her voice a blend of sweet and salty.

Cole frowned. Another nail in his incompetent coffin. He'd caused the collision by cutting her off. He'd been so surprised to see that sleigh—a freaking sleigh, with jingle bells and passengers singing a wassailing song and everything—he hadn't paid enough attention when he turned the van into the parking lot.

"It's just a ding," he said. A lie. It was more than a ding. A crease that would require body work and new paint. Blaine would chew him out over the damage anyway. And make him pay for the repairs. "Nothing to bother my insurance company," he added. *If* they'd accept Santa Claus joyriding in his sleigh as an excuse for an accident.

They stared at each other a minute, or maybe a week. Cole had no idea. He was still stunned to see her here. The woman who'd made him laugh at the supermarket, whose touch had been electric, whose teasing smile and soft brown eyes had coaxed him into flirting after vowing never again.

She shivered. She wasn't dressed for this cold weather. She wore a short skirt that displayed the nicest pair of legs Cole had seen in a long time, and all he wanted to do was cover them up. A biting wind rolled up from the Atlantic, whipping snowflakes around them in frozen tornadoes. The air smelled of wet and the nearby pine trees. A ferry horn bleated in the distance on Casco Bay, adding a mournful chill to the scene.

"We should get inside, out of the deep freeze," he muttered. "Your lips are turning blue." Not that he'd been looking at her lips. Not at all.

She cleared her throat, a stuffy, disapproving sound. "You're right. We'll exchange insurance information later, after the wedding." She glanced up at the gray sky. Snowflakes fell on her cheeks and eyelashes. "If there *is* a wedding. *If* anyone shows up."

That hit close to home. "As long as the *bride* shows up, we're good."

Her eyebrows shot up. "And the groom. He's an essential part of the equation."

"So he is, poor fool." Cole kicked at the snow that had clumped in the wheel well of the van's front tire. Cripes, bitter much?

Maggie studied him a few seconds, her thoughts unreadable. "Well, there's work to do before *anyone* gets married today," she said. "See you inside."

She spun on her boot heel and mushed through the snow to her car. The door closed with a soft thud. She tossed him one last searing look from behind the wheel then swung the vehicle around the van and into the parking lot.

He watched her go, his nerves jumping. For once in his life Blaine's judgment had been spot-on. The wedding planner seemed as prickly as advertised. What had Cole just been thinking about this wedding being fun? He suspected working with Maggie today would be anything but that.

He shook off the snowflakes that had piled on his head and jacket and got back in the van. He'd process his Maggie concerns later. Now he needed to check out his digs for the day and unload. He put the vehicle in gear and rolled toward the kitchen entrance.

Newell-by-the-Sea looked like something out of a fairytale. The only thing missing was a witch hanging out at the front door, offering candy to lure Hansel and Gretel inside. The place was old, but he'd heard the kitchen had been fully renovated to add space and also updated with state-of-the-art appliances. The only reason Blaine had agreed to take this job, Cole knew. The guy didn't like old equipment or cramped spaces. Cole didn't care about any of that. He'd cook on a camp stove in the middle of a desert, as long as he had a flame.

The van slid to a stop. He opened the side door and skimmed the carefully packed trays and boxes, glad to see nothing knocked out of place by the collision with Maggie's car. He hoped to have everything inside before his assistants and the waitstaff they hired through a third party arrived.

Not a ton to unload, anyway, since they were only feeding eighty people. A relatively small wedding, about the size he'd wanted, just family and close friends. Not the big shebang Celia had roped him into. He'd lost track of how many people they'd sent invitations to. Three, four hundred? Seemed like Celia had invited everyone she'd ever met.

He hadn't balked. That was the wedding she'd wanted. How could he deny her that? Even when she told him they'd gone so over budget her parents were tapped out and they had to sink their savings into the event, money he'd been putting aside for his restaurant, he hadn't complained.

Because he'd wanted her to be happy.

Funny thing, he still did. Even after she'd left him at

the altar, broke, broken, and bitter. He'd only seen Celia once since their spectacular breakup scene on the steps of St. Stephen's Church, and he had no idea where she'd gone from there. He didn't care to know. But he hoped she was happy. He truly did.

He propped open the kitchen door and returned to the van, slicing his gaze toward Maggie. She climbed the snow-covered front steps to the main entrance, where the old house and function facility joined, carrying a cloth bag bulging with supplies. She stopped on a wide landing under a portico with stout pillars at each end. A couple in their late sixties came out of the building to greet her. Both looked as if they were on their way to Christmas Town. The man wore green overalls, the woman, a red dress and red sweater.

As if she felt Cole's eyes on her, Maggie looked his way. Their gazes connected through the falling snow and his pulse kicked up. He wondered what she was thinking. Nothing good, the way she frowned at him.

He narrowed his eyes. And that bothered him, why? He wasn't here to meet women. That was Blaine's thing. Cole had come here to do a job. He needed to focus on his work. Focus on showing Blaine he could manage without him.

And show Maggie that too.

CHAPTER THREE

*N*ewell's caretakers, the husband-and-wife team of Hollis and Ivy Parker, adorable in their North Pole-chic red and green outfits, met Katy at the main entrance. They escorted her into a broad foyer, decorated with sparkling lights and mistletoe. Mr. Parker took her coat and hung it up, while Mrs. Parker murmured concern and sympathy over Maggie's illness and inability to be here today.

Katy hardly noticed. Barely heard a word they said. Only one thing, one thought filled her mind—*him*.

Blaine Dillard, whose gruff comments and alarming dimples at the supermarket had made her feel... Well, exactly as she'd felt gazing at him outside in the snow. Unsettled, unmoored, and with an unexpected flock of butterflies dancing in her belly.

No chance he felt the same way. Not even close. His growl when he'd discovered who she was and that unhappy look he'd leveled at her a moment ago said it all.

True to his temperamental self, Blaine had gotten into a snit when he found out Katy had to step in for her sister today. She cringed to think he feared the entire event would bomb with her at the helm.

"Snow's coming down at quite a clip," Mr. Parker said, busting in on her thoughts. He had an old-school Maine accent. The rest of him was old-school too, spare frame, bristled chin, and weather-beaten features, like a lighthouse keeper who'd been buffeted by ocean winds way too long. "The storm will probably mean lotsa no-shows today."

Mrs. Parker's lips pursed like she'd just bit into an extra-sour lemon. "Oh, Holly, don't be such a Gloomy Gus." As bristled as her husband, except for the curly mop of white hair that framed her face, she wore round-as-buttons glasses perched on the tip of her nose. "The forecast said only three to six inches. It'll clear up soon."

"Don't you be a Mary Sunshine, Ivy," Mr. Parker scoffed. "Those weathermen always say three to six inches, even when we get a nor'easter." He tapped his left leg. "I'm telling you, ever since my surgery, my knee aches whenever the weather turns. This storm's gonna be a whopper."

"You don't say?" His wife laughed and the trio of silver bells on the vintage-looking brooch pinned to her sweater jingled merrily. "I suppose your knee knows better than all that fancy weather equipment on TV?"

While the couple debated, Katy peeled off her wet boots, replacing them with her low-heeled, navy-blue pumps she pulled out of her tote bag. Now her efficient and competent event manager look was complete. Sober, professional. If she looked the part, she could *be* the part. Hopefully Blaine would agree.

The meteorology versus aching knees debate wound down with no winner declared, and Mrs. Parker turned to Katy. "Come and see what a nice job your sister did decorating the main room," she said.

Katy slipped her phone into her skirt's pocket and gathered up her clipboard, thick with papers detailing Maggie's battle plan for the day. She followed the Parkers across the foyer and under a high archway into the function hall, a long, spacious room with wood-paneled walls, a fan-shaped grand staircase to the upper level at one end, a stone fireplace at the other end, and plenty of room for tables and chairs in between.

A quaint New England setting, transformed into a shimmering Christmas wonderland. Glistening icicle lights snaked over the walls and windows. Garlands of green holly with bright red berries draped from the saloon-style bar, wound around the stairs' wooden banisters, and framed the wide doorway to the kitchen. Tall, potted poinsettias were placed around the room. A row of hand-stitched stockings hung over the blazing gas-powered fire and the mantelpiece held dozens of Santa Claus figurines of different shapes and sizes.

And mistletoe, the cherry on the festive sundae. From tiny sprigs tied with teeny red ribbons to the biggest ball of mistletoe Katy had ever seen, the kissing leaf hung everywhere. No one attending this wedding today would be able to move a muscle without getting kissed.

"This looks...amazing," Katy said, breathing in the Christmassy scents of pine and peppermint. Maggie had decorated the place with the vengeance of an elf determined to win a place on Santa's nice list forever.

Mrs. Parker grinned. "Your sister worked weeks and weeks to fix this place up. She's got an artist's touch, don't she?"

Katy nodded, not surprised at Maggie's diligence. Her sister always put in two hundred percent. And though everything was beautiful, and in order, *and* ready to go, the stress knot on the back of her neck tightened. It was up to *her* to see this wedding and reception through.

"There's more," Mrs. Parker said. "Come to the alcove to see the tree."

The bells on her pin rang like faraway church bells as she led the way, with her husband close behind. He moved with a pronounced limp, from the recent surgery he'd mentioned, Katy thought, and hopefully not a sign his prediction of a bad storm would come true.

She followed them both, taking in all the decorative details Maggie had added to the already sparkling holiday decor—snowflake-patterned white linens covered the tables, with Victorian-style caroling figurines and small, decorated Christmas trees as centerpieces, and place cards in the shape of Santa's hat, with each guest's name written in Maggie's elegant calligraphic hand.

The temperature dropped steadily the closer they got to what Mrs. Parker had called the alcove. The recessed area along the east wall had floor-to-ceiling windows and provided an expansive view of the grounds and the ocean beyond. In warmer months, the hinged windows folded open, allowing guests to move back and forth from the dining room to the manicured lawn and barbecue pit. Though the windows were shut tight today, winter's chill managed to slip between the cracks.

"What do you think of this beauty?" Mrs. Parker gestured to the Christmas tree set up in the center of the alcove. "Your sister decorated this herself, too."

Ten feet tall and almost as wide, the Nova Scotia balsam fir filled the area, its scent so fresh Katy could practically taste the sap. An angel in a flowing robe perched on the treetop, a red velvet tree skirt circled the base, and in between, shimmering tinsel, colorful bulb lights, and branches bent under the weight of dozens of clear ball ornaments with pictures of the bride and groom.

"Stunning," Katy said.

Mr. Parker chuckled. "You think that's something? Wait 'til you see the cake. Bakery dropped it off this morning. Took ten sturdy men to move it."

"Now, Holly," his wife chided, her pale blue eyes twinkling. "It's the cake the bride wanted. You shouldn't poke fun. Isn't that what I always say?"

"Is that what you always say, Ivy? I thought you always say to keep my feet off the furniture when I'm wearing my hobnail boots."

She let out a surprisingly girlish giggle and looked at Katy. "We put in a call to Roscoe, our plowman, as soon as the first snowflake fell. The parking lot and all else should be clear by the time the guests get here."

She then announced they'd be in the office if Katy needed them, took her husband's hand, and they left. Katy watched them toddle off, thinking they would win America's Most Adorable Couple contest in a landslide if such a competition existed.

She turned back to the tree and examined the picture ornaments dangling from the branches. Baby photos, the bride and groom as kids, hanging out with friends, graduation pictures, and the largest ornament, the couple's engagement photo. The bride, Lindsay Lathrop, looked like she'd been born with skis attached to her feet. A slim, fit, and tall woman with sun-kissed golden skin, she had silky blonde hair and sharp cheekbones. Her smiling fiancé, Todd Gaines, was equally tan, tall, and fit, also blonde, and with even sharper cheekbones. Their children would be born supermodels.

Katy checked her clipboard for the bios Maggie had pulled together. Lindsay worked as an accountant, Todd as an attorney. Neither had siblings. Todd's parents were together, but Lindsay's mom had passed away when her daughter was twelve. Katy found an ornament with a picture of young Lindsay and her mother at the beach. Grown-up Lindsay looked a lot like the willowy woman with the soft smile in the photo, hugging her daughter as if she would blow away.

Katy's throat tightened at the thought of Lindsay walking down the aisle without her mother to see her. Having lost her own mother, she knew the grief and longing the bride must feel today. And would feel for a long time to come.

A shriek of wind rattled the windows. Tucking her emotions away, Katy moved across the alcove to look out at the storm, which had intensified. Sleet ticked against the windowpanes. Snow squalls whipped across the broad lawn, tearing at the tarps covering outdoor tables and the barbecue pit. The branches of the pine trees that bordered the lawn sagged, weighed down with heavy, wet snow. A snowy haze obscured the view of the ocean at the bottom of the long, rolling hill.

"Volatile, but beautiful," a voice said, making her jump. Blaine strode up beside her, adding, "The storm, I mean."

Katy hugged the clipboard to her chest and shivered. From the chill air, she told herself. Not from him, standing so close. Close enough to feel his body's warmth. He'd taken off his jacket and changed from his jeans into his chef's uniform, dressy black pants and white coat. The clean scent of cotton mingled with his own unique scent. The coat's crisp white fabric offered a tantalizing contrast to his black hair.

"It *is* lovely," she managed to squeak. "But I think I prefer to be inside, out of the storm."

"Not much warmer in here." His breath steamed up the windowpane, punctuating his words and leaving a spiderweb pattern of ice on the glass. "But this is a heck of a facility." He turned and his gaze skimmed the room. He gestured to the Christmas tree. "That came out great. Everything did." He sliced her a glance. "Decorating this place must've been a lot of work."

"It *was* a lot of work." Maggie would be happy to hear how much Newell's had impressed him, but he'd left out one important compliment. "And the kitchen? Is that okay? You have what you need? Is there anything I can do?" she asked, nervous.

"No, everything's fine," he said quickly, and with so little enthusiasm Katy wondered if *anything* was fine. "I've got it under control." He hesitated. "Except... My support staff is running late. So are the servers we contracted for today. The snow's slowing everyone down."

A problem, certainly, but he sounded like the delays bothered him. Like she should be bothered too. "Well, couldn't be helped," she said coolly, completely unfazed.

"I guess not." He let out a gusty sigh. "If Mother Nature decides to gift us with a snowstorm for Christmas, what can a mere chef and a wedding planner do about it?"

"Event manager."

"Excuse me?"

"I prefer the term event manager." She knew that sounded patronizing, but she needed him to know she took this job seriously, despite stepping in at the last minute.

"Oh, right. I beg your pardon," he said with a rueful look. And a flash of dimples.

Their gazes caught. His eyes sparkled with light reflected from the Christmas tree, his expression open and pleasant. Could Maggie have been wrong about him? He seemed nice, like the Blaine she'd met at the supermarket. Not just good-looking nice, but *inside* nice. He had kind eyes. She shifted her gaze to his mouth. Nice lips, too. Well-formed, welcoming.

Kissable.

Warmth flooded her cheeks and just about every other

part of her body. All because of one simple word that had popped into her mind without invitation.

Blaine suddenly broke off his gaze and looked up. Katy did too and she swallowed a gasp. Just the thing she did *not* want to see, especially with the direction of her thoughts.

Mistletoe!

"MISTLETOE," Cole grumbled. His gaze flew to Maggie's face, and he scowled. He didn't want to kiss her. Didn't even want to *think* about kissing her. Yet he had. Every impulse, every nerve ending had urged him to take her into his arms and kiss her.

He placed the blame squarely on the mistletoe. It hovered over them like an annoying bug he couldn't swat away. Taunting him. Egging him on. That one bunch wasn't alone in its evil influence. Maggie had hung the stuff from every rafter, chandelier, and doorframe in the place. Small clumps, medium clumps, even a giant ball that looked heavy enough to crush a man. Cole couldn't escape it. How could he not fall under its spell?

The mistletoe had the opposite effect on Maggie. She eyed him, all twitchy, as if she found the idea of kissing him as appealing as eating rotten eggs.

"What is it you want?" she said, her voice frosting over. "As you can see, I have no wine for you to steal."

Still pissed about that, was she? "I didn't steal the wine, I simply—"

"Heisted it?" she said. "Pilfered it? Thieved it, perhaps?"

"All right, I confess, I stole the wine. But I have an explanation. I need it to cook the beef. You of all people wouldn't want the main course to be dried out and stringy."

She frowned. Cole ran a hand through his hair. He'd meant to appeal to her event manager's perfectionism. Instead, he'd offended her. Somehow.

"Fine," she said after pausing a few beats, hastily adding, "So, what do you need? You came over to ask me for something, right?"

"I need a key to the pantry. For some odd reason, it's locked," he said. A complete lie. He didn't need to get into the pantry. He always brought everything he needed to a job and today was no exception. But when he'd seen her standing at the windows, his feet had pulled him here before his brain could catch up. When she'd turned to him, so temptingly close, gazing at him with those soulful eyes, looking so beautiful and a little bit vulnerable, the key and everything else had fled from his mind.

Her frown deepened. "The Parkers, the caretakers, must have the key. They're in the office. I'll go get it."

Maggie fled. Cole watched her hurry across the room, her shoes clacking on the hardwood floor. He absolutely should get back to the kitchen where he belonged and far away from her. Far away from the mistletoe danger zone and the heated thoughts pushing him in all kinds of directions he didn't want to go.

Instead, he followed her.

Once he started something, he had to finish it. That see-it-through brand of determination was baked into his DNA. Whether creating a new recipe, taking on a job, or getting all the way to the altar when deep down he'd known something was wrong, he gave it one hundred and fifty percent, despite the outcome.

He'd started this ridiculous key charade and he had to see it through.

CHAPTER FOUR

*K*aty headed across the room toward the front entrance, so very aware of Blaine striding behind her, practically stepping on her heels.

She clutched her clipboard to her chest, wishing he'd go away. Had wished that since she'd spotted the mistletoe. She didn't know what had been more embarrassing, Blaine catching her gawping at him like a lovestruck girl aching for her first kiss or his scorching reaction. Like she'd personally hung up that invitation to smooch and lured him to the alcove to do just that.

She hurried her steps, annoyed with herself for losing control like that. She shouldn't be thinking about kissing anyone at the moment, not when there was work to do.

They reached the foyer and she steered toward the office. She peered through the open door into a small room that smelled of eggnog and was decorated with a couple of chairs, an old wooden desk, pictures of ships at sail dotting the walls, and Christmas lights strung everywhere. "Let It Snow" warbled from unseen speakers, as if the storm needed any encouragement.

"Did they run off to the North Pole?" Blaine said, scanning the empty room.

Katy's ears perked at the chatter of voices and scraping sounds from outside the main entrance. "Ah. Mystery solved," she said.

Blaine dove for the door before Katy and opened it to reveal Mrs. Parker on the landing. The bells on her brooch chimed from under her heavy wool coat as she swept away snow that had blown under the portico roof.

"Push from your knees, Holly, not your back," she shouted to her husband, who shoveled the steps.

"Be quiet, woman." Mr. Parker stopped a moment to shake a small pile of snow off his red and black checkered cap. "I've been shoveling for more 'n forty years. I know what I'm doing."

Forty years came out *fawty yee-ahs*, bringing a fond smile to Katy's lips. He reminded her of her dad, who'd been a huge fan of snow shoveling. Dad would have the sidewalk, front steps, and driveway cleared by the time the last snowflake fell. Would've shoveled out the whole neighborhood if they'd let him.

"Mrs. Parker," Katy called. "What're you doing out here?"

She stopped sweeping and swung toward Katy, standing in the doorway, with Blaine beside her. "I'm sorry, dearie. Our plow man just rung to say he's delayed. Got a dozen *pahking* lots and driveways ahead of us."

"I *told* you Roscoe was gonna be late," Mr. Parker grumbled.

"Did you, my love?" his wife said, gently teasing. "After nearly fifty years of marriage, you should know by now I don't listen to you." She looked at Katy and winked. "That's the secret to our success."

"The real secret is we work together," her husband said without pausing from his work. "Except when Ivy lollygags. Like *now*. Git back to it, little girl. We got to have the stoop and stairs cleared before people arrive."

Blaine's breath had puffed in and out during this exchange, building steam like the *Little Engine That Could* about to blow its top. Now he erupted with a sound that landed somewhere between outrage and offense.

"Mr. Parker, put down that shovel," he said, sounding like the hero in an old movie. "*I'll* do it."

Blaine took off to the kitchen to get his jacket before the caretaker could even open his mouth to argue. Not about to be outshone in the helping-her-elders department by Blaine the overachiever, Katy ditched her clipboard, put on her coat and gloves, and relieved Mrs. Parker of her broom.

The wind blew the snow sideways, coating the landing despite the protection of the roof overhead. Katy swept rapidly and had made some headway by the time Blaine popped outside, shrugging into his jacket. He'd removed his chef's coat, giving her a glimpse of muscled biceps and a black tee shirt that clung to his broad shoulders and solid chest before he zipped his jacket and hid them from view. Thankfully. His lips were distracting enough.

Blaine tugged on a pair of heavy-duty gloves and brushed past Katy to wrestle the shovel from Mr. Parker. He ordered both caretakers out of the cold. They obeyed, as meek as sheep. The ringing bells on Mrs. Parker's pin faded away as she and her husband stepped into the building and closed the door.

Blaine turned his bossy gaze on her. "I can take care of that. Don't you have a wedding to plan?"

"You mean an event to manage?" No way was he going to dismiss her too. "I need my chef back in the kitchen to get things moving. Clearing the snow will go faster if we work together."

He didn't argue, though he looked like he wanted to. Grumbling something that involved the words *stubborn* and *not my fault if you freeze*, he bent over the shovel and put his broad shoulders to good use.

Katy threw herself into her task with her usual focus and made fast progress sweeping the landing. Blaine had the bigger job, several inches of wet snow to be cleared from six shallow but long steps. They worked in silence. The only sounds were the scrape of the shovel, the brush of the broom, and the howl of the wind.

A merry jingle announced Mrs. Parker's arrival several minutes later. "This is for the young man," she said, handing Katy a small towel. "He'll be Frosty the Snowman by the time he's done and will need it."

She wasn't wrong. Katy had a roof over her head, but Blaine worked out in the open. He pushed the shovel, hunched against the storm, well on his way to turning into a snowman. Icy snow crusted his hair and stuck to his jacket and pants. A strangely endearing look that brought a grin to Katy's lips.

"Every time she moves an angel gets its wings," Blaine said when Mrs. Parker returned inside, bells ringing.

That surprised a laugh out of Katy. "Oh, I love that movie," she said, beginning to sweep again. "I'd be watching Jimmy Stewart look for Zuzu's petals and helping Clarence get his wings right now if I didn't have to work. It's number one of my top five favorite Christmas shows."

"Top five? *I* have a top ten," he said like they were in some kind of competition.

"Oh yeah? Name them." Katy held up a hand. "Never mind. If you don't say *It's a Wonderful Life* tops your list, you can keep that nonsense to yourself."

"Of course. It's first on my list. Family, drama, people falling into swimming pools, and some life lessons. What more could you want? I don't know why people call that film sappy. It's really kind of dark."

"Exactly." She'd finished the landing and moved to the ramp, starting at the top. The snow was heavier here, and wet. Harder to sweep. "I think that's why I love that movie so much. It's real, you know? Real people facing tough times, the struggle to maintain hope. We've all been there."

He nodded. "When I was a kid, we'd watch that movie as a family, like, thirty-five times from November to Christmas. I know practically all the lines."

"My family too. Well, we didn't watch it as much as yours, but my mom especially loved it. She'd cry every time." Wistfulness tickled her throat as it always did when she thought of her mom. And her dad. Especially this time of year. Focusing on clearing the ramp, she steered back on topic. "What's second on your list?"

"*Gremlins.*" He tossed a shovelful of snow onto a growing pile next to the steps.

Katy scrunched her nose. "That's not on my list at all. I'll admit those little creatures scare me to death. My dad thought I'd love *Gremlins*, so he took me to see it one year when I was about twelve. You know that cinema in South Portland that shows classic movies and anime? I love the theater's vintage look but did *not* like that movie."

"The Bijou? Been there more than once." He reached the bottom step. His shovel scraped the granite and the snow pile by the steps grew taller. "In fact, I practically lived there last summer. They showed all the *Star Wars* movies in order over the space of a week." He let out a rueful snort. "And now you know my entire nerdy history. What's second on *your* list?"

She didn't find that nerdy. She thought it was cute. "*Meet Me in St. Louis.*"

"Not noisy enough for me. Number three?"

"*Miracle on 34th Street.*"

"Original or remake?"

"Both," she said. "You?"

"*Groundhog Day.*"

"That's not a Christmas movie."

He laughed. "No, but there's lots of snow. And a holiday." Finished with the steps, he started at the bottom of the ramp, ratcheting up his speed, as if trying to beat her to the finish line.

"Fair enough." She picked up her pace too. "What's number four?"

"*How the Grinch Stole Christmas.* The original version."

"Oh yeah, that's on everyone's list." Funny, she'd expected him to be like the Grinch, opinionated, sour, full of *bah, humbug.* Getting to know him, Katy suspected there was more to Blaine than Maggie's negative first impressions. "How about Charlie Brown?"

"Definitely. Also, *The Nightmare Before Christmas.*"

"*A Christmas Carol*, all sixty-eight versions of it."

"Especially the Muppets one," he said. "*Die Hard.*"

"From the Muppets to *Die Hard*? Agree to disagree on that one. *Rudolph*?"

He paused, looking up. "Rudolph," he repeated with a nod, adding, "*The Santa Clause.*"

"*Last Holiday.*"

"*A Christmas Story.*"

They swept and shoveled and rattled off movie titles in no particular order, moving steadily toward one another along the ramp until they met in the middle.

"*Elf!*" they cried in unison as broom and shovel collided.

She laughed. He smiled down at her. Katy had forgotten about the stress knot at the nape of her neck. The tension and her worries about today had all but melted away. *Tell me again how he's supposed to be an unmanageable grump?*

Breathing heavily, and not just from sweeping, she returned to the sheltered landing, out of the driving snow. Blaine followed. She rested the broom against one of the fat stone pillars and handed him the towel she'd tucked in her coat pocket. He swiped the cloth over his face and hair, dislodging snow but doing little to dry off.

"You can probably put that down now," she said, gesturing to the shovel he still held in a tight grip. "Unless you're going to clear the whole parking lot?'

"If I have to," he said, kidding. Or maybe not. "The

steps will get covered fast and will need a redo." He aimed a glare at the falling snow that would've scared it into stopping if it had any sense. "Whoever wrote that song 'Let It Snow' must've lived in LA."

"Whoever scheduled a wedding for Christmas Eve in Maine must be from LA," she said.

He straightened at the far-off rumble of a vehicle. "The snowplow?" he asked hopefully, eyeing her. His wet hair spiked up in a thousand directions. His cheeks were ruddy and wet too. He looked cold to the core. And utterly hot.

Tempted to fan herself, Katy looked away from him and toward the source of the sound, two shuttle buses bearing the name of the city's most expensive hotel that rolled into the parking lot. "It's the wedding party," she said. "And they're *way* behind schedule."

The buses chugged toward the building, windshield wipers beating furiously back and forth, struggling to clear slushy snow so the drivers could see. Air brakes whistled as the vehicles pulled up to the bottom of the steps and slid to a stop. The doors on each bus creaked open and chaos ensued.

The groomsmen, eight young men of all shapes, heights, and races, spilled out from the bus in front. Dressed in Santa hats and black tuxes with red cummerbunds and bowties, they immediately scooped up snow and flung snowballs at each other, to a chorus of whoops and laughter.

The bridesmaids hopped off the second bus, chattering and laughing. Ten of them in all, a group as diverse as the groomsmen, they wore casual clothes and carried oversized purses, garment bags, boxes, and tote bags, some with champagne bottles peeping out of them.

Squeals broke out as the groomsmen aimed a snowball barrage at the women, like a broken tennis ball machine. The other guests getting off the buses were caught in the crossfire. Aunts, uncles, cousins, and everyone else had to duck and dodge to avoid the snowy projectiles flying left, right, and center.

Blaine looked like he wanted to join in, but Katy fretted over the messy scene. "This is getting out of control." She took a step forward. "I need to—" She cut off with a yelp as Blaine yanked her back. An incoming snowball hit the landing an inch from her feet with a gushy *splat*.

Blaine held her upper arm and gazed down at her, his expression both amused and concerned. "Need to what? Make yourself a target?"

She couldn't muster a response. His gentle grip on her arm, his protectiveness, and the intensity in his eyes set off a new round of fluttering in her belly, pushing all other thought from her mind.

Luckily, the groom popped into the bus doorway. Katy recognized Todd Gaines from the photo ornaments, and she silently thanked him for providing a distraction from Blaine's disruptive gaze. She shook off Blaine's hand and moved to a safe distance away, though at this point, she feared even Alaska wouldn't be far enough.

The snowball barrage abruptly ceased as the grinning groom loped down the steps. Groomsmen and brides-maids alike let out a cheer that turned to a gasp of horror as Todd slipped on the last step. His feet shot out from under him. His arms and legs flailed as he went airborne then slammed to the snowy ground. His head snapped back, and he hit the open door of the bus with an audible *thwack.*

Katy winced. Blaine swore. Twice.

The groomsmen dashed to their friend's aid before Katy could swing into action. They hauled Todd to his feet and brushed him off. He cradled the side of his head with his hand, looking sheepish and somewhat dazed. He must have hurt his leg in the fall, too, because he limped worse than Mr. Parker as his buddies steered him up the steps. Mrs. Parker met the guys at the door and ushered them inside. The bridesmaids followed, their giddy mood somewhat dimmed.

As Katy added Todd's injuries to her growing list of things to worry about, a thirty-something blonde woman with plump, pink cheeks bustled off the second bus. She carried a load so heavy a pack mule would complain—five or six tote bags on each arm and two garment bags slung over one shoulder. Undoubtedly the maid of honor, Jackie Frost, the bride's cousin. The thicker garment bag probably contained the wedding gown.

"Is Todd gone?" Jackie called out, her gaze landing on Katy. "He can't see the bride until the ceremony."

"If even then," Blaine muttered, not quite under his breath.

Katy shot him a puzzled look then turned back to the maid of honor. "Yes, Todd's inside," she said.

"The coast is clear," Jackie hollered at the bus. "You can come out now."

A vision of loveliness stepped out into the snow. As

tall and as graceful as a gazelle, Lindsay Lathrop wore no coat, just a lightweight, candy cane striped tube dress with cap sleeves, accentuated by knee-high black boots and a Santa Claus hat with a giant white pom-pom atop her golden hair.

"Here comes the bride," Blaine grumped. "At least she showed up."

Bitter words, with bitter sauce on top. Katy shot him a frown. What had happened to the guy she'd swept and shoveled and laughed with just a few minutes ago? Was there something about weddings—or brides—that set him off?

"May I remind you this is a *happy* occasion?" she said. "Keep your editorials to yourself."

He aimed a bruising scowl at her, but seriously, the man had chosen the wrong profession if he was going to get all prickly over anything to do with weddings.

Lindsay didn't seem to notice Blaine's scowls or anything else. Her hair and the Santa hat's pom-pom flew out as she twirled around and around, like a playful puppy chasing its tail. Showing no sign the frigid temperatures and blowing wind bothered her, she grinned, gurgled, and giggled, as excited as a kid on, well, Christmas.

"I can't believe it's snowing!" she cried. "Perfect! Perfect for my wedding day."

Her excitement was infectious. Katy laughed and the guests still making their way inside cheered and applauded. Not Blaine, though. He let out a supremely sour snort that tempted Katy to elbow him in the ribs.

Then she forgot all about Blaine, the bride, and everything else when she saw a Jeep Patriot she recognized all too well fishtail into the parking lot. She watched in growing dismay as the car roared across the snow toward the building then slide into a handicapped parking space near the entrance. Her dismay turned to alarm as her ex-boyfriend Ash Gregg climbed out.

Ash, here? *Not* possible. Then again, entirely possible. When not selling insurance, he worked as a deejay, and he had a history of taking gigs on Christmas Eve, including two years ago when they'd met. Katy whipped out her phone and quickly scrolled through the names of people contracted for this event. She let out a groan when she found Ash's name as the disc jockey.

About to curse her sister for not telling her, Katy remembered Maggie had tried. *I had the dickens of a time finding people to staff this event*, she'd said before the gluten attack had cut her off from explaining what that meant. Maggie knew Katy hadn't seen or spoken to Ash since their breakup eight months ago and had tried to warn her.

Ash headed for the steps, carrying a pile of boxes filled with his gear. Flustered, Katy dove behind a pillar before he could see her.

"What are you doing?" Blaine asked, coming closer, his eyebrows shooting skyward.

"Shh, quiet!" She pressed herself to the cold granite, trying to disappear.

He bent his upper body to the left, like a sinking ship listing to starboard, and craned his neck to peer at her around the pillar. "What's wrong?"

"Nothing's wrong," she hissed. Blaine was so tall, and

he looked so goofy contorted like that, Ash would surely notice him. And then notice *her*. "I'm trying to…"

"Hide?"

"I am *not* hiding. I just don't want to be seen."

He straightened to his full height and crossed his arms over his chest. "That's the textbook definition of hiding."

Katy sighed. He was right. She was doing exactly that. Cowering behind a post like a frightened fool because she did *not* want to make eye contact with Ash. She dreaded a face-to-face with the guy. Bad enough she had to deal with this gruff, wedding-hating, but somewhat irresistible chef today, without having to confront her ex for the first time since he'd dumped her.

Blaine flicked a glance toward Ash, now climbing the steps. "Who is that guy?" His voice rolled like far away thunder, ominous, building toward danger. "You need my help? What can I do?"

"Nothing. I've got this under control." No, she didn't. And the way Blaine stared at her, he knew it. "Okay, since you're not going away, could you step a little to the right?" That would put his broad back directly in the way of Ash's line of sight.

Blaine did more than step to the right. He spun around and crowded close to her, leaning casually against the pillar and blocking her completely from view. Her senses reeled as his warmth and enticing scent wrapped around her. The tendrils of his wet hair curled against his jacket's collar, tempting her to reach out and run her fingers through it. She gulped and closed her eyes, quelling the impulse.

The sound of voices and footsteps rang out, the thump

of people stamping snow off their shoes, and the hubbub slowly faded.

"He's inside. They're all inside. You can come out now," Blaine said, laughter in his voice. And a dose of sarcasm. Did the man ever speak in any other way? She mentally thanked him for reminding her that no matter how dizzy he'd made her feel, how many favorite Christmas movies they had in common, and how broad his shoulders were, he was insufferable.

Katy peeped around him. Ash and most everyone else had indeed gone inside. Including the bride and her maid of honor, who were probably scouring the place for the event manager.

Searching for *her*.

"Excuse me. I've got to get to work," she said and edged by him. Or tried to. The cold had turned the wet landing slick and icy. She slipped and fell.

Into Blaine's arms.

COLE CAUGHT HER.

Because of course he did. Though the devil on his shoulder told him to let Maggie bounce on her bottom, no way would his inner Sir Galahad allow that.

He snatched her to him, his right arm around her waist, his left hand pressed to her upper back. She blinked at him, her long eyelashes fluttering. Her breath warmed his cold cheeks. Her soft, fragrant scent warmed him too. She felt good in his arms. Natural, like two puzzle pieces fit together to complete the whole.

He shifted his gaze to her lips. The thought of kissing her slammed into his mind before he could shut it down. The second time today and no mistletoe out here to blame. What part of not ready for someone new didn't his brain get? He'd walled off his heart after Celia had shattered it into a thousand pieces. He'd made sure the dates he'd gone on since then went nowhere. No way was he going to risk the pain of letting any woman get close again.

It didn't matter that he was attracted to Maggie. Didn't matter that their bantering made him feel more alive than he had in a long time. Or seeing her cower behind the pillar had sparked the need to shield her from whatever had frightened her. None of it mattered. Because he wouldn't let it.

Couldn't let it.

Besides, she had zero interest in him. He'd known that the way she'd reacted to seeing the mistletoe by the Christmas tree earlier and how she stared at him now. Horrified, as if he were the kissing bandit and she was his next conquest.

Hot with embarrassment, he released her from his death clinch and set her on her feet so fast she almost slipped again. "You should watch your step," he said, more forceful than he'd intended.

Her cheeks went as red as fresh beets. "Whatever," she said, eyes flashing. "Now, if you'll let me by…"

He snorted. A fine thank you for catching her. Maybe he should've let her fall. He held up his hands in an *I surrender* gesture and got out of her way fast.

She skittered across the landing and into the building

without looking back, leaving Cole with her sweet scent and a mystery. He eyed the newly arrived Jeep, rapidly being blanketed with snow. Who was that guy? Why had she melted into the pillar when she'd seen him? He narrowed his eyes. And why should he care? Maggie's problems were none of his business.

Cole shivered. He should get back inside and dry off, but he turned his attention to the stragglers trickling off the buses instead. Mostly older folks, aunts and uncles in formalwear. A man with a tuxedo jacket that barely buttoned over his stomach clapped a cell phone to his ear, oblivious to the slim, silver-haired elderly woman who struggled down the bus steps behind him. She wore a fur hat and long fur coat over a floor-length gown. She carried a silver-handled cane in one hand and in the other, a large leather handbag with knitting needles sticking out of the top.

Fearing she would slip, Cole flew down the steps to the bus, nearly bashing shoulders with the guy in the tux.

"Tell Rudolph I want the package ready before the big guy takes off tonight," the Tux Man barked into his phone as Cole raced past.

"Need help?" he asked when he reached the old woman. He didn't wait for an answer and grasped her small, gloved hand in his own.

"I suppose I do," she said with a grateful smile.

The bus driver held her elbow and steered from behind as Cole guided her down the steps. Her fur-trimmed boots sank into the snow. Easily two inches had fallen since he and Maggie had taken on shoveling duties and the storm showed no signs of stopping. Neither did the wind. Looked like this Christmas Eve storm had turned into a surprise nor'easter.

The woman peered at him with bright blue eyes framed by a murder of crow's feet.

"Thank you, young man," she said, her voice soft, musical. "It seems everyone else forgot about me."

Including Tux Man, still yapping on his phone as he pulled open the heavy door and disappeared inside.

"How could anyone forget a lovely lady like you?" Cole said.

She laughed. "Aren't you a sharp one. I do adore flattery. Keep it up, and I might have to remake my will."

Cole tilted his head toward the ramp, already coated with snow again. "The ramp's pretty slick," he said. "Mind if I hold your arm so I don't fall when we go inside?"

She gave him an impish grin. "Well, if you insist."

Cole stuck out his arm and she slipped her hand into his crooked elbow.

"Hey lady, don't forget this," the bus driver called as they started to move. He snatched up a large bag from behind the driver's seat. He leaned out the door and tossed it at Cole, who caught it deftly, despite its weight.

"What is it?" Cole asked.

The man shrugged. "Dunno. Santa Claus's loot bag?"

He might not be so far off the mark. Made of thick brown canvas, with a white braided rope to tie it shut, the bag bulged with boxes Cole guessed were presents. Probably gifts for the bridesmaids and groomsmen. Another wedding tradition Celia had insisted on, another thing they'd spent an obscene amount of money on.

"We'll be back at eleven tonight to pick up whoever's

still standing," the driver said, then looked at Cole's companion. "Have a good time, lady, and stay warm!"

He tipped his cap and flopped into his seat. The door hissed shut and both shuttle buses rolled through the snow as they made their escape.

"They'll never be back, if this storm keeps up," the woman said, shivering.

"Hey, let's get you inside where it's warm, Mrs.—?"

"Lathrop. Carol Lathrop. I'm the bride's grandmother."

"Nice to meet you, Mrs. Lathrop. I'm the chef 'round these parts." Cole hoisted the bag over one shoulder. "But I guess right now you can call me Santa Claus."

She let out another lilting laugh and took his arm again. She leaned on both him and her cane as he steered her toward the ramp. Snowflakes settled on her fur hat and coat as they moved upward at a careful pace to avoid slipping. Cole estimated Mrs. Lathrop to be in her late eighties, maybe even ninety. Not very tall, but with a regal bearing that reminded him of his own grandmother.

"You're a fine, helpful young man," she said, pausing halfway up the ramp to catch her breath. "I wish you were the groom."

Cole chuckled, glad he wasn't. "I'm sure your grand-daughter's fiancé is a good guy."

"Oh, he is. Kind of a klutz, though. But Lindsay loves him, so who am I to judge? Come along, let's get this dratted thing over with," she added as they started to walk again. She flashed him a rueful look. "You must think me a terrible cynic, and I suppose I am. I used to love weddings, back in the day, when they were small and simple. Today, weddings seem like one of those business deals my son is always wangling on his phone. A merger, with a lot of folderol and fripperies, stress and nonsense. I must confess I'm not so fond of these big weddings."

"I'm not fond of weddings of any kind," Cole said.

Mrs. Lathrop eyed him shrewdly, as if she'd guessed every unhappy reason behind his words. She patted his arm consolingly. "Then I suppose it will be a long day for both of us."

CHAPTER FIVE

Katy rushed to catch up to the bride and her entourage, her mind whirling. Ash unexpectedly skidding back into her life had upset her. Blaine holding her in his arms had unsettled her in an entirely different way. A brief, electric, sizzling moment that had pushed that notorious *K* word—*kiss*—front and center in her brain again. And there hadn't been a single leaf of mistletoe in sight.

Stop it, Katy. Now wasn't the time for racing heartbeats and reckless thoughts of smooching grumpy chefs. She had work to do.

Katy found the bride and her bridesmaids clustered in the foyer. She led them up the stairs to the suite on the upper level in the main part of the house. The rooms had probably been the original owner's bedrooms when the place was built in the 1880s. With updates, the area had everything a wedding party needed to dress and primp—a full-length, three-panel mirror between the two dressing rooms, two hair-and-makeup stations with lighted mirrors, a bathroom, and a bright, spacious lounge area with plump armchairs and side tables.

The bridesmaids dropped their boxes and bags and hung up their gowns. They chattered, laughed, and snapped dozens of selfies and group photos. Champagne corks popped and the tangy scent of orange juice clashed with the scent of perfume as a couple of the women mixed mimosas and filled a dozen plastic cups.

Lindsay spun around and around like Julie Andrews on that mountainside in *The Sound of Music*. Katy half-expected her to burst into song, so the bride's giggly cry of, "It's my wedding day!" was almost a letdown. Not to the bridesmaids, though. They released a collective *woohoo*, and held their drinks high, sloshing a good amount of mimosa onto the carpet.

Jackie Frost, the pack mule maid of honor, had unloaded her burden and busied herself trying to maneuver Lindsay's wedding dress out of its bulky garment bag. Katy hustled over to help. She held the bag while Jackie unzipped it, and together they carefully removed the gown. Katy stood on tiptoe and reached up, securing the sturdy hanger on a hook on the dressing room door. The gown and train unfolded with a silky swish.

"Ooh, *gorgeous*," one of the bridesmaids said. The others echoed her gushing compliment. Jackie clapped her hands. Katy hoped no orange juice would be spilled anywhere in the gown's vicinity.

Lindsay floated over and smoothed the creases from the silky fabric, sighing in delight. So she should. Snow white, with a beaded bodice and a shimmery skirt, the gown had probably cost more than Katy would make in three years.

"It's beautiful," she said.

"It is, isn't it?" Lindsay glanced at Katy and her euphoric expression turned puzzled. "And you are…?"

Clearly not the event manager Lindsay had expected to see. That stress knot, all but forgotten while Katy had been with Blaine, came back with a vengeance. She hated to puncture the bride's happy bubble with bad news, but it had to be done. She introduced herself and quickly explained about Maggie's absence, horrified to see Lindsay's grin fade, her eyes widen, and her lips form an *O* of dismay.

"So, I'm the stand in for today," Katy finished, bracing for a bridezilla eruption. "Anything you need, I'm your girl."

"Oh no. Oh *no*," Lindsay moaned, pinning her in a teary gaze. "That's just *awful*. Poor, poor Maggie. I do hope she'll be okay. That poor woman, sick for Christmas, of all days!"

Well, that reaction came as a surprise. So did Lindsay's hug. A bruising embrace that left Katy breathless and certain the sympathetic bride had cracked three of her ribs.

"I'm glad you were available to fill in for your sister," Lindsay murmured, releasing her. "Today's going to be a lot of fun, a total party. But there's so much to do and to keep track of, I'm depending on you to make sure everything runs smoothly."

Katy cringed. No pressure there. "I'll do my best." Better than her best, she hoped.

"Oh, I *know* you will. Why else would Maggie send you in her place?" Lindsay squeezed her in another rib-shattering hug. "But we're going to have to do something about your outfit." Her gaze swept over Katy, from her hair coiled in a tidy bun to the tips of her sensible shoes. "You look so…sad."

"Excuse me?" Katy thought she looked professional.

"I mean, it's Christmas and it's my wedding day and everyone's got to be jolly and all that. Bride's orders. So, no, absolutely *no* with the funeral clothes." She beamed at her bridesmaids. "What do you think, guys? Can we come up with something merry for the wedding planner?"

"Event manager, actually," Katy said. "And I'm good with what I'm wearing—"

She cut off as the bridesmaids moved in like a mob of kittens descending on their mother at feeding time. After several minutes of pokes, prods, and even a pinch, their makeover turned her from a sober and serious duckling into a goofy yuletide swan.

Her hair came down from its tight knot. Someone peeled off her blazer, and her pumps disappeared. One of the bridesmaids, a petite, dark-skinned Asian woman named Joy, slipped a pair of chunky-heeled, candy cane striped shoes onto Katy's feet. Unlike Cinderella, the fit was far from perfect. In fact, they pinched her toes.

A pale, freckle-faced redhead named Candy moved in next. She tugged a baggy, knit sweater that reached almost to the knees over Katy's head. Neon red, it had a green Christmas tree design on the front, complete with red, yellow, and orange blinking lights. It had probably won awards in any number of ugly Christmas sweater contests.

Lindsay took her by the shoulders and pushed her in front of the tri-fold mirror. "You look adorable," she cooed.

Katy thought she looked like a Christmas tree gone wild. And so much less like the capable event manager she came here to be. Though, she had to admit, she looked better with her hair down, and despite the toe pinch, the shoes were charming.

"Only one thing's missing," Lindsay said. She removed her Santa hat and fit it onto Katy's head. It slid down over her eyes. Lindsay laughed. "Either I have a freakishly big head, or you have a tiny one." She straightened the hat so Katy could see again. "There. You look a *thousand* percent more festive."

Makeover done, the maid of honor shoved a mimosa into Lindsay's hand. Jackie's thoughtfulness earned her a one-armed hug and effusive thanks, as if the bride had just crawled through a desert and was beyond thirsty.

A bridesmaid named Eve, a tall woman with thick eyelashes and light brown skin, tried to hand Katy a drink, but she declined. She'd gladly run this event while dressed like an attraction at a Christmas theme park if the bride wanted her to, but she preferred to do it sober.

"Here's to weddings!" Lindsay cried. "Here's to Christmas! Here's to a Christmas wedding!" She hoisted her glass and took a gulp with each toast. The bridesmaids cheered and drank too.

"Hear, hear," Katy said, adding a sigh of relief. The

bride was happy, her attendants were happy, and the ceremony was only a few hours away.

"Oh no!" Candy, the redhead, cried. She squinted at her phone. "Got a text from Marla. She's not coming. Too much snow."

Katy bit back a groan. She'd relaxed too soon.

Lindsay sank into a swivel chair in front of one of the makeup mirrors. "Wh-what did you say?" she asked in a small voice.

Candy opened her mouth but before she could answer, another bridesmaid, Grace, a teenager with rosy, cherub cheeks spoke up. "I heard from Aunt Pauline and Jess," she said in a hushed tone. "They're not coming either."

The bride's giddy grin faded. Worry lines crinkled her smooth brow and her euphoric bride bubble burst like a balloon meeting a sharp pin.

Katy grabbed the pitcher and splashed more mimosas into Lindsay's cup. "Please don't worry. That's just one person canceling. Well, three people, but still, the rest of your guests will make it. They're Mainers. What's a little snow to them? They'll be here, you'll see."

Katy knew she sounded like a perky cruise director trying to distract a guest from spoiled food, but Lindsay bought every word. She brightened.

"I suppose you're right," she chirped. "And you know, what does it matter as long as my stylist gets here, and my photographer. And of course, Nick, my justice of the peace." She sipped her drink, eyeing Katy. "What time are they supposed to be here?"

Katy snatched up her clipboard she'd put on a nearby table and scanned the schedule. Her spirits sank. Both stylist and photographer were supposed to have already arrived. The justice of the peace, too. Everyone was late. Maggie's meticulous schedule had proved to be no match for Mother Nature.

"I'm sure they're on the way, just delayed a little," Katy said quickly, forcing a smile. "How about I give them a call and ask when they think they'll get here?"

The bride agreed and Katy fled the suite before any other problems could crop up.

She padded down the carpeted hallway. Potted poinsettias nearly five feet tall stood at attention on both sides of the hall like sentries on duty. Two more poinsettias bookended the broad landing at the top of the stairs. A mistletoe wreath tied with delicate lace dangled from the arch overhead.

Before heading downstairs, Katy stopped to make her promised calls. Shifting the clipboard to her left hand, she maneuvered through the folds of the sweater Lindsay and her bridesmaid elves had gifted her with to retrieve her phone out of her skirt pocket. Before she could punch in a single number, the phone vibrated. Maggie's picture popped up.

"Hey, you," Katy said, answering. "How are you feeling?"

"Much, much better." Her sister's voice croaked like a bullfrog with another bullfrog stuck in its throat.

"Liar. You sound worse, not better."

"Yeah, I'm lying." Maggie cleared her throat. "Remember when you were ten and our Chihuahua ate that bag of ribbon candy out of your Christmas stocking?

Remember how he barfed all over the house? I feel like that."

Katy grimaced at both the memory and the thought of Maggie suffering the same volcanic stomach as their poor dog that long ago Christmas day. "Then why are you calling me? Why aren't you trying to sleep?"

"I wanted to check in, and to warn you about—"

"Too late, Ash is already here."

"I'm sorry. I hated to dump him on you like this, but no other deejay was available. I hope seeing him hasn't upset you too much."

"Um…" Katy scanned the function hall below, looking for Ash. The small crowd of family and wedding party members who'd come in on the buses mingled, chatted, ogled the decorations, and made themselves comfortable all around the room. She couldn't see Blaine anywhere, but she found Ash, over near the bar. He fiddled with power cords and other doodads as he set up his equipment.

Her throat squeezed as bitter memories of the night they broke up flooded her. The nausea when she'd realized he'd been cheating on her. The knife to the heart when he told her he'd been seeing Sasha on the sly for months. The hurt and the anger. At him for humiliating her so thoroughly and at herself for her tears and words left unspoken.

"No, I'm good," Katy said, downplaying the emotions rolling through her. "Just would've been nice to have some kind of warning. Seeing him is like ripping a bandage off an extra sore spot."

"That's something Dad used to say." Katy heard a smile

in Maggie's voice. "It hurts for a second, but now you've got it over with, you can move on with your life."

Not quite. Katy still hadn't gotten a face-to-face with Ash over with, something she supposed would happen at some point today. Unless she wanted to spend the rest of Christmas Eve hiding behind pillars and sarcastic chefs.

"So, tell me how it's going with Blaine," Maggie said, as if she'd read Katy's thoughts. "Isn't he the worst? Doesn't he just make your blood boil?"

He made her blood boil, but not in the way Maggie had meant. "He's... Well, he's..." She trailed off, unable to come up with a proper adjective.

"Just say it. He's terrible. Ugh. Why are the hot ones always such jerks?"

"Wait, I thought you said you and Blaine never met, how do you know he's hot?"

"Duh, Katy. I've never met him, but I've seen pictures of him. He attends a lot of fundraisers and events, probably drumming up business. He's gorgeous."

Obviously, she and her sister had different tastes. Blaine had his appealing, boy next door charm, with the added incentive of those blue eyes and unstoppable shoulders, but she wouldn't exactly call him gorgeous. He was more interesting than that. Kind of scruffy, a little dorky, and with a presence that lit her up like the blinking lights on her ugly Christmas sweater.

But Katy would admit that only to herself. "Maggie, don't let your husband hear you drooling over another man."

"Oh, Jackson knows he's my hero. I'm just stating a fact. Blaine's hot, *and* he knows it, from what I hear. He's a big flirt, always on the prowl. A womanizer. A love 'em and leave 'em type, if the pictures are any indication. He's got a new squeeze on his arm every week."

A rock the size of Gibraltar thudded into Katy's stomach. "Maggie, are you serious?"

"I am. I've heard horror stories about Blaine's womanizing from my friends in the business and..."

A frustrated shout rolled up from below, drowning her out. Katy spotted the groomsmen swarming behind the bar, trying to pry open the locked liquor cabinet doors.

"Hey, gotta go," she said quickly. She'd deal with this disappointing revelation about Blaine and all the other drama later. She had a more pressing task at the moment, stopping those guys before they broke something. "Go back to bed. Doctor Katy's orders. Oh, and thanks for having the good sense to get married in July."

She put her phone away and dashed down the stairs. At the bottom, a large man in a tailored tuxedo leaned against the banister, talking on his phone. Katy recognized him from the photo ornaments—the bride's father.

"Yeah, the North Pole's the best," Mr. Lathrop said. "How could it not be, with all those goodies? That's why I want it."

As Katy darted past, he turned away and lowered his voice as if she were an inside trader listening in on his secret plans. Turning down his volume didn't help much. The man had a voice that boomed like a cannon.

Keeping her back to Ash, Katy waded into the group behind the bar, swarming around the liquor cabinet. "Come on, guys," she said. "Let's do this by the book and wait for the bartender, okay? She's on her way, probably slowed down by the snow. She'll be here any minute. She'll get the key and—"

Oh, the key! She'd forgotten Blaine had asked for the pantry key. She imagined him pacing the kitchen like a caged lion, cursing her name because he still couldn't open the locked door.

"Now go on, get out of here," she said. "If you're thirsty, have some water." Katy gave one of the grumbling groomsmen a shove toward the water dispenser then hustled to the office, where she found the Parkers relaxing with a glass of eggnog.

"Join us in a snort, girlie?" Mr. Parker asked, raising his glass in invitation.

She politely declined, then told the Parkers what she was looking for. Mrs. Parker pulled a silver key ring out of the pocket of her red dress. There had to be about a thousand keys on that ring, but she found the correct one right away.

Mrs. Parker unlatched the key and handed it over. "Glad to see you're getting in the spirit of the season," she said, with an approving nod at Katy's new couture.

Katy glanced down at the sweater. The lights flashed off and on like a broken traffic light. "You don't think it's too much, do you?"

"Nothing's ever too much at Christmas," Mr. Parker said. "Enjoy it."

Katy thanked them both and rushed back to the dining room, aiming toward the kitchen to deliver the key. Spotting the groom at a nearby table, she slowed, then stopped. Todd sat with an older couple who had to be his parents. Mom wore a red gown and a holly corsage that floated like a lily pad on her shelf-like bosom. Dad wore a tux and a red tie adorned with prancing reindeer. Todd wore a pained expression and an ugly purple bruise on the left side of his face.

Ouch. That bus door had really done a number on the poor guy. His eye was nearly swollen shut. Concerned, she headed over. "Is there anything I can get for you?" she asked. "A cold compress for your eye or something?"

"No, I'm good," Todd said with manly grit. His gaze flashed to the clipboard in her hand. "Are you the wedding planner? Have you spoken to Lindsay?"

The Santa hat slipped down to cover Katy's eyes again and she shoved it back. "I'm the event manager, actually, and yes, I have."

"How's she doing?" he asked.

Like an emotional ping-pong ball knocked back and forth at rapid speed, but she didn't want to worry the groom. "She's doing well. Calm and cool, just a tad excited."

A fond smile touched Todd's lips. "Highly unlikely. I know Lindsay. She's smart, crunches numbers like nobody's business, and could climb Kilimanjaro in heels. But one thing she doesn't do well is calm and cool. I bet she's bouncing off the walls. She's kind of intense."

Katy's hug-bruised ribs ached in agreement. Intense was an understatement.

"I hope the snow's not stressing her too much," Todd's dad said. The lenses of his black-rimmed glasses reflected the dancing lights of Katy's sweater.

"I suggested they get married in Greece or one of those other destination wedding places," Mrs. Gaines added.

"Some place warm. But who listens to a mother's advice?" She sniffed. "The lovebirds insisted they take the plunge tonight."

"You know why, Mother," Todd said patiently, as if they'd had this discussion too many times before. He looked back at Katy. "Lindsay's a Christmas nut. She *loves* the holiday. The decorations, the food, the music, everything. She lost her mother when she was twelve, you know. Christmas reminds her of her mom and happy memories." He glanced toward the alcove, where the tree's decorations and lights glimmered, giving the dimly lit area a warm glow. "I won't complain about a little cold and snow. My girl wants to get married on Christmas Eve, she gets her wish. I'd do anything to make her happy."

His voice thickened. Katy's throat got a little clogged too. She understood how Lindsay felt. Christmas was the toughest time for her and Maggie, remembering holidays gone by and missing the little things they did as a family, like watching the movies she'd talked about with Blaine or stringing popcorn and cranberries into garlands to put on the tree.

Katy pushed those emotions away before she started bawling. Though tears were the inevitable outcome when she thought of her parents and Christmas, this was neither the time nor the place.

"Anyway..." Todd noisily cleared his throat, also moving on. "Next time you see Lindsay, tell her I said take a breath and keep calm, Christmas is coming. I'd tell her myself, but I'm not supposed to see her before the ceremony. Strange old custom, in my opinion, but Lindsay insisted on it and, as an attorney, I know to step away when the case is lost." He peered up at Katy with his one good eye. "And...tell her I love her, too."

His cheeks blushed as pink as the dawn and Katy gave him a smile. She had no idea lawyers could be so sentimental.

"I think Lindsay already knows that," she murmured, then excused herself when she saw Blaine enter the room from the foyer. He still wore his jacket and he'd slung a large bag that bulged like a laundry sack full of bricks over one shoulder. A teeny elderly woman dressed in an elegant emerald-green, long-sleeved gown clutched his free arm for support as he steered her toward a table by the fireplace.

Squeezing the key in her palm, Katy hurried after them, Maggie's words buzzing in her brain. Could Blaine really be a womanizer, always on the prowl as her sister had claimed? If so, his seduction skills were poor. He was sarcastic, blunt, occasionally charming but more often grumpy. His jokes were ridiculous, his manner goofy. Awkward, even. His behavior in the supermarket had been more silly than smooth.

And yet... She'd kind of fallen for it.

Blaine swung the bag off his shoulder and set it on the floor, then took the old woman's arm and settled her into a chair as if she were a precious heirloom.

"You comfortable, Mrs. Lathrop?" he said, his voice more gentle than Katy had ever heard it. "Would you like me to whip up something hot for you to drink? Coffee?"

Mrs. Lathrop leaned her silver-handled cane against the table and waved that off. "Only if you put something with a little kick into it," she said.

He laughed and Katy's insides fluttered at the sound. It lightened him up in every way.

He noticed her then. "Nice hat," he said.

She pushed the Santa hat higher on her forehead, out of her eyes. "Thanks. Got it off some fat guy in a red suit."

"Daring. Was the guy driving a sleigh? Kind of want to get his insurance info if I can catch him."

She couldn't help a grin. "Sorry, he and the reindeer have headed back to the North Pole."

Blaine's gaze dipped lower to her sweater. "You're looking awfully *bright*," he said, the corners of his eyes crinkling in a smile.

Katy's internal thermostat cranked up the heat. Apparently, Blaine's Dad Joke brand of flirting hit her sweet spot. "I'm thinking of passing out sunglasses, so the guests won't be blinded by my dazzling presence."

The old woman cleared her throat. She'd been sitting there, watching them, her amused gaze bouncing back and forth between them.

Katy put her clipboard on the table and turned to her, dialing her giddiness way back. "You must be Lindsay's grandmother. Nice to meet you. I'm K—"

"The wedding planner," Carol Lathrop said briskly. "I can tell by the agitated look on your face."

Katy laughed. "Does it show? I'm afraid there's a lot to do, and with the snow and other things…" She trailed off, more heat flooding her as she looked at Blaine, *the* major reason for her agitation.

He nudged the bag on the floor with his foot. "What should I do with this?"

"What is it?" she asked, getting one of his sexy shrugs in reply. She *wished* he'd stop doing that.

"No clue," he said. "Bag got left on the bus. Must be gifts for the wedding party."

He spat the word wedding with an *ouch* in his voice that got her thinking. Was there something more than a chef's ego behind his grumpiness? Rain clouds closed over him whenever she mentioned brides and weddings. Had he been burned by someone? Not that it excused his bad manners. She'd been burned too, and she didn't go around grumbling about it all the time, scaring puppies and small children.

"I think the bride already gave out her gifts," she said. "Could these be for the groomsmen?"

He peeled off his wet jacket and tossed it on the back of a chair. "Only one way to find out," he said and hoisted the bag up onto the table, tugging at the corded rope.

"Hey!" Katy cried. "That's someone else's property. They might not want us poking into it. Maybe whatever's inside is a surprise."

"How will you know what's in here unless you open it?" He lifted his gaze from the bag and met her eyes with a devilish expression. A giddy tingle swept down her spine and her internal temperature shot up another ten degrees.

"And who's going to take the blame if we ruin someone's surprise?" she said, refusing to give in to his evil, and so very alluring, charm. "Not the almighty chef. It'll be me, the lowly event manager."

"*I'll* take responsibility," Mrs. Lathrop cut in. Cane in

hand, she stood and eyed the bag with a mischievous gleam. "Open it. Let's see what's in there."

Blaine untied the rope and the bag sagged open. Mrs. Lathrop craned her neck to look inside. Equally intrigued, Katy stepped closer. Or, as close as she dared, with Blaine's very presence wreaking havoc on her composure.

She peeped into the bag and saw dozens of gifts of all sizes piled inside, wrapped in shiny silver and gold foil paper, and tied with red ribbons. Each gift sported a tag shaped like a snowflake, with names written in red and green marker.

"Are these from you?" Katy asked, looking to Mrs. Lathrop.

"Me?" She clapped a hand to her breast, her many rings sparkling in the light. "Oh, my dear, no. I've long since given up on Christmas wrapping. My gifts these days come in thin envelopes."

Fair enough. Her sister could've planned this surprise. That would be so like Maggie, to add a little extra flourish to the festivities.

"Got to be some clue in here." Blaine stuck his arm into the bag and pawed around. A demand for him to stop died on Katy's lips. Why waste her breath? He clearly wouldn't listen, anyway.

He took out one of the gifts, a rectangular box with a red velvet bow. He peered at the snowflake tag. "This one's addressed to someone named Ashton."

Ash? Katy snatched the package from Blaine's hands. She stared at the tag. Gifts for the wedding party she understood, but who'd be giving the deejay a gift?

"Ashton?" Mrs. Lathrop said. "Now there's a solid, old-fashioned name. Sounds like a Victorian chimney sweep."

Blaine gestured to a slender elderly man seated across the room and wearing an old-style tailcoat and a top hat. "Must be that guy. He's dressed for the part."

"No, not him," Katy said. "And it's Ash, not Ashton." Her ex hated his full name, as he would explain in windy detail to anyone who tried to call him that.

Blaine popped an eyebrow. "And you know this...how?"

Katy looked toward where Ash had set up by the bar. He'd donned a pair of padded headphones and moved some dials on his soundboard, bringing up a sultry rendition of "Merry Christmas Baby."

Blaine followed her gaze, and his mood went from day to night. "Him? The guy you were hiding from?"

"For the last time, I *was not* hiding."

"Yeah, yeah. You just didn't want to be seen. Why? Who is he?"

"No one."

Blaine's eyes narrowed. "Not no one. You don't hide from no one."

Katy's shoulders sagged. Blaine was the persistent type. He'd probably find out sooner or later. "Not that it's any of your business, but he's my ex-boyfriend."

He stiffened like a guard dog on sudden alert. "Your ex? Is that why you got so jumpy when you saw him?"

"No, it's not like that. He's not the problem... I mean, Ash is a good guy." Well, not really. He was just okay. And maybe not even that. He'd cheated on her, hadn't he? "It's just that it's the first time I've seen him since—" She didn't want to say he'd dumped her. That would be admitting failure. "The first time we've seen each other since we broke up. It's kind of..." She shrugged.

"Painful," Blaine finished for her. Not a question. A statement. An admission. Suddenly, Katy understood his wedding grumpiness a little better.

"Yes," she murmured, meeting his steady gaze.

He shifted, eyeing her closely. The world around them stilled. Katy's breath stilled too. Tiny kitten paws seemed to dance along her skin and awareness shimmered through her. His fresh scent, like the outdoors and snow, enveloped her. His eyes gleamed with something Katy couldn't define. Something that turned her inside out. Drew her to him. Physical attraction, yes, but something more.

"Well now, look what we have here," Mrs. Lathrop said, poking Blaine in the side.

The bubble burst and Katy snapped toward her. She'd been so intent on Blaine she'd almost forgotten the bride's grandmother was there. Forgotten anyone else was there, too.

"Excuse me?" she said.

"What?" Blaine said at the same time, sounding equally startled.

Mrs. Lathrop gave them an odd little smile and pointed a slim finger upward, to the mistletoe dangling directly over their heads.

Katy swallowed a groan. Blaine coughed and choked like he had a piece of candy stuck in his throat. Like kissing her had to be the worst idea ever.

"I've got something to braise. I mean poach. Or whatever," he said quickly and nearly tripped over his own feet in his haste to grab his jacket and flee.

"What about the key?" Katy asked, somewhat annoyed by his reaction. Not that she ached to be kissed by him, or anyone, but him acting like he'd catch a terminal case of girl-cooties if his lips touched hers had stung.

"The key?" Blaine said as if he'd never heard the word before.

Katy sighed in exasperation and held it up. Its silver surface glinted in the overhead light. "The pantry key you asked for, like, twenty years ago?"

His scowl returned with a vengeance. "Oh, yeah, right. Thanks." He snatched it from her hand then tossed her a blistering look and dashed away.

Katy watched him shove open the kitchen's swinging door and disappear inside. She fumed. At him, and herself. For opening up to him. For thinking that blazing look between them had meant something. For blabbering away about her personal life as if she were hanging out with friends and not at work. To be fair, he'd asked. He'd insisted she tell him about Ash, actually. But she'd behaved in a thoroughly unprofessional manner.

"A crying shame to waste a convenient piece of mistletoe like that," Mrs. Lathrop said, glancing at Katy, that odd smile making a reappearance. "That young man seems like such a nice fellow. And there's something special about a man who can cook. If he washed dishes too, he'd be just about perfect."

Katy shot her a frown. Was this cunning woman trying to play matchmaker? She shouldn't waste her time. She'd admit to a smidge of interest in the man, but she couldn't let herself get sidetracked by him or his dimples or her own desire. Couldn't let herself soften on him because he'd listened to her like he really cared or because he'd gazed at her with such sympathetic, puppy dog eyes.

She needed to keep Maggie's words firmly in mind. Even though his very presence curled her toes, even if he could cook and clean and build a barn in his spare time, she could *not* let him in.

Blaine Dillard was a womanizer, a terminal flirt. Or even a cheater. Katy turned her gaze from the kitchen door to glare at Ash across the room.

She'd had enough of men like that.

CHAPTER SIX

*C*ole jammed the key in the pantry door lock. The key to a room he didn't need to get into. The key he'd all but forgotten in his hurry to get the hell out of the dining room and away from Maggie. Away from her and the mistletoe and the thoughts racing through his mind.

He'd been able to keep cool the whole time they'd bantered and bickered, but the moment she'd gazed at him when she'd talked about her ex, he'd lost it. She looked so wounded, had sounded so broken he'd ached to take her into his arms and hold her. Not to kiss her. To comfort her. Followed by a sprint across the room to Ashton, Ash, the chimney sweep, or whatever the guy's name was, to introduce him to Cole's fist.

Impulsive and inappropriate actions she definitely wouldn't have appreciated and would probably get him fired.

Then Mrs. Lathrop had jabbed him in the ribs, and he'd crashed back to earth. Caught under the mistletoe again, with Maggie an arm's length away. The woman who threatened to kick down that solid wall he'd built around himself. What could he do but run?

The lock clicked and the door creaked open. *There.* He'd fed his mulish need to follow-through and accomplished one thing today. And though he didn't need anything inside the pantry, he'd found a convenient space to change out of his wet clothes.

He grabbed his jeans and stepped inside a long, narrow room nearly identical to the pantry in his grandmother's vintage kitchen. The same wooden shelves loaded with dishes, linens and containers, an old porcelain sink, a single window, and a pull string light overhead. Even the smells were the same, cumin, tarragon and a hundred other spices that instantly time traveled him back to when he was eight and hanging out at Mémé's after school.

Except for that cinnamon scent drifting in the air. *That* reminded him of Maggie. All forms of her. The lighthearted woman he'd joked with about holiday movies, the tightly wound party planner, the complicated, vulnerable woman he'd glimpsed behind that clipboard she held like a shield, the woman he'd held when she'd slipped earlier and had longed to kiss.

And the woman who'd stood so close to him under the mistletoe a few minutes ago, eyeing him like she'd just swallowed curdled milk. Was the thought of kissing him that repulsive?

Get out of your head, Cole. You've got stuff to do.

Resolutely ejecting Maggie from his brain, he kicked off his soaked shoes, replacing them with his boots. He hung his wet pants and jacket near a heating grate to dry and put on his jeans and his chef's coat, glad he'd removed it before stepping out into the snow. He ran a hand through his wet hair and returned to the kitchen to wash up and get to work.

First things first, he placed his favorite side towel close at hand then unrolled his cutlery case on a countertop. The knives gleamed in the light. The leather case had been hand-crafted by his cousin Spencer, the knives and other cutlery inside a gift from his parents. Gifts for a wedding that never was, and unlike the blenders and coffeemakers that had been returned to sender, these were gifts he'd hung onto.

Next, he took his large, antique French skillet out of a box and brought it to the stove. The kitchen was impressive—two state-of-the-art ovens, two oversized refrigerators, a gas-powered, eight-burner stovetop built into a wide center island, and enough counter space along the walls to prep a meal for a thousand. Wouldn't be feeding nearly that many today. With this storm, they'd be lucky if the number topped forty.

He turned one of the burners on low and splashed olive oil into the skillet, swishing it around to coat the bottom. While the oil heated, he chopped several cloves of peeled garlic with frantic precision then tossed it into the simmering oil. The mixture sizzled and popped. The smell of garlic wafted up so strong it could kill a vampire at ten paces. He took a long-handled wooden spoon from a box and stirred with slow strokes, his thoughts drifting back to Maggie.

He could empathize with that raw, kicked-in-the-teeth emotion he'd seen in her expression and heard in her voice when she spoke about her breakup. But he couldn't imagine how she must feel to see her ex here today. Cole had bumped into Celia only once after she'd ghosted him, at a party at a friend's house, and he hadn't been able to get out of there fast enough. Their face-to-face had lasted only a few minutes. Maggie had to spend the whole day with the guy.

And Cole got to spend the whole day with her.

His phone buzzed, tossing ice water on that heated, and completely uninvited, thought. Grateful for the interruption, he placed the spoon in a lobster-shaped spoon rest, wiped his hands, and grabbed his phone off a chair where he'd tossed it.

"Daisy?" he said, relieved to hear his assistant's voice on the other end of the line. "Where are you? Everything okay, kid?"

"Kid?" Daisy laughed. "I'm ten years older than you, junior, show some respect."

That prodded a smile out of him. "All right, grandma, what's going on?"

"Well, what do you want to hear first, the good news, the bad news, or the *bad* bad news?"

"Since you're giving me a choice, hit me with the bad bad news first."

"Got a call from the service contractor," she said. "The waitstaff's cancelling. The turnpike's a mess all the way from Kittery on up to Portland and they can't get through."

"Cripes. This storm's caught everyone with their pants down. What's the other bad news?

"Liza's not coming either. Can't even get out of their driveway."

No surprise. His other assistant, Liza, lived so far out in the boondocks, snowplows wouldn't be able to dig out their street until June. "Bet that's not bad news to Sam and the kids. They're probably thrilled to be home together on Christmas Eve. Which is where we should all be."

Instead of here, with a brown-eyed event manager doing her best to wiggle under his skin.

"And the good news?" He shifted the phone to his left hand and gave the garlic a stir. "Has Maine outlawed weddings altogether and we can go home?"

"Now, now. You may be allergic to weddings, but I love them. Mainly because they keep me employed. You too, you sourpuss. Here's the good news. I'm inching along the highway, but happy to report I'm making progress. I'll be there. Even if I have to abandon my car and hijack a pair of snowshoes."

He grinned. "That's dedication." His mood dimmed as he thought of the conditions on the road. "But seriously, Daisy, turn around if you have to. I want you to be safe. I can handle things on my own. I doubt all the guests will show up, anyway. I expect a lot of leftovers." He eyed the wedding cake on the table at the center of the kitchen. "Including lots of cake. You've got to see this thing. It's a literal mountain. Too big to fit into the refrigerator, even with the racks removed. Could feed four hundred guests, maybe more."

Daisy whistled appreciatively. "Would you rate it a one, or a ten?"

Cole scanned the cake from top to bottom. Daisy was

the connoisseur, not him. As long as chocolate was involved, he was good. The one thing he'd insisted on for his wedding, and the one thing he'd gotten. But that had been an ordinary cake, a solid two stars by Michelin's culinary rating standards. *This* cake shattered every judging standard in the book and could make a Michelin Inspector consider hanging up their tasting fork for good.

Almost five feet tall and three feet wide at the base, the cake was frosted green and sculpted like a Christmas tree, complete with colorful fondant ornaments. A star the size of a dinner plate, possibly white chocolate, sat on the top. Around the base were candy cane red and white frosted cakes in the shape of presents, with green fondant ribbons.

Cole had worked a lot of weddings and had seen a lot of cakes, but never anything like this. He hoped it tasted good, at least.

"I prefer not to comment," he said. "You've got to see this thing to believe it—" A roar from the dining room cut him off. He put down the spoon and moved away from the stove to the swinging door, propping it open.

"Sounds rowdy there," Daisy said. "What's happening?"

"The groomsmen are happening." The tuxedoed horde surged toward the liquor cabinet behind the bar like a pack of rabid penguins. The limping groom with the ugly-looking black eye led the way as the guys tried to open the locked doors. "The bartender's not here yet and they're getting restless."

He shifted his gaze to Maggie. Still holding the deejay's gift, she paced in front of the Christmas tree, talking on her phone. Her sweater's blinking lights kept time with her steps. Cole's lips twitched. She looked like an adorable Christmas confection in that outfit and the red-and-white candy cane shoes.

Whoa. What was he thinking? He replaced his grin with a frown. He didn't want to find her adorable at the moment. Or attractive, or fun, or anything that could break through the barrier he'd built around himself.

"But lucky for us," he said brusquely. "The wedding planner's here."

"Ooh, that bad, huh?" Daisy said. "Now you've got me *really* curious. Looking forward to meeting this dragon lady, and seeing that cake, too. If I ever get there."

"Remember, be careful," he warned again, and they ended the call.

Instead of going back to work, Cole leaned a shoulder against the doorjamb, watching Maggie pace back and forth. Her outfit may have been festive, but her expression had shifted back into event manager mode. Serious, concerned, and worried, no doubt, about the weather and a dozen other things that could and probably would go wrong today.

A wave of defensive anger shot through him. Where did Blaine get off calling Maggie difficult? It took a lot of drive and a high level of perfectionism his boss could only wish he possessed to plan and run an event, especially a wedding. Especially a wedding during a nor'easter.

Maggie looked over and their gazes met. A hot, searing moment that got him cursing inwardly. Outwardly too. Why was he so drawn to her, when he didn't want to be? When *she* didn't want him to be.

A sharp, bitter scent assaulted his nose. The smell of olive oil and garlic burning.

"Son of a—" He shot to the stove and shoved the pan off the burner. He scowled at the charred mess and swore. What would it take for him to get his mind off Maggie and onto the job at hand? The whole place to go up in flames?

He wrapped his side towel around the skillet's scalding handle and carried the sizzling mess to the trash bucket, using the spoon to scrape every last bit of blackened garlic into the barrel.

"I hate weddings," he muttered.

Especially this one, thanks to a pair of brown eyes he couldn't seem to shake.

CHAPTER SEVEN

*K*aty hung up and breathed a sigh of relief. Not because of what she'd heard on the phone. That had been nothing but bad news. The stylist and photographer weren't coming. They had a valid excuse. The storm had increased in intensity and the state police were asking people to stay off the roads. She couldn't reach the justice of the peace, so he might be a no-show too.

Katy's relief had nothing to do with any of them. It had everything to do with Blaine. After standing in the doorway for what seemed like hours, distracting her, making it impossible to concentrate on her calls, he'd finally gone back into the kitchen.

To be fair, she'd been easily distracted by him. His hair had dried but was still enticingly tousled. Funny how she loved to make things tidy and organized but didn't mind those messy locks. Not one bit. He'd put on his white coat again and had changed back into those tight black jeans.

He'd looked as sexy and alluring as a romance novel hero. Making her so lightheaded she thought she'd swoon.

Thankfully, he'd popped back into the kitchen before that could happen, and now she could focus on more important things. Like the sticky task of telling Lindsay the bad news about her stylist and photographer. The stickier task of keeping the groomsmen away from the liquor cabinet. Figuring out the mystery of the bag of gifts she'd tucked, appropriately, under the Christmas tree.

She gazed down at the package in her hand. And what to do about her ex-boyfriend.

Ash had focused on setting up and playing the music since he arrived, giving no sign he knew she was here. How he'd missed the lighthouse beacon of her flashing sweater, she didn't know. Perhaps she could find a way to avoid him until the wedding and reception were over. She could hang out upstairs with the bride, out of sight. Or chill with the Parkers in the office.

Or... She glanced toward the kitchen. Or hide in there.

Blaine had left the door open, and she could see him puttering around inside. He squatted to remove something from a box, straightening a second later in a nimble motion that got her almost swooning again.

Okay, maybe she wouldn't hide in the kitchen.

What are you hiding from? What are you afraid of? What indeed? The worst had already happened between her and Ash. Time to put the past behind her and show him she'd moved on. If she could handle a wedding *and* a blizzard, she could handle a little discomfort seeing her ex again.

Hopefully.

Nerves jumping, she walked toward him. Bruce

Springsteen's "Santa Claus is Coming to Town" rocked from the speakers. Ash shimmied to the tune behind his soundboard, in his own little world, and didn't see her until she practically stepped on him.

"Katy!" he cried, his eyes lighting up, as excited as a puppy at playtime. He tore off his headphones and threw them down, coming in for a kiss.

Katy gulped. Ash may be thrilled to see her, but she hadn't reached that same level of seeing-your-ex Zen. She ducked away from his lips but too late. His mouth smacked her forehead full force, leaving a wet splotch and, she was pretty sure, teeth marks in her skin. Undaunted, he yanked her into a squeezing hug that threatened to crack every one of her ribs Lindsay had missed.

"Hello, Ash," she said, quickly freeing herself.

"Hello, yourself," he said in that butterscotch smooth deejay voice that had once tickled her spine. "What are you doing here?"

"I'm filling in for my sister. She's under the weather. I sure didn't expect to see *you* here."

"I always turn up where you least expect me." His gaze skimmed over her. "You look great. No, I take that back. You look *amazing*."

She did *not* look amazing. She looked like a shopping mall Santa's harried helper. "And you look…" Perfect. As usual. Just a hint of spicy cologne, his ashy-blonde hair artfully styled, his glossy, slightly tan skin and perfectly symmetrical features, slim physique, and tailored gray suit, red tie, and black Oxford shoes. Every inch of him flawless.

Not scruffy at all. Not interesting, either.

In fact, boring.

Katy stiffened. Where had *that* come from? Vindictive-ness? Or were her eyes open to the truth now that her relationship blindness had several months to clear up?

"It's *so* good to see you, Katy." Ash flashed his perfectly straight, perfectly white teeth in a grin. "Been a long time. How're you doing?"

A loaded question coming from an ex. She doubted he wanted to hear about her job or the physical therapy she'd needed because that stupid finger she broke in the great sledding disaster sophomore year in college kept acting up.

He wanted to know how she'd held up since he had cut her loose.

She gazed into his soft gray eyes. How *was* she doing? She'd missed him, a little. She'd cursed his name and everything about him, a lot. She'd given him ass kickings in her mind every night for weeks. In the beginning. The pain had tapered off. The anger had taken longer to fade, leaving a dull, melancholy memory in its place. Plus the wonderful parting gift he'd left her with, an active fear of ever getting hurt like that again.

Katy wasn't about to share any of that with him. "I'm doing well, Ash. *Great*, actually," she said, meaning it. Why had she worried so much about seeing him again?

She thought she saw disappointment flicker in his eyes, gone in a second. "Oh. Good. Still hanging out at the dog shelter? And the food pantry?"

"Of course." As if that would change. She'd been volun-teering at the shelter since her parents died. Getting drooled on and playing with dogs of all ages had been more comforting than she could have imagined. Her regular gig at Gray Street Food Pantry started around the same time, her way to give back for the help Katy and her sister had received after they'd lost Mom and Dad and they went through a rough patch.

Ash licked his lips and scrubbed his hands along his thighs. "It's strange, us being here together, today, of all days. Remember when we met? Christmas Eve, two years ago tonight."

She remembered, vividly. Her company had bought two tables to the Chamber of Commerce's *Jingle Bell Ball,* and she'd snagged a ticket. A single ticket at a table of couples. She had no date, hadn't had a date in a while and her last one had been a flop. Her sister and three of her friends had been married over the previous year and another friend had gotten engaged.

In short, Katy had been a little lonely. Not to mention a little tipsy.

And then she'd met Ash, all perfect smiles and purring compliments. He'd played "All I Want for Christmas Is You." Just for her, he'd said. He'd waged a flirty campaign for her attention. She'd felt giddy. Appreciated and noticed. Wanted. He'd offered her companionship and a cure for her loneliness.

Most important, he'd fit her life plan, even if he didn't fit her. She hadn't realized that at the time, but she knew that now.

"Ash, I don't have time to reminisce," she said abruptly. She shoved the gift into his hands. "Here, this is for you."

His eyes widened. "A Christmas present? Katy, you shouldn't have."

"Oh, it's not from me," she said, horrified. Why would she give him a gift? "Someone else brought this. I think there's one for everyone, not just you. Wasn't that a nice gesture?"

He tore off the wrapping paper and dropped it to the floor, along with the ribbon. He opened the box and pulled out a fancy-looking wireless microphone.

"Awesome!" he said. "I need a new mike. I need an upgrade to all my gear, actually. I've been getting so many deejay gigs, I'm planning to go full time next year. I can finally ditch selling insurance for good."

"Seriously? That's terrific. I remember you said more than once insurance wasn't the right path for you."

"You're kind, Katy. You always were nice to me. But I'm a crappy salesman and you know it."

She laughed, surprised by his honesty. "I guess you can say you've always preferred turntables to actuarial tables."

"That's clever. I might steal that. You know, it took me a while, but I finally realized it's time to break out on my own. I'm more than ready." He flashed a rueful smile. "I think my boss is ready too. He'll be glad to see me pack up my briefcase and go. He'll probably hold the door."

"Sounds like you have a great plan. I hope it works out for you." It probably would. A born performer, Ash came alive in front of a crowd, dancing to the tunes and leading the party guests in the latest line dance fad. Taking requests, schmoozing with grandmas, and flirting with pretty partygoers.

Katy lifted her chin. That was how they'd met—and how he'd met Sasha, the woman he'd dumped her for.

"Well, this reunion's been fun," she said, suddenly eager to get away. Away from his smooth voice and his perfect smile and his perfect perfectness, but mostly away from him, and the memories she would rather put behind her. "But I've got to go."

"Snooky-poo, wait. Stay another minute."

Ugh! How could she have ever thought that pet name was cute? "Sorry, Ash, I've got work to do."

"Katy…!" He chased after her as she walked away and grabbed her arm, stopping her so fast they bumped heads again.

"What do you want?" she demanded, rubbing her aching forehead. If this kept up, she'd be as bruised as the groom by the end of the day.

"Can we go somewhere more private?" He looked around the room, eyeing the guests with suspicion. "Somewhere we can talk."

Something in his voice touched her. Was it regret? Remorse? "Didn't we say everything that needed to be said the night we broke up? At least, you did."

She would never forget how he'd talked and talked, spewing all kinds of excuses, and even blaming her when he'd told her they were through. *Her* fault they'd grown apart, *her* fault he'd cheated on her with Sasha. It struck her that the only thing that had been her fault was not speaking up, not telling him how she felt. She'd kept it all in, to her regret.

He had the grace to look ashamed. "I said a lot of things back then. A lot of stupid things." He ran a hand through his hair. Every strand remained perfectly in place. "I don't like the way we left things. Give me the chance to make it up to you. Just two minutes. That's all I ask."

He took her hands, his gaze liquid and alluring. A smooth tactic he'd employed any time they'd had a disagreement, trying to coax her into forgiving him even though he could never utter the words *I'm sorry* himself. She'd been so determined to make their relationship work, to make the *plan* work, despite her misgivings, she'd let herself fall for his ploy every time.

But not now. "I'm sorry, Ash," she said with cool detachment. "I don't have two minutes."

She shook off his hold and swept away. Or tried to. She slammed into something, fast and hard. Not Ash this time. Something larger. One of the pillar posts, or a bridge abutment that had suddenly appeared in the middle of the room. Well, not a bridge abutment, but something equally solid.

Blaine.

He'd snuck up behind her and she plowed into him, her palms pressed to his chest. He held her by the waist to steady her, his grip gentle but firm. Katy's breath caught. She met his gaze and instantly forgot about Ash. Blaine didn't. He looked past her toward her ex with his eyes narrowed.

"Is this jerk harassing you?" he growled. He sounded winded, like he'd run over here in a hurry. "Want me to boot him out into the snow?"

Ash's perfect eyebrows drew down as he returned

Blaine's glare. "This is between me and her," he spat. "Why don't you shove off, fry cook?"

Katy suspected those were fighting words, but Blaine's gaze on Ash didn't falter.

"Did you know all chefs travel with their own knives?" he said calmly. "And they're all *very* sharp."

Ash gulped and looked at Katy. "We'll talk later," he said and skittered back to his soundboard.

"Don't count on it," she muttered to his retreating back then swung on Blaine. "That knife thing wasn't very nice."

"Who said I was nice?" He shifted his glower to her hands, still pressed to his chest.

She gasped in embarrassment and hastily pulled away, putting some distance between them. "What are you doing here?" she demanded.

"I thought something was wrong. Your sweater was sending out an SOS."

His words were light, but his expression flashed as stormy as the sky outside. Sexy, hot, and...heroic. Katy could take care of herself just fine, she didn't need him to save her, but she had to admit, his knight in shining armor act got her a teensy bit flustered. Okay, a lot flustered. Like, inner thermostat cranked up to scalding flustered.

"Well, thanks for your help," she squeaked. "But I had everything under control." Sure she did. She straightened her Santa hat and put on her event manager's voice. "Is there something I can help you with?"

"As a matter of fact, there is." He sounded reluctant to admit it. "The cake. It's hot in the kitchen. I've fired up the ovens and it's getting hotter. The cake won't fit in the fridge, so it's got to be moved before the icing slides off."

Another problem, but a teeny one, easily solved. Katy gestured toward the alcove. "You can put it back there, next to the tree. That area's almost as cold as a refrigerator."

Blaine shifted, looking uncomfortable. Still glowering.

She lifted an eyebrow. "Unless you can think of a better place for it?"

"No, that's good. But my kitchen staff's still not here." He paused a couple of beats before admitting, "I need help to move it."

Ah. Now she got it. Like George Bailey in *It's A Wonderful Life*, Blaine ran around helping everyone else, but hated to ask for help himself. A vulnerable admission that got her insides fluttering again.

Katy agreed with a somewhat heated nod and followed him toward the kitchen. A firm *tap-tap* of a cane on the hardwood floor caught her attention. Mrs. Lathrop waved to her from the groom's table, where she sat chatting with Todd's parents.

"Ask him if he does dishes," the old woman said, with the slyest of grins.

CHAPTER EIGHT

$\mathcal{C}$ole moved steadily toward the kitchen, hyper-aware of Maggie behind him. He could've waited until Daisy got here to move the cake. Had planned on that. But when he saw that jackass ex-boyfriend headbutt Maggie, then grab her, his blood had boiled with a protective fury he didn't know he possessed. He'd torn out of the kitchen, the superhero on a mission to rescue the fair damsel.

Bad move. She'd shaken the guy off like a mosquito before Cole had reached her. Reached her? He'd slammed into her like a speeding bus with no brakes and he nearly knocked her down. He'd only managed to pull himself out of the muck by making up a story about needing her help with the cake.

He'd left the door propped open and Maggie scanned the large room as they entered, checking out the open boxes and containers, bowls scattered on the counter along the inner wall, skillets and pans on the stove, his knives, utensils and cutting boards on the center island.

Her nose crinkled, maybe at the organized mess of his setup or the whiff of today's special in the air, burned garlic. The smell was fading, but still strong enough to seal the deal on everything Blaine had probably said to her about Cole's amateur status as a cook.

"What do you think of it?" he asked, distracting her by drawing her over to the cake.

She surveyed the sugary monstrosity, from the star on top to the base so wide it nearly spilled over the small table's edges. Her cheeks were a pretty pink, probably from the heat. Cole's face felt warm too, but not from the heat and definitely not pink. More like fire engine red. From excitement, anticipation, and a ton of other indescribable emotions that shot through him just being near her.

"It certainly is the biggest one I've ever seen," she said. Her startled gaze flew to his face and her cheeks got even pinker. "I mean, it's huge. Um, no, not that. What I mean is...ugh!" She threw up her hands. "You know what I mean."

She looked so adorably embarrassed he could barely stand it. "No, I don't know." He crossed his arms over his chest. "Please continue." She scorched him with a smoky look, and he relented with a laugh. "Did you mean to say it's *tall*?" he said, pulling her out of the double entendre hole she'd dug herself into.

"Yes! *Exactly*," she said with obvious relief. "I've got to say, it's the most unusual design I've ever seen. Do you suppose they'll save just the star or the whole top tier? You know, the piece of cake you're supposed to freeze and eat on your first anniversary. It's a tradition."

"It is? I wouldn't know," he said, hearing the hard note in his voice. He and Celia hadn't gotten that far. Their cake had come home with him to be shared with his family, but he'd never taken a bite.

Maggie flashed him an odd look, then back to the cake. "So, is it chocolate or vanilla?"

"Chocolate, I hope. It's not a real cake unless it's chocolate."

"We're on the same page there." Her expression turned curious and she tapped a finger to her lips, drawing his attention there. "I don't know, it feels like something's missing. It's got the star, and presents and ornaments, but it needs something more."

"How about a life-size Abominable Snowman sitting on one of the tree branches?"

She let out a little snort that morphed into a giggle. A laugh that stole his heart. "That would be *way* too much," she said.

"Too much? Have you even looked at this cake?"

"I mean it needs something more subtle, more old-school Christmas. Like a...train. You know, like under a real tree on Christmas morning? We had one when I was a kid." Her voice softened, sounding sad and a little wistful.

"We did too," he said, touched by a pang of nostalgia himself. "I think the only thing this cake needs is to be two feet shorter and a foot less broad. But who am I to judge?"

She cleared her throat. "Oh, you don't judge?"

The way she looked at him, even the fussy way she cleared her throat knocked him off-kilter, got him as jumpy as a kid on a date with the prettiest girl in class. He shifted into gruff mode. "I only judge deejays who get grabby with their exes. Now, you going to help me with this thing or not?"

"I suppose," she said and followed him to the pantry, where he'd seen a wheeled cart the right size for the cake against the back wall.

He rolled the cart forward at the same time Maggie squeezed by him to grab a white linen tablecloth from one of the top shelves. She brushed against him as she passed. Because why not? He was already about to go nova with her so near, why not add the feel of her body almost-but-not-quite touching his to complete the explosion.

Their gazes snagged a moment and his breath hitched. She smelled so good. He wanted to relieve her of that too-big Santa hat and run his fingers through her silky hair. Wanted to touch her, to hold her, kiss her, and much, much more. She quickly moved on and he closed his eyes, shoving those thoughts away.

A second later, something thumped him in the chest. He snapped his eyes open—Maggie had thrown the table-cloth at him.

"No time for a nap, sleepyhead," she said, with a myste-rious smile that lit him up inside. "There are cakes to be moved."

Struggling for control, he snapped open the tablecloth with a flick of his wrists. Maggie caught the other end, and they covered the top of the cart in one swift move-ment, as if they'd been doing this together their whole lives.

Cole pushed the cart out of the pantry as Maggie hurried ahead and pulled two of the four chairs away from the table. He pressed the pedal brakes on the cart's wheels with his foot, then turned to the problem at hand. The cake sat on a square of sturdy wood, covered with silver foil that shimmered like tinsel. With the cart about even in height to the table, it should be an easy thing to slide the cake over.

"Okay," he said, gripping the board. "We'll move it on my mark. Three, two—"

"Wait," Maggie cried and Cole froze. She stared at the cake with a worried look. "What if it breaks when we move it? There are enough things going wrong today. I don't want to upset the bride with a smushed cake."

"If it breaks, I'll fix it. It wouldn't be the first wedding cake to crumble on my watch. Some spackle and a putty knife will make it as good as new." She looked doubtful, so he added in a more serious tone, "But it won't happen. I've been at this catering thing for a while, and I've handled dozens of cakes. I haven't lost one yet."

"There's always a first time," she said.

"You worry too much."

"And you have too much confidence."

Not really. He just hated to see her so stressed, as if any problems that cropped up were her fault. "I guess we'll find out when we move it, right?"

She gave a reluctant nod and got into position again, holding her side of the board. Cole re-started the countdown.

"Wait," she said, and he jerked upright. She pulled off her hat and tossed it onto a chair. "I'd like to be able to *see* what I'm doing. Okay, now I'm ready."

"You *sure*?"

She ignored his sarcasm and focused on the cake. They each gripped the board and in one swift motion they dragged the whole shebang from table to cart. No breaks, no pieces toppling off, no fondant ornaments shaken loose, or even cracks in the frosting.

"There, what did I tell you?" Cole looked at Maggie and grinned. "Still in one piece. It may not be the most attractive wedding cake, but it sure is well constructed."

"And amazingly heavy. I'm glad we didn't have to lift it." She massaged her upper arm. "Guess I need to ratchet up my strength training. I'm a runner so I'm good with the cardio, but the other stuff, not so much."

"You run? I do too." He also trained with weights, but he didn't consider that news relevant at the moment. "Are you a rambler or a goal runner?"

She huffed like the steam radiator in Mémé's kitchen. "Certainly *not* a rambler. I have to know how far I'm going and when I'll be finished before I even start. I run five times a week on a track, four miles each time." She smoothed a tiny wrinkle in the tablecloth under the cake, then lifted her gaze to meet his. "How about you? I'll bet you run a marathon every day."

He laughed. She was teasing. And he liked her teasing. "I'm more about just getting out there than setting a goal. I run for an hour, two if I have the time. Unless I'm training for a race."

"Don't tell me, you do the Munjoy Monster run, don't you?"

"Oh yeah, every Halloween." A ten-miler that took runners through Portland's historical downtown, that race ended with a sprint up the city's only real steep incline, Munjoy Hill.

"Do you also run up to the top of the old Observatory tower?" she asked. "Isn't that part of the race?"

"Yup. I do all hundred and three steps. Double time. The view is amazing." He pressed the wheel locks on his side of the cart with his foot, releasing the casters, readying to move.

"I know, I've been up there." She freed the locks on the other side. "But I walked up, like any ordinary mortal would do. For running, I prefer the track. Nice and flat. Hills intimidate me."

"I don't believe it. You don't seem the type to let a little slope stop you."

"And you seem the type to *only* run up hills."

He laughed again. "Just Munjoy. It's a challenge too good to pass up. You ought to give it a try next year. I'll be there to cheer you on."

"Maybe I will." She flashed another mysterious smile then shifted gears. "So, are we ready to go?"

"We are." He angled the cart and began to roll it forward. "I'll push, you'll have to steer. I can't see anything with this giant 'O Tannenbaum' blocking my view."

She gave him a salute and they were off. Cole put his muscles into pushing the lumbering cart through the doorway and into the function space. Maggie's hips gently swayed as she marched out front, her sweater lighting their path like Rudolph guiding a certain sleigh on a foggy Christmas Eve. A hush came over the guests and they moved out of the way, watching them glide across the room.

All eyes were on the cake, except the deejay's. He aimed his attention straight at Maggie. Cole shot him a glare. She'd said the guy was her ex, but the gooey way he looked at her, Cole had to wonder.

"Did you give the chimney sweep his gift?" he asked.

Maggie aimed a puzzled glance back at him. "Chimney sweep? Oh, what Mrs. Lathrop said about Ash's name." She laughed. "That kind of fits him, with his ash-colored hair. And you know, it's supposed to be good luck to have a chimney sweep at your wedding."

A fond note touched her voice. A twinge of jealousy nicked Cole's heart, to his surprise.

They reached the patio area. Together, they slid the cart into a space to the left of the Christmas tree, where the guests could *ooh, ahh,* and go *huh?* over it for the rest of the day.

"Hopefully the groomsmen will keep their distance," he said. "Wouldn't want any of them falling into the cake."

"The one I worry about is the groom." Maggie nodded toward Todd, who stumbled and nearly face-planted merely crossing the room. "It's like he was born with a banana peel under his foot." She shot Cole a stricken look. "Oh, that was mean. Forget you heard me say that."

"Forget I heard you say what?" he said, earning a grateful smile. "Have you figured out who those are from?" He gestured to the bag of gifts at the base of the tree.

"Nope. No one's claimed them. I poked around inside the bag and found no note or instructions. I suppose I could call my sister M—"

"Don't sing me that Christmas carol," a man's voice boomed, drowning her out.

Cole craned his neck and spotted the tuxedoed man from the bus earlier behind the tree, on his phone again. Or maybe *still* on the phone, on the same call since he'd arrived.

"Who's that guy?" Cole asked.

"The bride's father, Buddy Lathrop," Maggie said.

"Negotiating a deal on Christmas Eve? At his daughter's wedding?"

"No, no! I don't want Donner," Lathrop bellowed. "It's *got* to be Rudolph on the lead, see? He knows the North Pole better than anyone up there."

"Sounds like he's doing a hostile takeover of Santa's village," Maggie said.

"Or he's Santa Claus, giving orders to his elves." Cole adopted a confused look and scratched his temple. "Shouldn't the guy be at the North Pole instead of yapping about it on the phone? He's got to get his sleigh loaded." He eyed Maggie. "You better watch out. He may demand his hat back."

"Are we back to that again?" She placed her hand on her hip.

"Would you rather we talk about the chimney sweep?"

She let out one of those adorable snort-giggles. "You're ridiculous. But certainly not boring."

Was that supposed to be a compliment? "I aim to please," he said.

"Congratulations, you two!" Mrs. Lathrop tottered over, her cane tapping the floorboards. Her gaze touched on Cole, then Maggie, then to the cart holding the cake.

"You managed to move that eyesore without major injuries. Well done. You make a great team."

Cole's good mood fizzled. *Team.* The word left a sour taste in his mouth. That's what Celia used to call them, *Team Celia and Cole.* Back before he discovered they were both supposed to be on team Celia.

Clearly Maggie didn't like the word either. The easiness that had grown between them the last few minutes slipped away. The light and laughter faded from her eyes.

"I suppose I should go check on how the bride's doing," she said, the harried event manager clicking back into place. She glanced at him. "Please let me know if you need anything else."

Cole nodded, feeling awkward. "You too," he said, like a bank teller thanking a customer. "Anything you need, you know where to find me."

She spun on her heel, snatched her clipboard off a table, and headed for the stairs. Cole watched her go. *Let me know if you need anything else,* she'd said. *You,* he thought. He needed *her.* He gulped in surprise. He hadn't felt anything like that since Celia. No, he'd never felt this way with anyone.

"I'm afraid I interrupted," Mrs. Lathrop said.

Cole stiffened, ashamed to admit he'd forgotten she was there. "Interrupted what?"

She eyed him the way his grandmother would when he'd done or said something she thought especially dense. "Weren't you two about to celebrate a job well done with a smooch?"

He flinched. "What gave you that idea?"

"The way you looked at each other. I could see the

sparks fly from all the way across the room. You nearly set the place on fire."

He frowned. One-sided sparks maybe. "You were mistaken."

"Oh, dear, seems I'm being presumptuous again. My apologies. You probably already have a girlfriend. Or a wife or a what do you call it, a main squeeze?"

"No, none of the above," he said quickly, hoping to shut down this awkward line of conversation. And fast. "No girlfriend, no wife."

She clucked in concern. "A handsome man like you, who can cook and everything, and you don't have a lady in your life? That's a crying shame."

"I'm doing okay," he said. "Single and happy that way."

"Are you sure? You seem to be trying *awfully* hard to convince me of that." She peered at him, watching him as closely as the lead administrator of Cole's culinary certification exam. Making him equally nervous. "Or perhaps… you're trying to convince yourself?"

She'd hit the nail on the head. No way would he admit that out loud, least of all to her. He squared his shoulders. Meeting Maggie may have put a crack in the armor around his heart. Maybe he was starting to like her, and possibly even a little more. But he'd just met her. He wasn't ready to surrender yet. Far from it.

He abruptly excused himself and beat it back to the safety of the kitchen, closing the door. Away from *her*. Both hers. Maggie *and* Mrs. Lathrop, the shrewd wolf in cuddly grandmother's clothing. Both women had gotten him wondering about his determination to stay firmly, emphatically single.

He scrubbed his hands and returned to work, starting with replacing the garlic he'd burned. He glanced at the windows, wondering if he should risk opening one to air out the lingering smell. Outside, the sky had turned silvery gray, the color of the snowstorm, inspiring dread and longing at the same time.

Kind of like how Cole felt right now.

His phone rang. Blaine's ring tone. *Great.* That was all he needed now. "Hey, Blaine, what's up?" he said, answering. Brisk and to the point.

"Yeah, checking in. How's it going?"

Cole bristled. Checking in? More like checking up on him. The guy was something else. Took off with a woman right before a big job, walked out on an event *he'd* signed the contract for, and yet he insisted on micromanaging. From another state. He *really* didn't trust Cole to run the show.

Or… Was Blaine worried he would run the show too well? Had he caught on to Cole's restlessness, his eagerness to get out from under his thumb and strike out on his own? Did he fear Cole as his competition? Blaine criticized him and put him down every chance he got. Did he feel threatened?

That would explain a lot.

"It's going okay," Cole said. No way was he going to mention the delays and the waitstaff's cancellation. The sooner he got Blaine off the phone the better. "Busy, but on track."

He regretted the words as soon as they spilled out of his mouth. Something else to harass Cole about.

"Busy?" Blaine snapped, going in for the kill. "It's a

small event. I could run it blindfolded. Are you sure you can handle this thing? I've got a reputation to keep up, you know. Don't want bad reviews because you can't manage a simple wedding."

It's all about you, isn't it, Blaine? Cole swallowed his anger, setting his mind on the day he had his own place and could say goodbye to the man for good. "I. Got. This," he bit off. "Everything's under control. Are we done?"

"Not yet. What about Maggie?"

Cole went still. "What about her?" he asked warily.

"She busting your butt? More important, is she hot?" He followed that with a sleazy laugh, like a leering cartoon character. "I could work with her if she's hot. Might even forgive her bitchiness if she's great to look at."

Cole balled his fist. First of all, could Blaine be a bigger ass? Secondly, Maggie bitchy? No. Not even a little. And finally, she *was* hot. A fact he hoped Blaine never got the chance to confirm in person. A tsunami of fury churned in his gut at the idea of him moving on her the way he did with all his women, seducing then dumping her.

"Goodbye, Blaine," Cole said, taking great pleasure in hanging up on him.

CHAPTER NINE

*K*aty hurried along the upstairs hallway, overwhelmed by what had happened downstairs with Blaine. Sure, the usual fever symptoms raged when she stood close to him, flushed cheeks, blood rushing through her veins, her belly flipping over and over. She'd almost gotten used to those sensations.

This time, she'd felt something more. Something that went beyond physical attraction. Something deeper. Startling.

She *liked* him.

She didn't want to, but she couldn't help it. Despite his scowls, or perhaps because of them, she liked him. Not only did they have a lot in common, but they also worked together well. She couldn't believe how much fun she'd had moving the cake and bantering with him like a couple in a romantic comedy. Then Mrs. Lathrop had come along and called them a team. Katy had fallen back to earth with a thud. She'd once thought she and Ash were a team. Look how *that* had turned out.

And, seriously, what did it matter? She had no time for romance with *any* man. Even if Blaine weren't a flirt, even if he were a saint who rescued baby ducks from storm drains every day of the week, she couldn't spare a second for him today. She needed to focus on this wedding day's many problems and get this event over with.

She reached the bride's suite and hesitated. The biggest problem of the moment was telling Lindsay she'd have no one to do her hair or take pictures of her big day. Maybe no justice of the peace since Katy hadn't been able to get in touch with him. She had no idea how Lindsay would take this news but suspected it wouldn't be pretty.

Bracing herself, Katy knocked on the door then entered.

Inside, the bridesmaids were in various stages of putting on their makeup and getting dressed. Some still wore their jeans and tee shirts. Some had already been zipped into their gowns, red velvet tea-length dresses with bell-like skirts and crinoline slips right out of the 1950s. A silky green sash around the waist and a head-piece adorned with holly and plastic candy canes finished the outfit. The style shouldn't work, but somehow it did. The dresses were lovely. And extra Christmassy.

The bridal party's giddiness of just a half hour ago had fizzled. A grim silence hung over the suite, broken only by the *ding* of cell phones and the groans of bridesmaids as they read texts Katy knew were delivering bad news. Lindsay stood in the center of the room, with two of her attendants helping her into a silky, full-length white slip. She flinched at every new ding and moan, like a boxer taking a barrage of blows in slow motion.

Katy made her way to the maid of honor. Jackie, wearing a red slip that fell to mid-calf, stood in front of the tri-fold mirror, applying mascara.

"How's it going?" Katy whispered.

"Not well," Jackie whispered back, meeting her gaze in the mirror. "Practically everyone's cancelled."

That would explain Lindsay's tragic expression. Katy touched Jackie's shoulder. "Hang in there," she said with more pluck than she felt.

"Oh, I'll be okay." She turned to Katy. "I teach first grade. I've lived through a thousand tantrums and bathroom catastrophes and that smartass kid who decides to tell the whole class Santa Claus isn't real." She jerked her chin toward the bride. "It's her I'm worried about."

You and me both.

The bridesmaids helped Lindsay put on a red dressing gown over her slip then ushered her to one of the makeup chairs. Katy followed but froze in her tracks when the bride speared her with a desperate look.

"*Where* have you been?" she demanded.

Everyone's attention snapped toward them. The room fell quiet. Even the phones stopped dinging. The muffled strains of the song Ash played downstairs was the only sound. "I'll Be Home for Christmas," exactly where Katy wished she could be right now.

"Did you get in touch with my stylist?" Lindsay asked hopefully. "What about my photographer?"

The bridesmaids twittered nervously. Katy wrung her hands and tried to swallow, but there seemed to be a giant stone stuck in her throat. She remembered what Todd had said about his fiancée's intensity. She'd felt it herself in that rib-cracking hug. Lindsay was stressed to the breaking point and what Katy had to say would no doubt push her over the edge.

But it had to be done.

"I spoke to them," she began slowly then delivered the rest in a rush. "I'm sorry, but they're both unable to come. The roads are really bad, with lots of accidents snarling traffic. The storm's worse than anticipated. The state police are asking people to stay home unless travel's absolutely necessary." Katy hauled in a breath, relieved she'd gotten it all out.

Lindsay's shoulders sagged so low they nearly touched the carpet. "What about my cake?" she pleaded. "Tell me *that* made it here at least. It was supposed to be delivered this morning."

Katy flushed as the cake-moving adventure and those breathless minutes with Blaine shot into her mind. Being near him, laughing with him, the feel of his chest against hers as she brushed by him in the pantry…

Lindsay let out a squeak of alarm. "You look upset. Don't tell me the cake's not here either."

Katy snapped out of her Blaine haze. Would she ever be able to focus her mind on anything but him? "No," she stammered. "I mean, yes, it's here. The cake's here."

Lindsay lightened up a fraction. "At least *something* is going right." She wrung her hands. "I can't believe it's snowing," she moaned, with a lot less enthusiasm than when she'd hopped off the bus a short time ago. "And now I've got no one to take pictures. No one to fix my hair."

She aimed another desperate look at Katy. Did Lindsay expect *her* to do her hair? She was no stylist and that would be a disaster anyway. She'd tried to style Maggie's hair once years ago and her sister had ended up looking like a circus clown who'd been attacked by a bear.

"*I* can do your hair," Jackie piped up.

"And we'll take pictures," Candy blurted. Lindsay swung her chair toward her. Candy trembled like a frightened Chihuahua but bravely rolled on. "We'll take pictures of you and Todd and everything. All of us will. We'll take tons and tons of pictures."

Katy jumped in. "Seriously, Lindsay, you have a lot of bridesmaids." Ten in all, counting Jackie. A veritable army of attendants. "Why are they here if not to help you? Put 'em to work. Let Jackie do your hair. Let Candy and Angela and Joy and everyone else take pictures."

Angela, a curvy white woman with towering blonde hair, shot Katy a *leave me out of this* look, but Joy and Candy nodded like agreeable bobble heads.

Lindsay hesitated. Her troubled gaze flitted around the suite, touching on each member of her attendant entourage before coming back to Katy. She seemed to teeter on a wire between quiet misery and a full-on volcanic eruption.

Time to play the groom card. "I spoke to Todd a little while ago," Katy said. "He says he knows the snow and everything else is probably stressing you out. He wanted me to tell you to keep calm, Christmas is coming. And that he loves you."

That did the trick. The sun broke through the storm clouds on Lindsay's face. She smiled the smile of a woman in love with a man who knew her inside and out. A throb of envy rose in Katy's throat. Even in their most compatible moments, she'd never felt such a connection with Ash. Or any other guy she had dated.

"Todd's such a good soul," Lindsay murmured. She dabbed tears off her eyelashes with her thumb and looked up at Katy. "And you're an angel. I'm so, so sorry I yelled at you. I don't know what came over me. Well, I do know. I just take everything too much to heart. Todd calls me his marshmallow. I think that's why I went into accounting. The numbers aren't soft. They're solid. They don't worry you or leave you or snow on you. If they come out wrong, you can fix it. No drama, no emotion. Do you see?"

Katy nodded. She did see. Lindsay had turned to math and crunching numbers the same way she and Maggie had become obsessed with planning. Something they could control in a world too frequently out of control.

Lindsay sat back in the chair and faced forward. "All right, ladies, time to get going. Jackie, let's see what you can do with my hair."

Everyone visibly relaxed as Jackie hurried over. "I'll need a hairbrush, hairspray, and some bobby pins," she called out, the seasoned teacher corralling her kids. "Oh, and a styling wand and blow-dryer. Does anyone have any of that stuff?"

A manic search through handbags, closets and drawers ensued, turning up twelve hairbrushes, thirty-five scrunchies, three eyelash curlers, two tubes of styling gel, one can of hairspray, and enough makeup to face-paint *RuPaul's Drag Race* for a year. But no styling wand or blow-dryer. No surprise. The stylist would typically bring that kind of equipment to a job.

Katy scrambled to solve this problem before the bride

crashed again. "Lindsay, why don't you do your makeup," she said. "I'll ask around downstairs. Maybe one of your aunties is packing a blow-dryer."

Lindsay agreed and Katy headed for the door.

"Wait a sec." Jackie rushed over and caught Katy before she could leave. "See if you can find more hairspray. This is almost empty." She shook a silver can labeled *Texturizing Spray*. "And *hurry*. We've got to get her dressed and ready. We're already a half hour behind schedule."

Forty minutes, actually. Katy hadn't lost track of that, despite the Blaine distractions.

She left the suite and headed down the hallway, wondering where she could find what Jackie needed. She didn't want to call Maggie again. Knowing her sister, she'd drag herself out of bed and brave the snow to drive up here with ten boxes full of styling supplies. She'd ask the Parkers. They'd know if there was a blow-dryer hiding anywhere in the building. If not, Lindsay would have to do without.

Katy dashed downstairs. A rumble of conversation and Elvis Presley's "Blue Christmas" rose up to meet her. The big room bubbled with activity as the guests moved about, socializing. Some of the table decorations had been knocked over. Todd had somehow ripped his tux and his groomsmen were pacing back and forth in front of the bar like sharks on the hunt.

She spotted Ash at his soundboard, chatting with two young women dressed like they'd just come from filming the movie *White Christmas*—low-cut red dresses trimmed in white, with a dusting of snowflakes across the skirts. Ash conjured a coin from behind one woman's ear and presented it to her with a flourish and a smile. Both women giggled.

Ash had pulled that magic trick on Katy the night they'd met. She remembered the feel of his fingers as they brushed her ear and slipped through her hair, and how special that smile had made her feel. Now she knew she hadn't been special at all. Now she knew it had all been an act.

She moved on before he could spot her and went on the hunt for Newell's caretakers. She found them both by the fireplace. Mrs. Parker sat at a table, playing gin rummy with Lindsay's grandmother. Mr. Parker had settled in for a long winter's nap in a nearby chair and not even the crackling, gas-powered Yule log or Lindsay's dad, talking on the phone, seemed to disturb him.

"That's great," Mr. Lathrop said, moving the Santa Claus figurines around on the fireplace mantel like chess pieces. "Tell Rudolph I'll shout with glee if he can get this thing off the ground."

Making a note to put the figurines back in proper order later, Katy interrupted the ladies' card game and quickly explained Lindsay's hair emergency. Mrs. Lathrop pawed through her handbag, a big blue satchel with a silver clasp. Katy wouldn't have been surprised if the old gal pulled a blow-dryer or even a three-ring circus out of the bag, but the only useful things she came up with were a comb, a vintage hairnet, and several holiday appropriate red-and-white striped peppermint candies.

"Try the junk room," Mrs. Parker said, picking up a card and discarding another. "It's full of lost and found items, mostly sweaters and party gifts and whatnot.

Things guests forgot and never came back for. You might find a curling iron or some such if you look."

Or maybe some hairspray. "And the junk room is…where?"

"You've got to go through the kitchen to get there. Down the hallway toward the back. *Aha!*" She slapped her cards on the table, jangling the bells on her silvery brooch and awarding more angels their wings. "That's gin! Pay up, Carol."

"Ivy, you devil!" Mrs. Lathrop cried. She scraped the cards across the table toward her and began to shuffle the deck. "Shall we go for best two out of three?"

Thanking the women, Katy left them to their competition and wended through the tables toward the kitchen. Excitement built with every step she took, so she paused at the now-closed door to get a grip on herself, vowing to stay cool in Blaine's presence.

Or at least attempt to.

She entered the kitchen and the door swished into place behind her. A hundred delicious smells enveloped her, including bacon and the buttery scent of some kind of bread baking.

Blaine stood at the island at the center of the brightly lit room, a mountain of vegetables on a cutting board in front of him. He'd slung a crisp white towel over his shoulder and put on his chef's hat. Katy had always thought those puffy hats looked silly, but not on him. *He* looked hot. Like a boss. A kitchen boss. Light flashed off the knife he held as he chopped green and red peppers so fast, she wondered how he didn't take his fingers off. He hadn't been kidding when he'd said his knives were sharp.

"What's happening? Anything I can help you with?" he asked without looking up.

"Do you know how to do a French braid?" she said, struggling to keep her vow. Hard to stay cool and detached when the mere sight of him got her pulse sprinting and her temperature soaring again.

"Is that some kind of pastry?" he asked.

"No. That was my way of saying the bride's stylist has cancelled and she's got no one to do her hair. I'm here to look for do-it-yourself supplies." Katy gestured to the hallway on the far side of the kitchen, determined to head that way. Her candy cane shoes had other ideas and moved her toward Blaine instead. "The photographer is out too. I'm also afraid the bartender isn't going to make it either."

Nodding, Blaine put down the knife and tossed the chopped peppers into a large skillet, then added sliced mushrooms to the mix. Spices and olive oil followed and within seconds the mixture simmered over the gas flame. The scent of cilantro and garlic drifted up, joining the rest of the kitchen's enticing smells.

"Probably not the best time to tell you the waitstaff's not coming," he said, stirring the bubbling mixture with a long-handled wooden spoon. "One of my assistants isn't going to make it either. Got stuck in the snow."

Katy sighed. "I think the snow's stopped everyone."

"On the bright side, the chimney sweep managed to get here," he said.

"Seriously? *That's* the bright side?"

"*You* seemed happy he's here."

Happy? That was the last word she'd use to describe

seeing Ash. Was Blaine teasing her again? Or trying to rile her? Both were skills he excelled at. Almost as much as his skill at making her knees go weak with a single look.

Eyes on the skillet, he said, "If it helps any, *I'm* here."

Definitely trying to rile her. "Thanks," she said, her lips twitching. "That's a *great* comfort."

"Ouch. That sarcasm bomb hit the target." He shifted and pinned his gaze on her. "What I mean is, I'm here to help, so don't panic. I can take on serving duties. And my assistant Daisy can help too when she gets here. So don't worry about the food. You focus on getting the bride and groom hitched."

"Oh, thanks, but I—" she began then snapped to a stop, cutting off her standard *I've got this under control* dismissal. Because truthfully, she didn't. She *needed* help today. All the help she could get. And Blaine had just the right size shoulders for her to lean on.

"Thanks, I appreciate that," she said, more genuine this time. "Though getting those two married might be a problem. The justice of the peace is late. If Nicholas Jolly doesn't get here soon, there won't be a wedding at all."

"Nicholas Jolly? You're kidding me. A guy named Nicholas Jolly, at a Christmas wedding?" His eyes twinkled. "Is Mr. Jolly old? Is he a saint? Do they call him Nick?"

She snorted a laugh. Really, he was the most unpredictable and ridiculous man she'd ever met. "I haven't been gifted with that information. I only know the man isn't here. And we can't have a wedding until he is."

"Good point. Have you tried calling him?"

"Yes, Captain Obvious, I've called him. Several times. He's not picking up."

"Could be a landline," he said. "Jolly Old St. Nick might've already left the house and missed the call."

"I—" She stared at him with wide eyes. Could she be a bigger dope? "I hadn't thought of that. Not many people have those kinds of phones anymore."

"Guess that confirms he's old. The jury's out on whether he's a saint."

Another gurgle escaped her lips. This guy had an amazing talent for making her laugh. And for keeping her from pushing the panic button. Not to mention making her heart go pitter-patter. Katy planned to have a long talk with her sister when she'd recovered. She'd totally misjudged the man.

A brief silence fell. She really needed to get to her task, but still didn't move. Outside, the wind blew in fierce gusts and sleety snow tapped against the windows, but inside, here with Blaine, everything felt cozy and warm. Comfortable. Except for the disorganized mess of his equipment and supplies strewn about the kitchen. *That* she itched to put in order.

Katy spotted the *Mistletoe* wine on the side counter, hiding between two stacks of salad bowls and she grinned. "I see you're flaunting your stolen goods in plain sight."

His expression turned apologetic. "I told you, the wine is for the beef tenderloin. An Italian recipe, a perfect winter entrée. Some rosemary and onions, and a splash of sparkling wine. The bubbles effervesce when cooked, and the beef's flavor pops."

"Well, if it's for today's event, I suppose I can forgive your thievery." She watched him swirl the spoon through the simmering mixture with slow, almost sensual strokes. "Where did you learn to cook like this?"

"Johnson & Wales," he said. "No, that's not right. I learned *technique* there. My grandmother taught me the art, taught me the true love of cooking. I spent a lot of time at her house when I was a kid since both my parents worked. Mémé cooked like a madwoman, as if she were feeding an army, instead of just her grandkids. Come to think of it, we *were* an army. Anyway, she taught me everything she knows."

"Your grandmother sounds amazing," she said, touched by the gruff affection in his voice. He obviously loved his grandmother and loved cooking just as much. "Can I tell you my most horrible secret?"

"What? You're a criminal on the run, operating under an alias?" His dimples flashed as he smiled. She hadn't seen them in a while. In this instance, absence truly made the heart grow fonder.

"Worse than that," she said, ignoring the shimmer that skipped down her spine. "I can't cook. Not at all. My parents tried to teach me when I was young, but I didn't have the skills. I burn water, even with a recipe. My sister's the cook in the family. Everything comes out perfect. She makes these Portuguese sweet rolls that are to-die-for. A recipe passed down on my dad's side of the family. But me? Well, when the smoke detector goes off, I know that means it's done."

"Not everyone's cut out to be a cook," he said. "Which is a good thing for people in my business. We need someone to eat the food we make." He adjusted the flame under the skillet. "What do you do when you meet up with friends and have to bring a dish? Takeout?"

"Oh, I just bring wine. White wine, of course. When it's not being stolen from me." He rumbled a laugh that got her spine shimmering again. She quickly turned her attention to the mixture he stirred with great care. "What *are* you making?"

He drew himself up and his good humor dimmed. "This is filling for one of the appetizers. Vegetarian tortilla cups with portabella and a touch of garlic, one of my specialties. I usually make it with carrots but went for red and green peppers in the spirit of the season. The pastry cups are in there." He tilted his head toward one of the two ovens. "The bacon-wrapped lobster bites are in the other oven. When they're ready, I'll brush them with maple syrup. *Then* I'll start on the cranberry chicken, risotto, and the beef." He gestured to two big silver bowls full of greens on the side counter. "The salad is already prepped."

His voice bordered on prickly as he went through the menu. Katy couldn't figure out why. Everything seemed to be coming along nicely, and he was mostly on schedule, unlike the rest of today's wedding spectacle. He had nothing to get defensive about.

"Sounds good." She leaned forward and inhaled the tantalizing scents floating up from the skillet. "Smells good too."

"Good?" He shot her the most delicious scowl she'd seen yet. "Good is what you call fast food and frozen meals. What I cook is not *good*." He sputtered, endearingly frustrated. "That's not what I mean." He stopped again. "I mean… Let me show you."

He scooped up a spoonful of veggie mix, circled around the island, and moved in so close to her, Katy's insides twittered in alarm. And delight.

"Here, taste it," he coaxed. "Then tell me it's just *good.*"

She heard uncertainty in his voice. He'd been so brash when it came to taking charge of the shoveling, running in to save her from Ash, and ordering her and everyone else around, his defensiveness now surprised her. Was he really that insecure about his cooking skills? Maggie had said his company was one of the most sought-after caterers on the Maine coast. Perhaps that success wasn't enough to wash away his self-doubt.

She knew how that felt, though after the way her year had gone, she was unfamiliar with the *success* part. But the insecurities she understood. Didn't she always blame herself when a plan fell through?

"I'm sure it's delicious," she murmured as he lifted the spoon to her lips.

Delicious turned out to be an understatement. An explosion of flavor filled her senses as she took a bite. Cilantro, garlic, and other spices she couldn't name bombarded her taste buds. An indescribable blend of sweet and spicy. She felt the warmth of his hand as he held the spoon to her mouth, his other hand cupped beneath her chin to capture any drips. He watched her, seeming to hold his breath as she ate.

"Oh, my, that's…good," she said. He frowned and she relented with a giggle. "I mean, *really* good. *Immensely* good. *Enormously* good."

"Wise ass." He flashed a smile so pleased and so lusciously hot her toes threatened to curl. "The secret is to lightly spice the veggies, chop them fine and top the whole thing with a dollop of sour cream. Wait, you've got a..."

He touched the corner of her mouth with his thumb, dabbing away a spot of juice. His thumb lingered. His smile faded, replaced with a smolder that scalded Katy from head to toe. Champagne bubbles skipped along her skin and all inhibition abandoned her.

That all-powerful K-word invaded her brain. She longed for him to kiss her. Willed him to kiss her. *Invited* him to kiss her, with a slight tilt of her head and the merest parting of her lips. She shivered, anticipating. Excited and terrified at the same time.

"Damn it," he growled, breaking the spell. He sounded stern, and not at all pleased. "That stuff must be following us around."

Katy didn't have to look up to see what had set him off. *Mistletoe.* Right overhead. Again. And Blaine completely uninterested in answering the call. While she'd practically thrown herself at him.

All thoughts of kissing fled, and Katy flushed in embarrassment. How could she have lost her head like that? Horrified, she backed away slowly, as if she could rewind the last few minutes and start again. She bumped into one of the chairs at the table.

"Excuse me," she said. To Blaine or the chair, she couldn't be sure. "I'm sorry, I've got to get back to...to..." To what? Why had she come into the kitchen in the first place?

Blaine's blue eyes blazed. "Yeah, I've got to..." He waved toward the stove. "To whatever."

Katy didn't stick around to hear any more. She dashed down the hallway toward the junk room, her thoughts whirling. Had she imagined that aching expression on his face? As if he wanted to kiss her as much as she wanted to kiss him. Had she been mistaken? Had she let her imagination run away with her? Maybe. Probably. Her emotions were a mess, what with Christmas and the inevitable longing for her parents, and Ash here, bringing back bitter memories. She was vulnerable, not to mention stressed.

And yet...

Something had sparked between them. She'd call it chemistry except she didn't have a clue about how that worked. She'd done so poorly in the subject in school her teacher had thrown up his hands, gave her a D+, and promptly retired to Arizona. So yeah, not so keen on chemistry or any of the other combustive sciences, but that had to be the only explanation for the heat she felt building between them. He'd felt it, she knew he had.

The rational side of her brain tossed cold water on the bonfire of her thoughts. It didn't matter if he was as attracted to her as she was to him. Or if she'd felt herself warming to him, connecting to him in a way she never had with any other man.

If Blaine was anything like Ash, she knew she could never trust him.

CHAPTER TEN

$\mathcal{C}$ole watched Maggie disappear down the narrow hallway, barely able to think. Barely able to breathe.

What in hell had just happened? An electric moment, sizzling with energy. The sensual way she'd pulled those veggies off the spoon and into her mouth, her rapturous expression. He'd never been so turned on watching someone eat as he had been watching her. That it was something *he* had cooked made it even more amazing.

The urge to kiss her had nearly overwhelmed him. And when he'd touched the soft corner of her mouth to wipe off some liquid, he almost had. The way she'd gazed at him, the way she'd parted her lips, seeming so warm and willing, he could've sworn Maggie wanted to kiss him back. But he was so out of practice with women he couldn't be sure. He could've sworn Celia wanted to marry him, too.

And then, damn it all, the mistletoe. The shrubbery that encouraged a man to sweep a woman into his arms and kiss the living daylights out of her made him do the opposite. He'd pushed away and shut down.

Why? Because his pulse jumped when he looked at her. Every time she smiled. She made him laugh. That absurd sweater and her even more ludicrous shoes tugged at his heart. The way she stressed over every little detail activated his inner fix-it man, the part of him that never saw a problem he didn't want to move heaven and earth to fix.

And he liked her. A *lot*. That explained his mistletoe aversion. He wanted to get to know her better. Wanted a kiss, if it ever occurred, to be more than just him acting on impulse. He wanted it to mean something.

If she was even interested.

Cole had seen the way the deejay had looked at her, as if she were a plate of freshly baked baklava served up especially for him. When Cole had busted in on Maggie and Ash earlier, thinking she needed his help, she clearly hadn't appreciated the interruption. Cole suspected they wouldn't be exes for long.

He stomped back to the stove, pushing her and her tempting lips out of his brain. He had a lot of tasks to focus on today and not one of them involved kissing the event manager. He turned down the flame under the veggies and covered the skillet. He checked on the lobster bites then went to mix up the salad dressing so it could chill. Blueberry vinaigrette. Couldn't have a Maine wedding without lobster and blueberries, even in the winter.

Good is fast food and frozen meals. Had he really said that to her? What an egotistical thing to say. A Blaine thing to say. Cole had never needed his ego pumped up like a tire with a slow leak, like Blaine did. Why had he felt the need to prove himself to Maggie?

He stuck the salad dressing in the fridge and went back to the stove when he heard jingle bells. Not the song. The deejay was playing something non-holiday at the moment, music that didn't jingle, but jangled the nerves. Especially at such a high volume. Poor Mrs. Lathrop's eardrums had probably exploded.

The jingle bells came from outside and were getting closer. Had the sleigh driver from earlier come back to wreak more havoc? Or Santa Claus searching for that sack of gifts he'd misplaced?

Cole stepped to the door and flung it open to see not Santa on the doorstep, but Daisy, who had, to his relief, finally made it here through the storm. A petite Black woman with laughing eyes, she'd gone all-in for the holiday, dressed head to toe in an elf's costume—green tights, green handbag, a peaked green cap over her short black hair, green elf shoes with curled toes, and a candy cane striped scarf and belt circling her slim waist. Plus, tiny silver bells that dangled from every part of her outfit.

"Ho-ho-ho!" she gurgled, grinning from ear to ear.

"Isn't that Santa's line?" He ushered her inside before the storm winds could blow a snowdrift into the kitchen.

"Oh, Cole, must you be a grouch all year round?" The bells on Daisy's costume jingled as she brushed snow from her shoulders and stamped her feet. "Don't you have any Christmas spirit?"

"Not at the moment. I'm fresh out."

"You're a regular old Scrooge, you know that?" More

jingling as she unwound the scarf and tossed it alongside her handbag on a chair by the door.

"Bah, humbug," he said, then lightened up. "I'm glad you made it, safe and sound." To punctuate his relief, he pulled her into a quick hug. He had to reach down because she was pretty short. She was also ice cold. "Why aren't you wearing a coat?"

"I wanted you to get the full elf effect." She checked out the kitchen with an approving gaze. "Nice digs. What do you want me to do first?"

Cole didn't hesitate. "Check on the tortilla cups." He gestured toward one of the ovens. "You can start stuffing them as soon as they're ready."

Daisy went to the sink to wash her hands. "Whatever you say, you're in charge."

"Today, anyway."

"What do you mean?" She glanced back at him over her shoulder. "You run the show *all* the time. Think I'd take orders from Blaine? He doesn't know a scallion from a scallop."

Cole quirked a smile. He and Daisy had worked together at a restaurant before signing on with Blaine. Cole had recommended her, in fact. He fully intended to take her with him—and Liza too—when he got his own place. When and if that dream ever became a reality.

Daisy tugged a red apron dotted with Christmas trees out of her purse and put it on. "Where's the cake?" she asked, tying the apron strings. "Got to get a look at that sucker."

He jerked his head toward the door. "It's in the dining room. You can admire it later. Let's get this party started."

He went back to the stove. She jingled to the oven. She opened the door and heat wafted out. So did the smell of the pastries inside, three trays full, one tray on each oven rack.

She peered inside then closed the oven door. "Oops, these guys aren't ready to party yet. Not quite done."

Cole tensed at a tapping sound coming from the hallway. Maggie's shoes on the tile. She popped into view a second later, carrying a small cardboard box with what looked like a blow-dryer on top.

"Did you find what you were searching for?" he asked, watching her move gracefully across the kitchen toward the door.

She stopped and gazed at him. "Um, yes, I did," she said, cool and distant, as if they hadn't almost locked lips seconds ago. She turned to Daisy and spoke in a much warmer tone. "I see Santa Claus has sent us one of his elves. Glad you got here safely."

"It was a heck of a trip from the North Pole." Daisy shook the bells on her belt. "But I made it."

"Armed with enough bells to give a thousand angels their wings today," Cole said, his eyes on Maggie. She responded with a hint of a smile. More than a hint, actually. Enough to whip up his pulse rate again.

"Those are some sassy shoes," Daisy said to Maggie, then shifted her gaze toward the windows. "The parking lot's awful empty. Did anyone else show up? Any of the guests?"

Maggie shook her head. "Not since the buses from the hotel dropped off the wedding party. Not a single person."

"Hey, it's not like *you're* personally responsible for the

weather," Cole said, too gruff, but he couldn't help himself. She took the *manager* part of event manager way too literally and tended to blame herself for things she couldn't control. It frustrated Cole to no end—because he couldn't do anything to fix it.

Maggie shifted the box under her arm. "Well, I better get back upstairs."

Cole beat her to the door and yanked it open, holding it so she could pass through. "Let me know if you need anything or if I can do anything," he said, feeling awkward, and acutely aware of Daisy watching them.

"Yes, I will," she said softly, a guarded look in her eyes, and then she was gone.

"*That's* the event planner?" Daisy asked as soon as the door swung back into place. "I expected to see her riding a broom, from the way you sounded on the phone." She arched an eyebrow pierced with a tiny silver bell. "And you sure don't act like you think she's a witch."

"Leave it alone, Daisy." Cole moved back to the stove, his expression as placid as he could manage. He didn't want her to see him so unsettled. He didn't want to feel so unsettled.

"You like her, Cole," she said, giggling.

"I do *not* like her." He frowned. He sounded like a sixth grader denying he had a crush on the teacher, when he absolutely did.

"Yes, you do. And want to know something? I think she likes you too. I mean, you talked to each other like distant relatives, but the non-verbal stuff between you was off the chain. So hot, I almost grabbed the fire extinguisher to put you out."

"You're imagining things—" *Wait.* What did she say? Could Maggie like him? Did she feel the same way he did? *Had* she wanted to kiss him moments ago? No, not possible.

"How can I imagine something right in front of my eyes?" Daisy took a number of serving trays out of a box and brought them to the counter along the inner wall. "I think there's some chemistry going on there."

Cole scoffed. "I don't have time for that kind of thing. We're in the middle of a job."

"Yeah, okay. I've heard that ever since Celia. You're always in the middle of a job. Or wrapping up the last job or planning the next one. Truth is you're afraid to take a risk on someone new. News flash, Cole, not every woman is Celia. Thankfully."

"What does that mean?" He grabbed the spoon to stir the veggie mix, though it didn't need stirring.

"No offense, you almost married her, but she wasn't all that. Kind of on the selfish side. And totally wrong for you. Plus, none of us liked her, especially your grandmother."

That was news to him. His grandmother had seemed to welcome Celia with open arms. "Why is this the first time I'm hearing about this?"

"I think the veggies are done." Daisy came over and relieved him of the spoon, replacing the skillet's cover. "Your grandmother didn't want you to find out she felt that way. Afraid you'd be hurt, I guess. Grandmothers are like that, you know."

Cole grimaced. His grandmother didn't like Celia, but she'd kept her mouth shut about it? Daisy, Liza, his parents, no one from his family had said a word. He wished they had. Could've saved him from making a huge mistake.

Or would it? That likely would've made him dig in more. Before Celia, he'd never been serious with anyone. Sure, he'd had fun dating. A lot of fun. But Celia was the first woman he'd been with long-term. They had their problems, but he'd been determined to make the relationship work. His inner mule wouldn't let him accept failure. That's why Blaine's criticisms sparked his anger, why he'd gotten so defensive with Maggie about the menu. And why he'd been dragging his feet on moving forward with his restaurant.

Cole straightened. Was that the real reason he'd backed off from kissing Maggie? Fear she'd reject him?

"So, there you have it, my two cents." Daisy returned to the side counter and switched on the heat lamps that hung overhead then began to line up the serving trays in a neat row. "Time for you to move on. You need more than your dog for companionship. And speaking of Lily, what did you do with her today? You didn't leave her home alone—" She broke off as shouting erupted in the function hall and frowned at Cole. "What's that about? Did the Patriots just lose a big game?"

Cole rushed to the door and flung it open to see a bunch of the groomsmen tossing a football around. "Not exactly."

"I'm open," Todd called as he darted between two tables. One of his buddies flung the ball and Todd leapt up, reaching for it. He missed, colliding with a chair as he came down. Both the groom and the chair crashed to the floor.

Gasps shot around the room. Cole winced. The guy hadn't been born with a banana peel under his foot, as Maggie had said. An entire banana tree seemed to be stapled there. Todd already had a limp, a black eye, a bruise on the side of his head, a torn tuxedo, and now a new injury—he cradled his left arm to his side and grunted in pain as two of his friends helped him up.

Cursing under his breath, Cole moved back to the stove and turned off the flame under the skillet. "Daisy, mix up the sour cream and get those apps ready to go as soon as the pastries are done. Things are getting out of hand out there. We're serving the appetizers now."

"Before the ceremony? Blaine would lose it to hear we'd gone off schedule."

So would Maggie, Cole figured, but speeding things up would be in service to a good cause. "Who cares? I'm in charge, right? The schedule's shot anyway. We need to get some food into those boneheads to settle them down. Especially the groom. He's on track to end up in a body cast before he can say I do."

"Sounds like a plan." She hurried to the oven and every bell on her outfit rang like a jingle bell chorus. "Want me to go tell the wedding coordinator about the change in plans?"

"No. *I'll* go tell her." He pulled off his *toque blanc* and dropped it onto the table.

"Oh, really? Aren't you too busy for that kind of thing?"

Yes. Yes, he was. So why was he so eager to run an errand his elf assistant could handle? Why did he find himself heading for the door, with anticipation flooding his veins, making his pulse race at a marathon level?

Because he wanted to be near her again.

"Oh, yeah, Cole. There's *nothing* between you and the event lady at all," Daisy said, and her laughter followed him all the way across the dining room.

COLE TOOK the stairs two at a time. He moved swiftly past a jungle of poinsettias and down the hallway toward the bridal party's ready room. When he heard voices coming from the closed door, uncertainty gripped him. He slowed his steps.

"Bad plan," he muttered. Beyond the chance to see Maggie, he hadn't thought this through. The bride might not appreciate him barging in on her territory. He started to pivot when the ready room's door flew open and a mass of bridesmaids spilled out, bringing with them the smell of perfume and orange juice.

Cole froze in his tracks. The women were a vision in Christmas red—red headpieces speckled with tiny candy canes and berries, the same red-and-white striped shoes Maggie wore, and red gowns with puffy sleeves and an even puffier skirt. They looked like red velvet cupcakes.

"Over there, near the flowers," a tall, freckle-faced redhead said, waving the others toward a massive poinsettia at the hallway's end. "The light's better there."

The cupcakes arranged themselves around the plant. The redhead aimed her phone in their general direction, ordered them to smile, and clicked off a bunch of pictures.

"Oh, hi there, cute stuff," a pretty blonde in the middle of the scrum said, noticing him. "What brings you up to no man's land?"

All eyes turned to him. He flinched, uncomfortable. He would have tugged at his coat's collar if it had one. "I'm the chef," he said. "I need to see Mag—"

"Ooh, the chef!" the redhead cried. She dove at him and latched onto his arm, tugging him toward the others. "Come on. We need a picture with the chef. Lindsay will *love* it."

He went, dragging his feet. Blaine lived for this kind of stuff, especially if it involved hot bridesmaids. Cole, not so much. He wasn't fond of schmoozing, even less fond of getting his picture taken. He posed stiffly as the women arranged themselves around him.

"Aw, don't look so glum," Redhead coaxed. "This is for Lindsay. You don't want a picture of her chef frowning in her wedding album, do you? How about a smile?"

He supposed he could put his inner introvert on hold and do as instructed. Considering it practice for when he had his restaurant and had to promote himself, he straightened and plastered a big, happy grin on his face. Suddenly, a slew of arms latched onto him like an overly friendly octopus. The blonde grabbed his arm and hugged it to her chest so tight she nearly cut off circulation. Her hat bounced on top of her hair mountain and repeatedly bopped him in the jaw.

The rest of the mob squeezed in close, grinning and giggling, as the redhead took about a thousand pictures. Cole's cheeks ached from smiling and he counted the seconds until he could break free from this red velvet torture.

"Having fun?" he heard from the suite's doorway.

Maggie stood there, her gaze lasered on him. Their almost-kiss shot back into his mind. Heat infused his blood, going from simmer to sizzle in two seconds flat. *Chill, Cole.* No matter what Daisy said, he had to remember that near kiss had been completely one-sided. Maggie had looked at him then as fiercely as she did now. Clearly *not* happy to see him up here, when he should be at work in the kitchen.

He shook off the blonde woman's ironclad hold and tried to escape the rest of the velvet octopus, but the redhead had other ideas.

"Let's get the wedding planner in the picture too," she trilled.

"Event manager, actually," Maggie said. "And no, Candy, I've got work to do."

"Relax for half a second." Candy pushed her toward the group. "We promised Lindsay we'd take pictures, and that's what we're going to do." She shoved Maggie next to Cole. "Now, everyone get cozy."

The cupcakes squished in again, jamming Maggie against Cole's side. The top of her head reached his ear and strands of her silky hair tickled his cheek. Even with all the other scents whirling around him, he found hers. His heart slammed against his ribs.

"I can't get everyone in," Candy said. "Get closer. Put your arms around each other."

Cole had wanted to put his arms around Maggie all

day, but here, with an audience, wasn't what he had in mind.

"Don't be shy," Candy scolded, her eyes on him.

Groaning inwardly, he slid his arm around Maggie's waist, bringing her soft, warm body against his side. He looked at her and their gazes caught. The bulbs on her sweater blinked steadily, lighting her face in a rainbow of color, drawing his attention to the smooth curve of her neck, her blushed cheeks, her eyes. Her lips, inches from his. A roaring blaze tore through him and his heartbeat nearly went nuclear.

"Ooh, that's the perfect pose," Candy said. "Now, say *mimosas!*"

No way could Cole manage a smile now. Not with Maggie pressed against him and the thoughts that raced through his brain.

She seemed unable to smile either. "*What* are you doing up here?" she demanded under her breath.

"Came to see *you,*" he bit off, wishing he'd stayed in the kitchen. Or had never left the house today. "But I got caught in a maze of bridesmaids."

"So I noticed." Her eyes snapped at him.

"Come on you two." Candy pouted. "Try to at least *pretend* you like each other. I want nothing but smiles for—"

A high-pitched shriek tore through the air. Bloodcurdling, worse than anything Cole had heard in a horror movie. It came from the ready room. Everyone abandoned their poses. Skirts swished and headpieces bounced as the bridesmaids sprinted into the suite.

Maggie ripped from Cole's embrace and ran after them. So did he.

Inside, the cupcakes swarmed around something in the far corner of the room. Maggie pushed through a wall of velvet to the front. Cole followed and saw the bride, seated in a chair in front of a mirror. She wore a slinky red bathrobe—and an expression of abject horror.

Cole's jaw dropped. Lindsay's hair was green. Bright, neon, St. Patrick's Day green.

"Jackie, what…what did you *d-o-o-o-o*…?" Lindsay wailed at the woman standing behind her, holding a can of hairspray.

"I-I don't know," Jackie cried, eyes wide in shock. "I don't know what happened!"

Lindsay leapt out of the chair and snatched the can from Jackie's limp hand. "You used novelty spray! You sprayed my hair with green gunk. It's my wedding day and my hair is *green*!" She hurled the can into a trash barrel with an angry huff.

"I thought it was just hairspray," Maggie whispered, mortified. She flashed to Cole. "Why didn't I look at the label more closely?"

Wouldn't have mattered. The spray can's label had worn away. Anyone could've confused it with the regular stuff. Maggie shouldn't blame herself for an honest mistake. He opened his mouth to tell her that when a bright light flashed off the mirror. Candy had snapped a picture.

Lindsay lost it. Her face flared as red as the robe she wore. "Candy! No pictures! Don't you dare Instagram that!" she shouted. "This is the *worst* day of my life!

Nobody's coming to my wedding. My hair's green, and... and..." She balled her fists and stamped her feet. "And I can't believe it's snowing!"

She burst into tears and fled into the bathroom, slamming the door.

A second of stunned silence before the drama kicked up again. Bridesmaids began to yell at each other. Drinks spilled, so did tears. Jackie glared at Maggie then stomped to the bathroom and pounded on the door, begging Lindsay to come out. The bride shouted at her to go away.

Cole ground his teeth. He gazed at Maggie. He felt bad for Lindsay, but he felt *really* bad for her. She looked like a cornered mouse.

"I suggest a strategic retreat," he said, close to her ear. "Let's get out of here."

"No, this is my mess, I have to fix it. I'm sure I can wash that green out of her hair. Or something."

Cole took her gently by the shoulders and turned her to him. Worry clouded her eyes and unshed tears balanced on her long lashes. "Hey," he said softly. "Don't be doing that. It was an accident. It's not your fault. No one's to blame. It's *not* your fault."

She leaned into his hold and her anxious expression softened some, but only for a second. She straightened and stepped back. "You'd better go now," she said.

Cole dropped his arms to his sides. She hadn't heard a word. He supposed he knew how she felt. After Celia had dumped him, he heard that *not your fault* line a hundred times, from his parents, his sisters, his grandmother. He hadn't listened to any of them. Whose fault was it, if not his? He'd spent two years blaming himself, as Maggie did now. Kicking himself for the mistakes made and his inability to fix whatever went wrong. He still was, in a way.

Maggie led him across the room, skirting handbags, makeup cases, and boxes on the floor, then turned to him at the door. "Thanks for coming up," she said. "Oh, wait. Why *did* you come up?" She braced, as if expecting a sucker punch.

Cole didn't hesitate. "I think the best way to keep the groom from killing himself, and his buddies from helping, is to get some food into them. I thought Daisy and I could serve the apps now, before the ceremony, instead of after. That might keep everyone occupied."

Maggie rubbed the back of her neck, something he'd seen her do before. She was stressed and trying not to lose her cool. "Sure, if you think that'll help," she said with a sigh. "Go ahead. Serve the appetizers as soon as you're ready."

"Which will be in just a few minutes." He smiled into her eyes. "You going to be okay?"

She gazed back at him, her expression alive with a hundred emotions he couldn't decipher. "Yes. I think I might be."

Suddenly, she hugged him. A hug so fast and fleeting he barely felt it, but powerful. Stunned and somewhat terrified by the feelings coursing through him, Cole gave Maggie an encouraging smile.

Then, though he hated like hell to abandon her, he did the only thing he could.

He left.

CHAPTER ELEVEN

"**Y**ou are *not* touching my hair again," Lindsay snapped, backing away from Jackie. She spun toward Katy. "And neither are *you*."

Katy's belly roiled with guilt. She'd spent the last ten minutes helping Jackie wash Lindsay's hair and trying to calm her down. The washing part had worked, the green was gone—mostly—but calm had not been restored. The bride was in a full-on meltdown and no amount of soothing or reminding her how much Todd loved her could stop it.

Lindsay sank into her chair and stared wanly at her reflection in the mirror, teardrops poking her eyes. She lifted the straggling ends of her wet hair. "Candy, see what *you* can do with this mess."

Candy gulped and crept over to the chair like a condemned woman. Jackie sighed in relief and retreated to the corner where the rest of the bridesmaids huddled. Katy retreated altogether. Because, what else could she do? She'd already done enough.

She went into the bathroom, gathered up the wet towels they'd used on Lindsay's hair then made her escape. The once white towels were now green. Katy had noticed a sink downstairs in the kitchen pantry. She'd soak the towels there, hoping the stains would come out. It they didn't, she'd pay for replacements. Which wouldn't be cheap, based on the plush thickness of the cloth. She did *not* want her sister to take the blame for her mistake.

Chuck Berry's "Run, Run Rudolph" blasted up from below as Katy hurried down the hallway. She clutched the soggy ball of towels, completely shaken by everything that had just happened. The green hair debacle. The odd possessiveness that bit her when she'd seen Blaine snuggle up to the bridesmaids. Then getting smushed against him during the photo shoot, the heat of his body against hers, his hand resting lightly on her back. His eyes burning with bold intensity.

The way he'd spoken to her after the hairspray incident had been the most unsettling thing of all. Calm, considerate. Caring. Different from the scowling chef who insisted his food was more than good. Or the funny guy who teased and joked with her or the sweet guy who'd spoken with such fondness about his grandmother. Or even the man whose nearness set her blood on fire.

In that moment, the steadiness of his gaze and the strength in his voice, something had shifted within her. Something beyond attraction or the impulse to kiss him whenever he got close. It went deeper than that. It felt almost as if she could trust him.

Her head spinning, she rushed downstairs and immediately thought about turning around when she saw Ash waving at her, bouncing up and down like he'd just spotted Santa Claus coming in for a landing on the Island of Misfit Toys.

Katy rolled her eyes. Hadn't *any* other deejay in all of Maine besides him been available to work today? Someone who wouldn't keep bothering her, desperate to get her attention. If only Ash had been more interested in being with her when they were dating, instead of turning his wandering eye on Sasha.

No, that wasn't entirely fair. They *both* could've paid more attention to each other, could've made their relationship more of a priority, instead of dead last after their jobs, Ash's weekly poker night and Katy's volunteering. She knew that now. When he'd ended it, Ash had said they'd grown apart, when in reality, they'd never been completely together.

Green water drops dripped from the towels, plopping onto her candy cane shoes. Katy needed to get them to the pantry and into the sink before she left puddles everywhere. Time to put Ash and all that emotional baggage in the past where it belonged and move on. Not such a difficult task, considering how her heart thumped like a happy dog's tail every time she thought of Blaine.

"I know what you're thinking," Mrs. Lathrop said, coming up to her, a wry grin on her face.

Katy flushed. "You do?"

"Your expression says it all."

"It does?" She should've known this shrewd matchmaking grandma would pick up on her growing interest in Blaine. Could anyone else see it?

"You're thinking that boy is the clumsiest young man that ever walked."

Oh. She meant Todd, not Blaine. Katy followed Mrs. Lathrop's gaze to see the groom stroll over to where Ash had set up his equipment. He limped like a peg-leg pirate, his arm propped in a sling of tied together cloth napkins, and the rest of him looking as rumpled and messy as Katy did after playtime with the rowdiest dogs in the shelter.

"He does seem to have more than his share of accidents," Katy said, trying to be diplomatic. And with relief —Todd was a problem out of her control.

Mrs. Lathrop gave a dainty snort. "An understatement, my dear. I sincerely hope he doesn't try to carry Lindsay over the threshold tonight. I'd fear for *both* their safety." She patted Katy's arm. "But complaining about my soon-to-be grandson isn't why I stopped you. May I beg a favor? I'm feeling a bit peckish. Famished, actually. Woozy, even. I barely ate a thing at the hotel earlier. You know that hotel food, so greasy and full of starch. Do you suppose the chef that tall, dark and good-looking chef could rustle me up a wee snack?"

"Of course. We'll be serving appetizers any minute now, but I'm sure he wouldn't mind giving you a preview. Come with me." Katy nodded at the bundle in her hand. "I'm headed to the kitchen to rinse these anyway. I had to mop up after some spilled drinks," she added quickly before Mrs. Lathrop could ask what happened. Katy didn't want to stress her any more than she had to. The bride was stressed enough for them both. For everyone.

"Splendid." She took Katy's free arm and tugged her forward with surprising strength for such a tiny thing.

As they reached the door, it swung open and the devil Mrs. Lathrop had just spoken of burst out, with a tall, pretty, athletic-looking woman of about thirty-five in tow. She had tawny skin, delicate facial features, and straight black hair with blue highlights, and she wore a heavy wool coat over black pants, a white dress shirt, and a red and green bowtie.

The anxiously awaited bartender, Katy thought, with an inner sigh of relief. One problem solved.

"Hi, I'm Natalia," the newcomer said, stuffing a pair of red mittens into her coat pocket and shaking Katy's hand. "Sorry I'm so late. This storm is brutal. If I had a sleigh, I would've been here an hour ago."

"Guess all the sleighs are spoken for tonight," Blaine said, flashing Katy a dimpled grin that would've made her sizzle if she wasn't trying so hard to be cool. She'd admit an attraction to him, and so much more, but she didn't have to advertise it by drooling over the man every time she saw him. Especially when Mrs. Lathrop watched them both with the intensity of a terrier waiting for a treat to drop.

"I'm glad you made it here in one piece," Katy said, focusing on Natalia and not those disarming dimples or those strong arms that had held her for too short a time upstairs. She gestured to Todd and the pack of groomsmen huddled around Ash's soundboard, bombarding him with music requests. "I have a feeling those guys will be extra glad to see you."

"I guess that's my cue." Natalia rubbed her hands together in anticipation. "Off to the bar." She shot Blaine a saucy smile. "I'll see *you* later. We need to catch up."

They bumped fists and he watched her go. "I know Natalia pretty well," he said, turning to Katy. "We've worked together before. She's a former marine. She'll keep those guys in check." His gaze dipped to the wet towels. "Looks like the de-greening went well." He held out his hands. "Let me take those."

"No, I'm good. Just point me toward a soak sink."

He dimpled again. "I think I can do that."

Mrs. Lathrop cleared her throat, a sound both annoyed and amused.

Katy bit her bottom lip, embarrassed. She'd forgotten about her companion's request for a snack. "Mrs. Lathrop's blood sugar is a little low and she needs something to eat. I was hoping you could help."

"Absolutely." Blaine leapt into action. He shoved the kitchen door inward and kicked the stopper into place to hold it open, then took Mrs. Lathrop's arm and escorted her to the table. Katy followed, feeling giddy and warm and melty all over. She loved how Blaine's inner George Bailey activated the moment he heard that someone needed help.

"I'm sorry to be such a bother," Mrs. Lathrop said, settling in her chair.

"No bother at all." Blaine went to the sink and washed his hands then headed for the stove. "How about a taste of the beef tenderloin? Lightly seasoned with a touch of white wine." He put on his chef's hat and tossed a couple pieces of beef into a small skillet, turning on the flame. "You also need to hydrate. Daisy, there's some bottled water in the fridge on your left."

Daisy, at the counter filling the cup-shaped pastries

with the vegetable mix, wiped her hands on a towel and moved to one of the refrigerators, jingling all the way.

"You see why I like him?" Mrs. Lathrop said in a low voice, looking up at Katy. "He's kind and thoughtful. And funny and friendly. I want to squeeze those dimples right off his face. And as I said, a man who can cook is a keeper."

Katy glanced at Blaine and couldn't hold back a smile. She agreed with everything on that list, except the dimples thing.

They belonged exactly where they were.

IN THE PANTRY, Katy dumped the towels into the sink. She plugged up the drain with the old-fashioned rubber stopper and twisted the spigots. Cold water gurgled as the tub filled, drowning out the conversation in the kitchen. She couldn't hear much beyond Blaine's deep rumble and the murmur of the women's voices.

The sink quickly filled. She swished the towels around, watching the water turn a festive Christmas green, her body humming with an excitement she hadn't felt in a long time. Mrs. Lathrop had sounded like the president of the Blaine Dillard fan club as she sang his praises moments ago. Giving Katy that sly look, as if trying to recruit her as the club's newest member. No need for the hard sell, she'd been a fan since the supermarket.

But was she ready to jump onto the Blaine train completely?

Leaving the towels to soak, and that question unanswered, she dried her hands and returned to the kitchen. Daisy focused on filling the pastry cups. Blaine worked at the stove, monitoring the pots and pans on the burners while drizzling maple syrup onto the bacon-wrapped lobster bites with the skill of a surgeon performing a delicate operation. The liquid hissed and popped as it hit the hot pan and a steamy maple smell wafted through the kitchen.

He glanced up and gave her a look that melted her insides like a snowball under a hot August sun. Would she *ever* have an interaction with the man that didn't involve some part of her sizzling, melting, or bursting into flames?

Mentally fanning herself, she turned to Mrs. Lathrop, who looked comfortable in her chair at the table, holding a bottle of the pricey designer water Maggie had insisted on keeping on hand.

"You good?" Katy asked. "I'm headed back up. Just want to make sure you're okay before I go."

"Won't you stay a bit? Chat with me a moment." She pushed out a chair with her foot. "Have something to eat. I'm sure our obliging chef will whip something up for you, too."

"Already on it," Blaine said, putting the appetizers aside and reaching for two plates. He carefully deposited a piece of beef onto each then tipped his gaze at Katy. "Sit down."

Well, if the chef insisted... She sat. "I'll stay for only a second. Lindsay needs me back up there." Not really. The bride would probably be glad if she never saw Katy's face again.

Blaine's arm brushed against hers as he placed a plate and some silverware in front of her, setting off internal fire alarms again. Katy mumbled something that might have been *thank you* as she struggled to get her raging thoughts to heel.

He moved on to Mrs. Lathrop and set the plate in front of her as if he were the palace chef and she was the queen.

"Thank you, young man." She picked up her utensils. "It looks scrumptious."

He brushed off her compliment with a wave and went back to the stove, but Katy saw him watching them both closely as they began to eat. She sliced into her beef, releasing a flood of simmering juices and a delectable aroma. She popped a piece into her mouth, savoring its tenderness and rich flavor, with just the barest hint of the wine.

Her stomach gave a grateful gurgle, and she gave Blaine a grateful smile. "This is good." She waited a beat. "*Enormously* good."

His lips quirked and he seemed to blush, but that could've been the heat. There were a lot of pans and skillets bubbling on that stove.

"Now don't you feel better?" Mrs. Lathrop asked, her eyes on Katy. "Steering a wedding can be exhausting and you can't do it if you die of anemia before the bride puts in an appearance. Speaking of the bride, how is my granddaughter doing? I'd go ask her myself, but I can't manage the stairs."

Blaine caught Katy's eye. A slight shake of his head and she knew they were on the same page about the green hair disaster. The less said about it the better.

"Lindsay's doing okay," Katy said. "She's a little stressed. A lot of people have cancelled because of the snow." And some were just missing, like the justice of the peace, who Katy feared had plowed into a snowbank on his way here.

"Poor Lindsay," Mrs. Lathrop said. "I think she got so wrapped up in the magic of a Christmas wedding, she never thought of the downside."

"She should've gotten married in Hawaii," Blaine said.

Mrs. Lathrop chuckled. "With Lindsay's luck, it would snow in Hawaii too." She popped the last bite of her beef into her mouth and pushed her plate away. "Ah, now that's what my mother would've called plate food. Fills the plate and fills the tummy." She dabbed at her lips with her napkin. "A shame only a few of us are here to enjoy it. There'll be so many leftovers. A terrible waste of food."

"Including a metric ton of cake," Daisy put in, loading the filled pastries onto trays lined up under a row of bright warming lamps.

"I can arrange to have whatever's left taken to a food pantry or soup kitchen," Blaine said. "If the bride okays it."

Katy lit up. "That's a great idea. I volunteer at Gray Street Food Pantry. I know the manager. I can contact her and see what she can take."

"When you speak to Inez," he said. "Tell her I can cook up whatever's left over from today or freeze it, her choice." Before Katy could ask how he knew the manager's name, he cut her off with a grin. "I volunteer at Gray Street too."

"Huh," she said, surprised yet not surprised to hear that news. There were so many layers to this man, each one more interesting and compelling than the last. Each layer drawing her closer.

"Quite commendable," Mrs. Lathrop's admiring gaze touched on them both. "It's inspiring when you young people take time from your busy lives to volunteer."

Always uncomfortable with praise—or pity—Katy flushed. Blaine looked equally uneasy.

"I don't do much," he said. "I pitch in for a few fundraisers, Thanksgiving, a couple other times of year when they need me." He kept his gaze pinned on the lobster bites he moved from the pan to a large silver serving tray. "Working in the food service industry, I see people struggling. Volunteering's my way of helping out in some small way. The true heroes are the food pantry's staff. They make a real difference in people's lives."

He glanced at Katy before going to retrieve another tray of lobster bites from the oven. Her throat went tight. She rarely talked about what Gray Street had done for her and Maggie. She'd never even mentioned it to Ash. Not because she was ashamed of needing help, but because she never knew how people would react. There were a lot of judgmental folks in this world.

Blaine wasn't one of them.

"Figures we'd have a storm today." Mrs. Lathrop cast an annoyed look at the windows, speckled on the outside with icy snow. "Lindsay planned this wedding for more than a year, but never a word about possible snow. It's been all about the big, splashy party. Lindsay thinks I'm old-fashioned, but I ask you, what's wrong with a small affair, a simple ceremony? When Wilfred and I got married at St. George's church, I had one bridal shower and seventeen people at the ceremony. Well, seventeen and a half since my sister Miriam had a baby on the way. Afterward, we had a lunch at my folks' house. Everything was simple, plain. A special day without much fuss."

"Bet you were a beautiful bride," Blaine said, ladling maple syrup onto the new batch of lobster bites.

"You're darned right I was. I wore a suit, bought from Filene's on sale. The color of cream, with pockets in the jacket." Mrs. Lathrop patted her hips, her face scrunched in thought. "No, perhaps there were no pockets. I don't remember. It was so long ago, and that suit is long gone. The hat's gone too, but oh, I remember it! A darling, shell-shaped thing, trimmed with cream-colored rosettes, and a puffy veil that brushed my nose." She squared her shoulders. "We wore *hats* back then, you know."

"My grandmother still wears a hat everywhere she goes," Blaine said. "She says it's more convenient than dyeing her hair." A corner of his mouth tugged upward. "She's a blonde. Has been a blonde for eighty-two years."

Katy smiled, picturing Blaine's feisty blonde grandmother, a little envious he had someone like her in his life.

"A wise and, I'm quite sure, fashionable woman," Mrs. Lathrop said. "We must meet up for tea."

"I bet she'd like that, but gotta warn you, she'll talk your ear off."

"Not if I talk first."

Laughing, he returned his attention to the appetizers.

"You about ready to get those out there?" he asked Daisy, nodding to the trays she had just about filled.

"In two shakes of a reindeer's tail," she said. "Hey, you never told me what Lily's up to with you gone for the day. She's not stuck at home?"

"No, she wouldn't stand for that," Blaine said. "She's getting pampered all day, then going to my grandmother's party tonight."

Katy stiffened. Lily? Who was Lily? Someone special, judging by the affection in his voice, the tender smile on his face. Could she be the woman who'd called him at the supermarket?

"Lucky girl." Daisy hoisted the trays and headed for the door. "I wish I could be partying with your family, instead of working Christmas Eve."

"I don't know. There's some perks to being here today," Blaine said, aiming those sparkling and oh-so-blue eyes at Katy.

She resolutely turned her gaze away. She had no claim on the guy, she barely knew him, but her belly stung with disappointment. Like he'd failed her somehow. She could kick herself for getting so wrapped up in her blistering thoughts and growing interest in him that she'd forgotten about his reputation. And what about Lily? Did she know Blaine had been running around here all day flirting with the bridesmaids? Pouring on the charm with Katy until she'd melted into a puddle at his feet?

"Are you all right, dear?" Mrs. Lathrop leaned toward her, her gaze keen on her face. "You look ill. Didn't something upset your stomach—?"

A loud *pop* and the kitchen went dark before she could

finish her question. Before Katy could cobble together an answer from her confused and confusing thoughts. Lights blacked out in the dining room, too. The Christmas tree lights winked off. So did the icicle lights draped along the walls and windows. The music from Ash's speakers abruptly died.

Cell phone flashlights popped on as disappointed cries rang out. Mrs. Lathrop let out a curse no respectable elderly woman should know. Lindsay's faint shriek of frustration echoed from the bridal suite upstairs. Katy wanted to shriek too. Or laugh. Hysterically. A power outage. What was next on the list of today's disasters? An alien invasion?

The muted gray light of the storm seeped through the snow-splashed kitchen windows. Katy's sweater and the stove's gas flame provided the only other illumination. Eerie shadows flickered over Blaine's scowling face. His expression shouted his thoughts loud and clear.

I hate weddings.

Katy sagged, beginning to think she hated them too.

CHAPTER TWELVE

*C*ole's glare took in the darkened kitchen. *Great.* As if a snowstorm, a wounded groom, a green-haired bride, and an absent JP weren't enough, now the power had gone out. The heat lamps they used to warm the food went cold. At least the gas stove still worked.

Cold comfort for Maggie, though. She drooped in her chair as if the weight of a thousand bridezillas sat on her shoulders. Her sweater's happy, dancing lights seemed to be mocking her. He wanted to go to her, gather her in his arms and whisk her away from this insanity. Take her somewhere warm and quiet, where he would cook her a sinfully creamy lobster mac-and-cheese and watch her face as she ate.

And try to figure her out. Why did she smile at him one second and shoot icicles the next, like he'd done something wrong? Whipping him around like a confused carnival ride.

Daisy hurried into the kitchen, bells ringing. "The power's out," she said, tossing her empty trays onto the counter with a clatter. She rushed over to Maggie. "Is there a way to fix it?"

"She's an event manager, not a mechanic," Cole said.

Maggie pushed back her chair and stood. "I'm sure there's a circuit breaker or some other way to get the juice going again," she said, sounding far from certain.

The maid of honor dashed into the kitchen, madly waving her phone's flashlight. "The power's out," she cried, out of breath from her run down the stairs. She shot toward Maggie. "Lindsay is *fuh-reaking* out! Can you fix it?"

A spot of light followed her through the doorway. The deejay, clutching his phone. "Hey, snooky-poo," he said. "Did you know the power's gone out?"

Snooky-poo? That nickname alone was reason enough for her to break up with the guy. Cole narrowed his eyes. Or had the chimney sweep been the one doing the breaking up?

The groom came in next, tripping over the doorstopper, with Natalia right behind him. They joined the group swarming around Maggie. Everyone peppered her with questions, drowning her out with their suggestions and demands. She held up her hands as if trying to stop a stampede at an all-you-can-eat dessert buffet—a valiant effort, but futile.

That was it for Cole. "Quiet, everyone," he bellowed, and the roar of voices ceased.

He threw his *toque blanc* on the counter and stomped over. Pushing through the crowd, he elbowed the deejay out of the way and took Maggie by the shoulders, as he'd done upstairs. She gazed at him with a distressed look that practically wrecked him. He wanted more than anything to make her worry go away.

"I'll fix this," he said, with a gentle squeeze before letting go. "I'll call the city's power company and get a truck up here right away."

"That won't work," a voice said from the doorway before Maggie could respond.

Cole spun to see Mr. Parker limp into the kitchen, followed by his wife. They wore their winter coats. She'd tied a kerchief over her hair, and he'd donned a cap.

"If the power's out here, it's probably out everywhere," Parker said, nearly blinding Cole with the beam of the heavy-duty flashlight he carried.

"Repair crews will be overwhelmed and won't get here for a while," Mrs. Parker added.

Maggie looked like she wanted to hurl some plates and not care who they hit. "Lindsay ought to be out of her mind by then," she muttered.

"We're not out of options yet." Cole turned to the Parkers. "Does this place have a generator or a backup system of some kind?"

Mr. Parker nodded. "Ayuh. A generator. It's supposed to kick in when the power blows."

"Not this time, though," his wife said, wrapping a scarf around her neck. "It must need a kick start."

"The generator craps out sometimes, especially in the cold," Mr. Parker said. "She's a cranky old gal. Sometimes don't like to start when she's most needed."

"Just like me," Mrs. Lathrop said from her chair at the table.

Cole scowled, not at her, at the Parkers. The way they

had bundled up, he knew there was more to the story. "And the generator's not in the basement, or the hallway or the next room, is it?" he asked warily.

Mrs. Parker let out a bark of laughter. "Oh heavens, no. It's outside, of course. Got its own special shed. We'll get to it. Holly will jimmy the whatchamacallit and get the power back on in no time. I'll hold the flashlight."

"Gotta get it done fast, before the heat's gone," Mr. Parker said. "An electric fireplace is a fat lot of good when there's no juice to power it. Ivy said as much to the owners when they had it installed."

"Indeed I did. I told Chris and Rudy the fireplace is quaint and all, but we're out of luck in an outage. They wouldn't hear of it. Didn't want the mess of a wood-burning fireplace. Didn't want Holly having to tote in firewood, either, not with his bum knee needing surgery and all. So, they converted it over."

"The generator's in an outbuilding. Not far from the side door, fifty yards or so," Mr. Parker said. "You folks sit tight and we'll get this thing fixed right up."

Maggie looked as winded as Cole felt by the time the couple finished their tag-team tale. This wasn't a job for them, or at least not a job for Holly. Traipsing through a nor'easter would put a lot of strain on his bum knee.

"Why don't you two stay put? I'll go," Cole said, only to be cut off by Maggie, blurting the same thing. He tossed her a glare and repeated, "*I'll* go."

"No, let me go," the deejay said, oozing closer to Maggie, all Mr. Congeniality and sympathetic simpering. "*I'll* take care of it for you."

Cole ground his teeth. Every time he'd seen Ash today,

he'd been staring at Maggie with an *I want* expression on his face. Now, the guy hoped to play hero for her. To impress her, maybe enough that she'd consider taking him back. That made him boil, though hadn't Cole been doing the same thing? Trying to impress her?

"If anyone's going to fix this, it's going to be *me*," he said, ignoring that thought and focusing on the problem at hand. "And this is how it's gonna go." He swept his gaze around the room, stopping on each person as he spoke. "Daisy, keep an eye on the food. Natalia, go back to the bar. Mr. Parker, take care of your knee. Go put your feet up. Mrs. Parker, bring him a hot water bottle. Mrs. Lathrop, stay put and eat something else. You—" He pointed at the groom. "Go sit down and don't move a muscle." He swung on the maid of honor. "And you go massage the bride's feet, or whisper sweet nothings in her ear, or whatever you have to do to keep her calm, while *I* fix the generator."

"And me?" the deejay asked in icy tones.

Cole sized him up with a hard look. *Get away from Maggie*, he wanted to say. But he had no right to be jealous, no right to butt into whatever was going on between them, so he settled for an almost pleasant, "Get back to your post."

Everyone got busy. Daisy went to the stove. The maid of honor left. The deejay followed her, but not before giving Maggie a longing look that made Cole want to grab him by the ears and pitch him out into the snow.

"You sure about this?" Natalia asked. "I saw some wicked weather when I was deployed. This storm would be cake. And you've got food to cook."

"You've got liquor to guard. Daisy can handle things while I'm gone."

Nodding, Natalia gave him a good luck fist bump and headed for the door. Cole turned to Maggie, who glowered at him, her hands on her hips.

"And what about me, Mr. Bossypants?" she said. "*I'm* perfectly capable of fixing the generator."

"Not sure you've noticed, but the weather outside is frightful. Your sweater may help guide the way tonight, but the rest of you isn't dressed for the part." His gaze dipped to her legs, and her short skirt, lingering appreciatively for a couple beats before he met her eyes again. "You'll get frostbite the second you step out the door."

"I can find something warm to wear. I saw tons of clothes in the junk room. Problem solved. And seriously, do you even know anything about generators?"

"Sure. I know a lot, including how to reboot them." Thanks to summer jobs when he was in college and culinary school. "So, logically, *I* should go."

He knew he sounded like a mansplaining jerk, but her determination to freeze her butt off bugged him. Couldn't she just let him do this for her? Did she have to be in control every second? He stiffened at the thought. *She* had to be in control? *Look in the mirror, Cole.*

"Sorry, but you *both* gotta go," Mr. Parker interrupted. "It's dark out, even darker in the shed. It's a two-person job. One of you to reset the generator, the other to hold the flashlight."

"Yes…you *must* go out there together, just the two of you," Mrs. Lathrop said, as subtle as an extra-spicy Texas chili. Her sly gaze bounced from Maggie to Cole. "You know the saying many hands make light work."

Maggie set her chin and shot Cole a challenging look. "I'm in."

"All right," he said, surrendering, vowing to wrap Maggie in twenty blankets and fifty scarves before they set a single foot out into the snow. "The two of us will go."

Mrs. Lathrop grinned, looking as satisfied as the cat that ate all the cream. "There, that's how you get things done. Didn't I say you two make a great team?"

It took a few minutes to get going. Maggie went to the foyer to exchange her shoes for her boots, while Cole retrieved his jacket and gloves from the pantry, both finally dry from his shoveling adventure earlier today. Only a few hours ago, but it seemed like weeks.

Daisy ran over as he put on his jacket and looped her elf's scarf around his neck. "That ought to shield you from the wind," she said.

The scarf was so thin it would barely protect him from a baby's breath. But as his grandmother liked to say, it was the thought that counted. He jingled the bells dangling from the tassels, his way of saying thanks, then picked up the flashlight Mr. Parker had left for him, ready to go.

All he needed was Maggie, who'd yet to return.

Concerned there might be another bride crisis or groom injury slowing her down, Cole popped into the dining room to investigate. He skimmed his gaze over the guests mingling at the bar or slumped at tables, finding Maggie near the entrance.

With the deejay.

The guy stood close. Too close. He ran his hand up and down her arm, talking to her. Talking *at* her. Maggie shook her head. Ash flashed a smarmy grin and talked some more, the smooth operator working his target, so much like Blaine the two could've been separated at birth.

Cole's blood boiled. The guy sure didn't act like an ex-boyfriend. More like making his case for a reunion. And damn it, a big clump of mistletoe looked on from above the couple, cheering the guy on. Encouraging Maggie to say yes.

Her gaze flicked toward Cole and she stiffened. Shaking off Ash's grabby hand, she abandoned him and hurried over.

"Glad you could finally tear yourself away," Cole said, as frosty as the storm outside.

She shot him a pretty scowl. Her cheeks were rosy, and she seemed flustered. Had the chimney sweep convinced her to give him a second chance? Were they getting back together?

Cole's breath caught to think that, though why should he care one way or the other? He liked her, but there were plenty of other women out there he could like, too. Plenty who would fire him up the way she did. Women who would tease him and make him laugh. Who would push back like she did when he went all *I'll save the day* intense. Many, many women who were as beautiful and caring and as full of fun as she was.

"Let's go," he said, determined to make himself believe that.

He steered her back to the kitchen and their next task before they could go out—finding warm clothes for her to wear. Mrs. Parker had loaned Maggie her coat, a heavy wool thing with enormous buttons, but she still needed a hat and something to cover her legs.

"Be careful out there. Don't get lost," Mrs. Lathrop called after them as they made their way down the hallway to what Maggie had called the junk room.

The smell of wool, bug spray, and perfume spilled out when Cole threw open the door. The light from Maggie's phone flicked around the small, wood-paneled room as she scanned several shelves and the long table pushed against the wall. What had probably been a laundry room or the servants' breakfast nook a hundred years ago was now a graveyard for forgotten clothes, shoes, feather boas, plastic tiaras, and other items left behind by partygoers' past.

"Probably too much to hope we'll find a pair of snow-shoes in here," Maggie said as they waded in. "Then we could get to the shed and back again in a second, job done."

"Just one pair? What are you going to do, ride on my shoulders?"

She let out a surprised laugh. "You're ridiculous, anyone ever tell you that?"

"All the time," he said, determined to ignore the way his pulse pounded at the affection that laced her voice. "Okay, we both need hats." He pointed his flashlight at her legs. "And you need twenty-five more layers."

She snatched a sparkly, stiletto-heeled shoe off a shelf and held it up. "How could anyone forget this? I mean, who leaves just one shoe behind? What happened to the other one?"

"Left all on its own, poor *sole*," he said, and she groaned at his pun. He fished a pirate's eye patch out of a box. "This is perfect for the groom. Could cover up that black eye."

"Ugh, don't remind me. I'm dreading when Lindsay gets a look at the poor guy. What I wouldn't give to be home, where all my troubles would be out of sight, as the song says."

In a strange way, Cole was glad she wasn't home. Glad she was here. With him.

She pulled a pair of *University of Maine* sweatpants out of a box and held them to her waist. "These seem warm enough, if a little big." She draped them over her arm and continued searching. After a brief silence, she asked, "Do you really think you can fix the generator?"

"Watch me. I can use a pair of pliers as well as I can a spatula. I'll get it done." He knew he sounded boastful, but he heard doubt in her voice, and he didn't want to let her down.

She nodded, seeming reassured, then picked up a red hunting cap and put it on. It swallowed up her head. The ear flaps dangled over her shoulders like a basset hound's floppy ears.

"That hat is way too big," he said. "I should wear it."

He held out his hand and she stepped out of reach. "Nope. You're not stealing anything else from me today. Find your own hat."

Cole blurted a laugh. "I'm never going to live that down, am I?"

"Not if I have anything to say about it." The hat slid down over her eyes. She pushed it back. "It's the Santa hat all over again. I won't see a thing, but it'll keep snow off my head. And *so* stylish. My sister would die to see me in this. She doesn't dare leave the house unless she's draped in designer brands, even in a snowstorm. She's all about those labels. I don't care much, as long as the clothes fit and are comfortable."

Cole thought she looked damn good in that simple suit she wore today, designer label or not. Hell, she looked good in that blinding sweater and Ivy Parker's wool coat.

"All my sisters are the same way." He aimed the flashlight into a box filled with pacifiers, combs, and a pair of what he hoped were toy false teeth.

Maggie stopped pawing through a box and glanced up. "*All* your sisters? How many do you have?"

"Too many." He shifted his hat hunt to the upper shelf. "Four of them. Two older, two younger, with me stuck in the middle."

"Oh, poor you, surrounded by all those girls." She didn't sound like she felt bad for him. "Did they torture you when you were growing up?"

"I didn't give them the chance. I bossed them around. What about you? Sisters, brothers?"

"Just one sister. Not as big a family as yours." A moment of hesitation, like she was trying to get over a speed bump. "It's just the two of us, actually. Well, except for a great aunt who lives in Florida, but that's it. We lost our parents in a car crash."

Cole's heart wrenched. He couldn't imagine how painful that loss must be. And could he be a bigger fool? That hadn't been nostalgia making her sound so bitter-sweet when they compared notes on favorite Christmas movies earlier. That had been raw emotion—she missed her parents.

"I'm sorry," he said, the expected words at a moment like this, but inadequate. How could two words ease the hurt he saw in her eyes? A hurt he'd seen in his grand-mother's eyes when anyone spoke of his grandfather, who'd died when Cole was a kid. An ache of memory and sorrow that would never go away. "When did they... How long ago did you lose them?"

She kept her eyes focused on the clothing box. "Just over ten years. I was in high school. My sister was in college."

"Must've been tough." He winced, saying that. Of course it had been tough. Gutting, probably.

"It was. We didn't know what to do. Took a while to get the financial stuff straightened out and money was tight." She gazed at him now, her eyes shiny in the muted light. "We needed help. That's how I got to know Inez at Gray Street. That's why I volunteer there."

He felt for her, but he sensed she didn't want his sympathy, or admiration, or to hear him say how brave she was. He settled for a simple, "I get it."

She nodded. "We muddled through. Things got better. Took a while, and I don't know if I would've made it except for my sister. She was my rock. She held me up and helped me through it all." She pulled in a decisive breath and straightened, as if closing the door on the subject. "And now, here I am today, missing my gazillionth re-watch of *It's a Wonderful Life*."

Cole wished there was something more he could say, some way he could comfort her, but he followed her lead and moved on. "Spoiler alert, an angel gets his wings, Zuzu's petals are found, and George Bailey learns he's the richest man in town."

She laughed softly, her sadness washing away. Maybe he'd said the right thing after all.

She shifted her gaze and let out an *eep* of surprise. "*Oh! Will you look at this!*" She wrenched a giant rawhide dog bone out of the tangled mess in the box. The ends had been seriously chewed. "I have no idea how this got in here, but I'm stealing it."

"For what? Christmas brunch? I know you don't cook, but that's just sad."

She smacked him on the arm with the bone. "No, you doofus. I'm going to bring it to Canine Rescue League. It's a dog shelter downtown. I help out there as often as I can. I love dogs."

And dogs loved her, Cole thought, remembering that mop dog Maggie had petted outside the supermarket earlier today. The pup had jumped around in excitement and wagged its tail at a speed that had threatened to send the thing airborne.

"I can picture you at the shelter, with your clipboard," he said. "Making a list, checking it twice, organizing all the dogs into play groups."

"Not at all. I'm a soft touch where dogs are concerned. I let them walk, and drool, all over me." She put the bone down on the corner of the table. "Good thing my apartment building doesn't allow pets, or I'd have adopted twenty of them by now."

He laughed softly. "That's nineteen too many for me. I've only got the one. I adopted her from where you volunteer, about two years ago."

"Oh? Maybe I saw you when you were there. What breed is she?"

Cole knew he hadn't seen her. He would've remembered. "Border collie."

"Border collies are great dogs. Frisky, but good watchdogs." She slanted him a glance. "Completely loyal."

"Completely slobbering you mean, *and* constantly trying to herd everyone."

"I wanted a border collie when I was a kid in the worst way. Or a black Lab, but we ended up adopting a Chihuahua." She dug through another box. "Dad got her for my mom one year for Christmas, because the breed was her favorite. A nervous little peanut with a tan coat and nails that always had to be trimmed. Mom named her Kris Kringle and dressed her up in a little Santa suit every holiday. I thought the outfit was *most* undignified, but the dog tolerated it."

Cole watched her, emotion clutching his throat. Her voice dropped an octave as she spoke of her parents, resonating with grief. He longed to take her into his arms, to try to fix a pain he knew he couldn't mend.

"Seems your mother was as Christmas crazy as Lindsay Lathrop," he said, his voice low.

"She was." Maggie sighed. "And she loved that dog. After the accident, I went to live with my sister. We couldn't take Kris Kringle, so my great aunt Florida drove up from Florida and brought her home, where she lived the rest of her days in dignified comfort."

"Wait. You have an aunt named Florida who lives in Florida?"

She grinned. "Isn't that hilarious?"

It was. So was she. She seemed to love wordplay as much as he did. Seemed to love a lot of things he did. And with everything she'd been through, she could still laugh, could still smile. Or maybe because of it. Whatever, her loved her smile. He felt he could live for weeks on just one of her smiles.

He checked himself. *You're stepping into dangerous territory, Cole.* She wasn't interested in feeding him her smiles. She had the deejay for that. Or did she? He wished he knew what was going on between them but didn't want to ask. He doubted he'd like the answer.

Irritated, he snatched a ratty-looking *Colby College* knit hat from a box and jammed it onto his head. "This will do," he growled. "Let's get moving."

She put on the sweatpants. Standing on one leg, she wobbled unsteadily and reached out to him for support. He moved closer, offering his arm and she clung to him. He didn't even think about it until it happened. Instinctive movements, automatic, as if they'd been a couple for years, supporting each other in small ways.

She released his arm and pulled the sweatpants up over her skirt, hiding those perfect legs. She tightened the drawstring, tucked the cuffs into the top of her boots, and put on her gloves.

"There. How do I look?" she asked, holding out her arms for his inspection.

Cole ran the flashlight over her mismatched clothing —a borrowed coat that brushed her knees, baggy sweatpants, a way too big hunting hat, and a pair of leather gloves that should keep her hands from freezing for about five seconds. She looked like a demented scarecrow. And as sexy as hell.

An unexpected tenderness curled around his heart. He felt close to her in a way he never had with any other woman, even Celia. It didn't seem possible, but Maggie Costa, the woman he'd vowed to stay away from at all costs just a few hours ago, had now become very important to him.

"You look warm," he said, suppressing that thought. Suppressing *all* those thoughts.

Gripping the flashlight, he led her to the end of the hallway and the side door, a solid slab of wood with a snow-crusted window. His breath fogged up the windowpane as he peered out into the gloom. Visibility was poor. The snow came down at a fast clip, caught by the wind and blown in sixteen different directions. That couple-of-inches snowfall predicted for the Maine coast had become a foot and growing. No wonder none of the other guests had showed up. Impressive that Daisy and Natalia had been able to get here at all.

Cole eyed Maggie. "Last chance to back out. I'm sure I can do this on my own."

"So you get all the glory? No thank you. I'm all in." The hallway darkened as she buttoned the coat over her blinking sweater then knotted the scarf around her neck. "Besides, you think I'd pass up the chance to get away from this dumpster fire of a wedding for a few minutes?"

"Okay. If you're intent on freezing, I won't stop you."

"As if you could."

Cole turned the doorknob, pushed the door, and... Nothing. The damned thing wouldn't budge. Snow blocked it shut. So much for a quick exit.

Maggie's brow furrowed. At least he thought it did. Couldn't see much of her face behind that hat. "Should we go out the kitchen door and around?" she asked.

Not a great idea. This place was huge. Going out that way would mean circling the building in foot-deep snow when their destination was much closer to this door.

"Let me give it another try." He put the flashlight on the floor, pressed his palms to the thick wood, and shoved. The door didn't budge. He tried again, using all his weight. The door moved, just barely. The heavy, wet snow on the other side proved an effective doorstop.

"Let me help," she said.

I've got it, Cole was about to say. The words were half out of his mouth when he realized he didn't have it. He needed her help. They *needed* to work as a team.

He agreed with a grunt, and she got in right next to him. Her scent surrounded him, mixed with the smell of wool and a trace of mothballs emanating from her borrowed clothes.

"Ready?" he said. "One, two, three. *Go.*"

Shoulders braced, they pushed. The door inched open until, finally, success. Chill wind and icy snowflakes gusted into an opening just wide enough for his big frame. She slipped through with more ease.

Out in the cold, he reached for Maggie's hand.

CHAPTER THIRTEEN

*B*laine aimed the flashlight's beam toward their destination, a copse of pine trees about fifty yards ahead, hard to see through the pelting snow. Katy directed her phone's light downward at their path as they pushed forward. She shivered. The temperature had dropped, and dropped a lot, since she'd sparred with Blaine over the dent in his van.

She leaned into the biting wind, holding onto his hand for support. She didn't know how his hand had found hers, but she was happy it had. His steady grip made her feel both protected and wanted. Part of a team again. Or maybe for the first time. She couldn't remember ever feeling this way with Ash.

She stole a glance at Blaine out of the corner of her eye. Snow lashed his face, clinging to his eyelashes. More snow stuck to his clothes. His nose had turned as red as a cherry. He'd set his chin and plowed through the foot-high drifts with purpose. Katy would melt at the sight if she hadn't already melted down to a puddle earlier, when they were hunting for outside clothes.

She'd never felt so close and comfortable with anyone. Comforted, too. She rarely shared what had happened to her parents and the dark days that had followed. The wound was too raw. But the kindness in his voice, and the understanding way he'd looked at her had touched her deeply. She'd hesitated only a moment before opening up about her grief and pain.

Looking at him now, affection surged. Her heart cried, *I'm in, all the way*. But her brain still had its doubts.

"Why is this generator shed so far from the house?" she asked, raising her voice to be heard over the wind.

He gestured to the left, toward the tarp-covered barbecue pit area and the lawn that slanted down to the ocean. At least, she *thought* the Atlantic was out there. The storm obscured the view of the water. The horizon looked like a murky void.

"I think it's so outside guests don't have a building in their sight line," he said, and a cloud of condensation puffed from his mouth. "More likely to meet fire codes." He bent close to her ear. "It's a real slog mushing through this mess. You don't want to turn around, do you?"

His teasing had the desired effect—she picked up her pace and they soon reached the relative shelter of the pine trees. The snow wasn't as deep here and the wind somewhat less intense. In the distance, Katy saw a white Cape Cod-style cottage where the Parkers must live, and just ahead, their destination, a small building with aluminum siding and a shingled roof.

Suddenly, Katy stumbled over a small tree stump hidden under the snow and she pitched forward. Abruptly releasing Blaine's hand, she flailed as she tried to stay upright. He hooked his arm around her waist and held on as if landing a particularly wiggly fish. That tipped him off balance. The bells on his scarf jangled as he flopped into the snow on his back.

Katy fell on top of him.

She felt his hard chest and solid legs beneath her, even through thirty layers of clothing. He'd lost his grip on his flashlight. Still lit, it poked out of the snow, spreading a soft light over his face. He gazed at her, his jaw clenched, a scowl firmly in place. And his eyes... If she looked up the word *smoldering* in a dictionary, she'd see those eyes gazing out at her.

His arms tightened around her. His warm breath brushed her face. Her whole body went as hot as a bonfire's blaze. Her blood thundered in her ears and the butterflies that had danced in her belly all day erupted into a full-scale Broadway show.

His lips were *so* close to hers. Lips she longed to kiss. *Needed* to kiss. The wind and the snow faded from her mind. So did her doubts. There was only him. Only her. Only...

A deer?

A deer, a doe, in fact, crept up beside them and stopped about five feet away, breaking into their heated moment. The creature's ears twitched as she stretched her long neck toward them and sniffed in curiosity.

"Hey, Blitzen," Blaine said, his voice rumbling under Katy's breasts. "Where's Comet and Cupid?"

Blitzen didn't take kindly to that. The doe flinched and kicked snow into his face as she dashed off into the trees.

Laughing, Katy shifted off of Blaine as gracefully as she could and stood. She waited for him to get up. But he didn't.

"Are you taking a nap?" she asked.

"Nope." He stuck out his arms and swished them up and down in the snow. He did the same with his legs. Katy giggled. The adorable goofball was making a snow angel.

A second later, he hopped to his feet, snatched up the flashlight and pointed the light downward to survey his artwork. He frowned. Understandably. The snow was too wet and sticky for a proper angel. He'd created a snow blob instead.

"I'm sorry but no amount of bell ringing will give that poor angel wings." She patted him on the back, dislodging clumps of snow. "Cheer up, even *you* can't do everything."

He shot her a *wanna bet?* grin that called those butterflies in for an encore. Katy liked this goofy version of Blaine. Almost as much as she liked the scowling version. Or the dog lover. Or Mr. Bossypants. Or the man who'd spoken to her so tenderly about her parents.

Yeah, time to admit it. She liked *every* version of this man, and her feelings grew stronger by the minute.

They moved on. He didn't take her hand this time. They finished the final steps to the shed without incident. They stepped onto a small porch with a snow-dusted wood plank floor and a rectangle of metal jutting out overhead, shielding them somewhat from the storm.

It took some time to get the door open. The hook latch had frozen in place. Blaine had to bash the hook upward with the flashlight several times to force it to come loose. Finally, the door swung inward with an ominous creak of cold hinges.

Blaine entered first. Katy followed him into a small, cramped room smelling of some kind of fuel. A tiny window and their flashlights provided the only illumination. It was marginally less frigid in here than outside. Blaine stamped his feet and brushed snow off his pants, like a snowman shaking off his outer layer.

He skimmed the light beam over the generator, a rectangular metal box three feet tall and about five feet long, sitting at the center of the little room.

"Take this." He thrust the flashlight into her hand and turned to the machine. He flipped a handle and the generator's metal lid popped up.

Katy pointed both lights at the machine's inner workings, making the metal parts, wires, and other components glimmer. Blaine peered inside like a math professor pondering a tricky equation.

"I think the battery that powers the whole thing isn't getting a charge," he said after a few seconds.

"Can it be fixed?" she asked, reality pressing down on her again. In all the pulse-racing, falling into the snow excitement, she'd forgotten about Lindsay and the guests huddled together in the rapidly cooling building. His grim diagnosis brought it all back. What if the generator was completely broken?

"I can fix this with my eyes closed." He flashed a brash grin. "Okay, one eye closed. I guess I have to see what I'm doing. The generator's just cold and needs to be primed. Carburetor probably could use a push to get going, too."

He straightened and reached for her. Well, that was what she thought until he dropped a sultry, "Excuse me," and brushed by her. He picked up a large plastic toolbox tucked into the shadows and began to slip by her again but stopped and gazed down at her. Close. Close enough that visions of sugar plums and kisses danced in her head.

"I've got this you know," he said, less cocky, more warmth. "The important thing is for *you* not to panic."

"Easier said than done," was all she could manage at the moment.

He nodded and went on his way, as if nothing had happened.

He placed the toolbox at the foot of the generator then shook off his gloves and opened the lid. Katy shifted the lights so he could see inside. The tools had been dumped in there in such a haphazard manner she itched to dive in and organize them properly. Blaine found what he needed with minimal poking around, though, and pulled out a screwdriver.

"Okay, confession time," Katy said, aiming both flashlight and her phone light at the generator again. "How do you know how to fix this thing?"

He began to loosen the screws holding an inner panel in place. "My oldest sister and her husband own a small engine repair company. Outboard motors, snowmobiles, lawn mowers, and generators. I picked up a few non-kitchen skills helping out in the summer when I was in college." He flashed her a glance. "How about you? How'd you learn?"

"Huh?"

"Earlier you said you could fix this machine."

"Oh, that." She flushed, embarrassed. She'd lied and his smirk told her he knew she'd lied. "Yeah, I don't know squat about generators."

"And you said you did because…?"

"Because I couldn't resist the chance to freeze my bottom off out here with you." She laced her voice with sarcasm, though the words were kind of true. "Actually, I think I just panicked. This day hasn't exactly gone according to plan, and I hate more than anything when that happens. Makes me feel…frustrated. Like why can't I keep this mess under control? Keep *all* the messes under control. Then there you were, telling everyone what to do and taking charge and taking over my job and, well, you sent my event manager's ego into a snit. I'm kind of a control freak, you know."

He laughed. "*You're* a control freak? Have you even met me?"

"Well, I won't argue with you there."

"That's a first. You seem dedicated to arguing with me like each fight has a million-dollar prize on the line."

And she'd enjoyed every moment of it, much to her surprise. "I wouldn't bother if you weren't so eager to fight back."

He gave her a strange look then loosened the last screw and removed the panel. He put it down on the cement floor with a soft *ting* and reached into the toolbox again, taking out a spray can she hoped wasn't green hairspray.

"I need light right there. On the carburetor." He pointed to the generator's upper left corner, and she did as he asked. He pushed a metal flap aside with the screwdriver and squirted liquid from the spray can into a small opening. "What you said about me jumping in and taking over. I'm told that's my number one flaw, especially by my sisters. I guess I've never met a problem I didn't think I could fix. I think I can handle everything with no help, and I'm determined to prove it. Even when no one wants me to."

She let out a soft laugh. "Control freaks, assemble! We're scarily alike in that way. Though I don't beat a problem into submission. I approach it more logically."

Maybe too logically. That straight-forward, stick-to-the-plan approach had helped her cope after losing her parents, but it had also gotten her locked into a relationship with a guy she had nothing in common with. Had kept her plugging away at a job she didn't like. Because both were in her plan. She blinked in surprise at the realization. Maybe it was time to put the plans aside and just *be*. Time to do what made her happy, rather than what she thought was expected of her.

"I guess logical wouldn't have cut it in this situation," Katy said, brightening. "I would've waited hours for the power company, stressing out every second, while you and your screwdriver and your take-charge approach came out here and saved the day. I guess that kind of drive and dedication is what makes you such a good cook, too."

"Don't you mean such an *immensely* good cook?" His humor faded, morphing into an uncertainty she'd never seen on his face before. "I'm glad you think so. I hope the rest of the world thinks so too. I plan to open my own restaurant."

"That would be fantastic," she said with decisive pluck,

since he sounded so doubtful. Where was that confident, take-charge attitude now? "I know you'll be a success. You certainly will be if you put that control freak attitude into action."

He gave an unconvinced grunt, his eyes on his task. "Not everyone has that kind of faith in me. My family does. They believe in me no matter what I do. But some of the people I work with sure don't, not to mention my former fiancée."

Those last two words banged into Katy's head, drowning out everything else he'd said. "*Former* fiancée?"

He stopped spraying and sat back on his heels. "Yeah, former. I was engaged a couple of years ago. It did *not* end well." He flashed her a rueful grin. "A classic story, actually. Boy meets girl, boy wants to marry girl, girl leaves boy at the altar."

"That's awful," she said. And it completely explained his wedding hate. Katy had been dumped, badly wounded, but he'd been *nuked.* Spectacularly and publicly.

"Yeah, it was," he said. "I raged like a tornado for a long time. Still stings, but I get it now. We weren't right for each other. Celia's lack of confidence in me was proof of that. She did me a favor." He shrugged. "I couldn't be happier."

He didn't sound very happy. Could that be the reason for his fickleness with women? Blaine didn't want to get burned again, so now he did the burning. Understandable, if not very admirable, but still... She felt for him. She wanted to reach out to him, to soothe the bitterness and hurt. To tell him she understood.

He tossed the spray can back into the toolbox and grabbed the screwdriver. "What about you? What happened with you and the deejay?"

"Another classic story." Katy shrugged, trying to brush away her own bitterness. "Boy meets girl, girl thinks boy might be the one, but she was wrong. Spectacularly wrong. He cheated on me with another woman."

Blaine's expression turned as dark and unsettled as the sky outside. "Your chimney sweep sounds like a real jerk."

The protective heat in his voice touched her. And made her glad Ash wasn't within punching distance. "Couldn't agree more," she murmured. She met Blaine's gaze for a brief, blistering moment. "I've moved on."

"Good," he said, his voice low, husky. His hands seemed to shake as he fit the carburetor's protective metal panel back into place and began tightening the screws. "Done. All I need to do now is prime it."

Metal clanked against metal as he flung the screwdriver into the toolbox. He stood and pressed a rubbery orange bulb inside the generator, three times in quick succession. Then he moved a lever up, stepped back and looked at her.

"Here we go."

He flipped a switch and the machine shuddered to life. It groaned and moaned. Katy held her breath, fearing it would die an ignoble death.

"Come on, girl," Blaine coaxed and patted the machine's side, like burping a baby.

A hum, a shifting sound and a second later, the machine kicked into action. Through the shed's small window, Katy saw the sky brighten as the floodlights in the parking lot and around the property popped back on.

She cheered and Blaine grinned. "*Told* you I could do more than cook," he said.

"For which Lindsay is no doubt grateful." Katy put her hand to her ear. "Hark! I think I hear her shrieking with joy from here." She eyed Blaine and did a silly little curtsey. "Thank you, almighty chef mechanic control freak. You saved the day."

The light made it hard to see, but Katy could have sworn he blushed.

He closed the toolbox lid and pushed it against the wall. "You ready?" he said, his voice extra gruff. "We'd better get back before they send a St. Bernard and a rescue party looking for us."

"Do we have to? There's probably ten more disasters waiting to happen back there."

"And we'll take on each disaster one at a time, as a te—" He snapped his jaw shut then spun away to snatch his gloves off the floor.

Katy shivered. Had he been about to call them a team? An hour ago, that word had made her shudder. Now, her pulse thrummed in excitement at the thought.

The door's hinges squealed again as Blaine opened the door. He gestured for Katy to go first, as if he were escorting her into a fancy restaurant and not outside into a blizzard. She felt him close behind her as they stepped onto the little porch under the protective overhang.

Blaine took off his gloves so he could re-latch the door, shoving them into his pocket. Katy put the flashlight on the narrow rail. Peeling off her own gloves, she switched it off then did the same with her phone and tucked it away. No need for additional illumination. The floodlights beamed across the entire compound. More light spilled from Newell's many windows, looking festive and welcoming. A spotlight on the shed's roof lit the path they'd taken to get here. She could see a vague outline of their footprints and Blaine's misshapen snow angel, almost obliterated by the wind-driven snow.

Blaine finished locking the door and came to stand beside her.

"Look—" Katy directed his gaze to the Parkers' house, about twenty yards away. Multi-colored Christmas lights ran along the eaves, buffeted by the wind. A deer, probably the one who'd disturbed her intimate moment with Blaine earlier, made a meal out of a leafy wreath hung on the front door. "It's so pretty."

A brief pause before he murmured, "Yeah, beautiful."

Her gaze flew to his face. He wasn't looking at the scenery. He looked at *her*. Not with a scowl. Or a smile. His dimples were nowhere to be seen. She saw something new in his expression, something primal and powerful. So intense Katy could barely breathe and, she suspected, neither could he.

They stood there, lost in each other's eyes. The wind sighed and the trees creaked, gentle, lush sounds that filled the stillness around them. His masculine scent invaded her senses. His eyes glimmered with longing. Heat pooled in her belly. Her heart seemed to pound a thousand beats a second and desire flooded every part of her, demanding one thing and one thing only.

His kiss.

Eager to satisfy that demand, she moved closer. In a moment, their lips came together, blending as one. Her gloves slipped from her fingers. She barely noticed them fall. She noticed only his lips on hers, warm and soft, gentle yet demanding. He tasted sweet and tangy, the chef who sampled his own wares. He shifted and his arms came around her, pulling her against him, deepening their kiss. She trembled and every nerve ending sizzled with awareness and need.

She slid her hands over his shoulders, feeling their strength under her palms, then looped her arms around his neck and, with a soft moan, fully sank into his embrace. She feathered her fingers through the thick hair that touched his collar, as she'd wanted to do all day. She touched his face, traced the contours of those dimples, and caressed his strong jaw.

They broke apart for the space of a breath and smiled into one another's eyes.

"Let's get this out of the way," he murmured and pulled off her hat.

Their lips joined again. She sighed against his mouth and tilted her head. Their tongues danced, tasted, and explored. Savoring the moment and each other. Oblivious to the snow and the cold and the world around them.

This was the kiss Katy had wanted since she'd met him in the supermarket. The kiss she'd been waiting for since their gazes met in the alcove. The kiss that had simmered between them all afternoon into the evening, every time they had looked into each other's eyes. The kiss the mistletoe that seemed to follow them around had been promising.

The two of them, a team, here together. Inevitable, and so, so right. Katy and Blaine. Blaine, the wine-stealing goofball, the supposedly bad-tempered chef who could fix any machine but was terrible at making snow angels. Blaine, who scared off reindeer and made Katy sizzle.

Blaine the flirt. The womanizer.

The words screamed in her brain like the shrill of an alarm and she wrenched out of his arms.

"What is it?" Blaine glared in all directions, as if he expected an axe murderer to jump out from behind one of the trees. He focused back on her with deep concern. "What's wrong?"

Everything. She'd kissed him. She'd listened to her heart and not her head and kissed him when she shouldn't have.

"I—I... Tell me..." The questions whirled through her mind as fast and fierce as the storm's driving wind, but she couldn't get them out. Was he a flirt as her sister had claimed? Who was Lily? His girlfriend? And what if the answer was yes? Was Lily waiting patiently at his grandmother's house for Blaine to arrive, as Katy had waited so many nights for Ash? Thinking he was working, only to discover he'd been kissing another woman.

Icicles rocketed through Katy's veins, freezing every drop of heat and warmth in her blood as the cold truth set in—*she* was that other woman.

"Hey," Blaine said, reaching for her again. "Talk to me."

She shook her head and stumbled backward, away from him and his tempting lips. Away from his kind eyes and his strong arms. Away from his dimples and smoldering looks and her own mixed-up feelings.

Away from his kiss.

Her stomach churned with guilt and remorse. Hurt and anger seared her throat. Tears poked her eyes, and she did the only thing her muddled mind and aching heart wanted to do at the moment.

She fled.

CHAPTER FOURTEEN

"*M*aggie, wait!" Cole cried, but the wind snatched his words, and she didn't hear him. He watched her run, moving as fast as she could through the deep snow. His fists clenched and so did his gut.

What happened? They'd been getting along so well, with all that joking and back-and-forth and sharing of relationship war stories. And earlier, when they'd fallen in the snow and she'd nestled on top of him, he hadn't cared that the cold seeped through his clothing and the wind bit his cheeks. He'd only cared about her, and how much he wanted to kiss her. Then that deer had stuck its nose into their business, not preventing the inevitable, but delaying it.

Turned out, their kiss had been worth waiting for. Electric and electrifying. Full of passion and searing heat. She'd tasted as sweet as he'd thought she would. They'd fit together perfectly, blended together as if fated for it. As if they were soul mates.

He'd felt as if they were moving toward…something. Something that had finally pushed him forward. Finally smashed that defensive wall he'd built around himself wide open. He didn't want to be alone anymore. He *wanted* to be part of a team again. With her.

And then she ran.

Frustrated, Cole grabbed the flashlight from the rail and snatched Maggie's hat and gloves from the porch floor where they'd fallen. He trudged through the snow back to the building, following her footprints.

Why had she bolted? Was it something he'd done? He could swear Maggie had wanted him to kiss her. She'd made the first move, even. Or had she? Had he overstepped, pushed her into it? He shook his head, confused. He had no idea how the kiss had started. It had just happened.

And then she'd ripped out of his arms. Had gaped at Cole as if he'd given her food poisoning. Why? Cole groaned inwardly as the obvious answer shot into his mind.

The deejay.

The guy had been eyeing her all day, clearly still into her. Was Maggie still into him? She'd said she had moved on, but had she?

Cole's head spun. If Maggie was still interested in her ex, despite the guy cheating on her, then that kiss she had shared with him meant…what? Nothing to her? Cole touched his mouth. He could still feel her warm lips on his, could still taste her cinnamon sweetness. Still feel the thunder of his heart and the need and desire that had filled his every pore.

That kiss sure hadn't meant nothing to him.

Scowling at the pelting snow, he pushed his anger, hurt, and confusion onto the back burner and pumped up his pace. He reached the building and shoved inside, blasted by the heat and nearly blinded by the bright light. Maggie had shed her outerwear like a snake shedding its skin—her boots, the sweatpants, Mrs. Parker's borrowed coat, and her scarf were strewn along the floor.

Guilt pinched at him. She must've been really upset for such a tidy and organized person to leave a mess like this.

He tossed her hat and gloves on top of the rest of her things then put the flashlight on a table by the door and peeled off his own outside gear. He hung his jacket on a coat hook to dry. He stomped snow off his boots as he stomped down the hallway to the kitchen.

He would never understand women if he lived a thousand years. Never understand Maggie in particular. Or what she'd done to him. What he'd done to himself. He'd let her in. After he'd vowed not to get close to a woman ever again, he'd opened the door and let her waltz right in.

"Hooray for you, Cole," Daisy said when he got to the kitchen. She stood at the counter, filling more trays with appetizers. "The lights are on and everything's back to normal. More important, we have heat."

Cole didn't need heat. He burned in so many ways he generated his own. "Daisy, I'm not in the mood," he said, heading into the pantry to change into dry pants for the second time today.

He opened the door minutes later to find her waiting for him, her hands on her hips, a supremely annoyed elf.

"Come on, out with it. What went on out there?" she

demanded. "The event lady flew through here like her hair was on fire. Now you roll in, looking like the one who lit the match."

"Let's just say my track record with women is zero for zero," he muttered and moved to the sink. He turned on both faucets full blast, drowning out any further questions.

Hot water pulsed. He soaped up and scrubbed his hands hard, washing away every speck of grease and gunk from his Mr. Fix-It adventure. He wished he could scrub away the memory of those moments with Maggie just as thoroughly. How natural she'd felt in his arms, pressed full against him. Her silky hair as he'd run his hand through it. Her touch as she'd traced her fingers along his jaw. The way her soft, pliant lips had felt against his.

How he'd never wanted the kiss to end.

Done washing, he reached for a fresh towel when Daisy materialized beside him and handed him one. She peered at him, her usual teasing expression now serious and concerned.

"Won't you tell me what's wrong, Cole?" she asked, her voice soft, coaxing.

A direct question, with only one answer. He was stuck on Maggie. A woman who'd run from his kiss. *That* should tell him everything he needed to know about her interest in him. He gritted his teeth. No time for that, he had to get back to work. He grabbed the towel from Daisy and quickly dried his hands.

"Nothing's wrong. Absolutely *nothing*," he said with finality. He put on his coat once again, shifting back into chef mode. "How's it going here?"

Daisy hesitated and he hoped she wouldn't press him. He did *not* want to talk about it.

"Fine and dandy," she said. "Good thing everything's gas-powered. No interruption in our flame while the juice was out. I put the apps in the oven to fire 'em up."

"Great." At least *something* was going right. Cole buttoned his coat and put on his hat. "What about the justice of the peace? Any sign of him?"

"Nope. Not yet. I suppose that means no wedding."

"Seems like it. I don't want to be anywhere near the bride when she finds out." Cole frowned. "For now, let's keep things calm with food." He nodded toward the dining room.

"On it." She went to the counter, slid two trays out from under the warming lights then turned for the door.

"Wait," he said, stopping her before she could go. He sprinkled more cilantro on the veggie cups and dropped an extra splash of maple syrup on the lobster bites. "That'll do. Listen, I'll handle the mob down here. You get those up to the bride's ready room. I bet they're hungry, and some food will ease the pain when they find out about the JP. Hopefully."

Daisy jingled across the kitchen, pushed through the door, and disappeared.

Cole did a quick check on the dinner items in various stages of preparation. The beef simmered nicely, and the chicken was plugging away, too. He finished up by sprinkling the blueberry vinaigrette over the mixed greens then laying out salad plates along the counter, ready to fill when Maggie gave him the go ahead to serve dinner.

Whenever that would be. *If* she ever spoke to him again.

He picked up a tray in each hand and headed for the door. Pausing to brace himself for an awkward post-kiss encounter with Maggie, he stepped into the dining room.

A HUNGRY HORDE ENVELOPED HIM. Bacon juice and sour cream splattered every which way as the guests snatched appetizers from the trays like ravenous wolves. Devouring without tasting, it seemed.

Cole scanned the room for Maggie but couldn't find her. Probably a good thing. Seeing her, he'd be torn between the urge to pull her into his arms or demand she answer the only question that mattered right now. Why did she run?

The deejay stopped by and elbowed his way into the hungry mob, seizing a handful of appetizers. Cole watched him cram a vegetable pastry into his mouth and his mood went thunderous. The man had cheated on Maggie, breaking her heart. Whether she'd forgiven him and considered getting back together with him was beside the point.

Cole's inner caveman itched to punch the guy's lights out.

A couple of people waiting in the line at the bar signaled for him to bring the food their way. A timely distraction. He shot Ash a death glare and hustled away before he could give in to temptation.

The bar, a thick slab of mahogany that looked custom

made, stretched about eight feet long. The double-door liquor cabinet behind the bar was equally impressive, with claw feet like a lion's and so tall Natalia had to use a step stool to reach the less frequently requested liquors on the top shelf.

At the moment, she snatched bottles from all the shelves and mixed drinks like a pro. It was an open bar, but the guests had come armed with cash and her tip jar overflowed. The groomsmen were being especially generous, and Cole could almost forgive them for all the grief they'd put Maggie through earlier.

He went down the line of people waiting to buy drinks, and more devouring of appetizers occurred. The groom stumbled by and picked up a lobster bite. He bit into it and syrup and bacon juice dribbled onto his snowy white tuxedo shirt. Even the bride's father paused long enough to snap up a snack before resuming his never-ending business call.

"You bet they'll need a sleigh," Lathrop bellowed into his phone. "It wouldn't be Christmas without one, would it?" He laughed heartily, and Cole didn't think he'd ever see such a sight in real life, but the man's belly shook like a bowlful of jelly.

Both serving trays were severely depleted by the time Cole reached the front of the line. "Hey, you hungry?" he called to Natalia. "I'll save a few lobster bites for you."

"Yay, my favorite," she said, handing the groom's father what looked like a glass of ice milk topped with cranberries but was really a Christmas margarita. "Just leave them. I'll get to them when I have a second."

Natalia greeted her next customer, Mrs. Lathrop, who'd cut to the front of the line.

"I'll have a martini," she said, resting her cane against the bar. "Dry. No olive, no twist. Nothing fancy for me." Natalia started on her order, and the old woman turned to Cole. "My doctor says I shouldn't drink, but what he doesn't know won't hurt him." She skimmed her gaze over him. "Well, here you are. You made it back safely, and you got the lights switched on in record time. What did I tell you? You two make a fine team."

His jaw clenched at that word, but not like before, when the idea of being part of a couple again made him want to jump out a window. He'd done a one-eighty because of that kiss. No, earlier than that. He'd gone all-in the moment he'd seen Maggie in that absurd hunting hat. He'd known then his days of team-avoidance were over.

Except... The person he wanted to team up with wanted nothing to do with him.

"If you say so," he muttered.

She frowned. "Oh dear. What's the matter? Did something happen between you two out there? I should've suspected it. That girl just flew by when she came in. Dashed upstairs, wouldn't even stop to shoot the breeze with me. Now here you are, with a face as droopy as a bloodhound. What did you do?"

"Me? *I* didn't do anything. She's the one who ran away —" He shut his mouth. He did *not* want to rehash his humiliation. He thrust a tray under Mrs. Lathrop's nose. "Want one?"

"Ooh, don't mind if I do." She daintily stuck out her pinky and picked up one of the few remaining veggie bites. She polished off the treat in two big gulps. "Superb! Five stars, my boy. Though I suppose I should expect nothing less from a talent like yours."

Cole handed her a napkin, mentally patting himself on the back for his successful distraction. As Mémé liked to say, when all else failed, change the subject to food. "Thanks," he said. "I plan to put that talent to work in my own restaurant someday."

"Really? A fine ambition. I'm sure you'll be a huge success."

That's what Maggie had said, in the same impressed tone of voice. Cole gave a cool nod, but inside he flushed with pride at the compliment.

Natalia returned and set a vintage-looking martini glass on the bar. Mrs. Lathrop pulled a bill sporting Ulysses S. Grant's whiskered face from her gown's sleeve like a magician and added it to the pile of cash in the tip jar.

"Merry Christmas," she said, and hoisted her martini glass in a toast.

Natalia sputtered her thanks then lunged for a brass bell fixed to the wall. She gave the clapper pull-rope a sharp tug and a happy *clang* rang out. The guests cheered this traditional bartender's celebration of a large tip.

Cole laughed. "Sounds like you're giving out wings, Nat."

Natalia's forehead crinkled. "What?"

"Never mind." He handed her the tray with the last of the lobster bites. Maggie would've gotten the reference. She seemed to get everything about his nerdy self. He eyed Mrs. Lathrop, who'd certainly earned her wings today. "You seem to be enjoying yourself."

"You know I am." She sipped her drink with a satisfied smirk. "Ah, delicious. As dry as the desert. You must hire that young lady for your new restaurant. With your culinary skill and her martini mixing talent, you can guarantee I'll be your first and most loyal customer. When do you plan to open?"

Cole shifted uncomfortably. "Yeah, that's the thing. I don't know where and when. I need to scrape up the cash first, find some investors. But I'll do it, someday and somewhere."

"I understand. Starting out is difficult." She took another sip. "Wilfred and I had some lean years in the early days. Took my late husband a while to get his business going too. But we did well, and he left me comfortable, so if you're looking for investors, look no further than me. I'd be happy to oblige."

Cole winced. He hadn't blabbed about his troubles to get her sympathy. Or her charity. "I can't let you do that."

She speared him with a look so sharp he felt its barb. "*Let* me? My boy, never tell a woman you will or won't let her do anything. And don't tell me what I should do with my money. If I say I'd like to invest, I mean it."

Her kindness touched him, almost as much as her scolding terrified him. "Thanks. I'll have to think about it."

"Don't think too long. You've got to get started on your dream soon. Life's too short to waste time." She chuckled. "Listen to me. I sound like a fortune cookie, spouting all sorts of clichés."

"Clichés stick for a reason."

"Indeed." She placed her martini on the bar and took the last veggie cup off his tray, nibbling contentedly. "Now, once we get you going with your restaurant, you'll need someone to help you."

"Don't tell me you want a job as a line cook?" He pictured her stirring a pot of clam chowder and peeling potatoes.

"While that could be fun, I was thinking of someone more suited to the job." A sneaky smile curved her lips. "Someone like the wedding planner, perhaps."

"Event manager, actually."

She waved her hand. "Yes, yes, whatever. Her experience will make her invaluable. She's a hard worker. Smart, caring. And she's beautiful. She would be ideal for you, in all ways."

She was. He didn't need Mrs. Lathrop or anyone else to convince him of that. But… "I don't think she wants the job." She'd made that clear outside. "I think there's someone else. Someone she has a history with." He tipped his head toward the deejay, boogying to a disco version of "I Saw Mommy Kissing Santa Claus." "He's her ex-boyfriend."

"Oh, please," Mrs. Lathrop scoffed. "Sure, he's an attractive fellow, but not worthy of a girl like her. He seems to think he is, though. Men like that *always* think they're the lord's gift to the women of the world. He pesters her every time she comes into the room, his attention unwanted and uninvited, like that fruitcake nobody wants but keeps showing up at Christmas parties. She's *not* interested. In fact, I don't think she even likes him.

Body language says it all." She side-eyed Cole. "For instance, *you* like her. That's crystal clear."

Cole had no answer for that.

"If you ask me, and mind you, nobody has, if you're in doubt how she feels, there's one way to know for sure. *Ask her.*"

"Sure," he said doubtfully. Asking Maggie about Ash would get him an answer. Probably not the answer he wanted.

Mrs. Lathrop tapped his ankle with her cane. "Don't waffle, son. I get it, that busted engagement hurt you and you don't want to get hurt again, but you've got to take that chance."

"How did you know about—?" Duh. *Daisy.* He knew he shouldn't have left those two in the kitchen together when the lights went out. Daisy loved to talk, and Mrs. Lathrop seemed to be on a matchmaking frenzy.

"Son, I've been around a long time. How many years I don't care to share. A woman never tells her age, you know." She took Cole's hand. "But one thing I've learned in all the time the good lord has granted me is love is the only thing that matters. The thing that keeps us going, and what gives us hope." She squeezed his hand then released it, letting out a musical giggle. "There I go again, talking like a fortune cookie. I guess what I'm trying to say is, if you like the girl, don't wait. Go get her."

Dazed, Cole returned to the kitchen. He checked on dinner and began to load up with more appetizers, weighing Mrs. Lathrop's words. He'd never had trouble taking charge, plowing in, and getting stuff done. But this task almost paralyzed him. He could ask Maggie how she felt, and she might fall into his arms for a repeat of that amazing kiss in the snow. Or she might tell him to take a hike.

If she rejected him again, that'd be twice in one day. He didn't think he could take that.

His heart had finally defrosted. Could he risk having it iced over again?

CHAPTER FIFTEEN

Katy padded along the upstairs hallway toward the bride's suite, scuffing her candy cane heels on the carpet. As soon as she'd gotten inside and discarded her wet clothing, she hurried up here. Partly to check on Lindsay and the rest of her entourage, but mostly to get as far away from Blaine and his oh-so-tempting lips as she could.

Her emotions rocketed in all directions, up, down, and sideways. How could she let herself lose control like that? How could she have kissed him?

She blamed her foolishness on the banter, his enticing smiles, his warmth, and the connection she'd felt growing between them. She'd been pulled in by the way he made her heart sing and how he seemed to know everything she was thinking. The man who'd offered her a broad shoulder to lean every time a new crisis erupted. A man she'd thought she could depend on.

Had it all been an act? A womanizer's game designed to get her to let her guard down and fall into his arms?

Then why had he snarled at her when he realized they were standing under the mistletoe? Twice. Would he have been so vocally anti-kissing if his goal was to seduce her?

Katy's head spun and she'd gotten no closer to any answers by the time she reached the suite. She knew only one thing for certain.

That kiss had been *the* most amazing kiss of her life.

She paused at the door to compose herself, then knocked softly and slipped inside an eerily quiet room. The bridesmaids were finishing up their hair and makeup, almost ready for a wedding Katy felt ninety-nine percent sure wasn't going to happen.

The bride wasn't even close to dressed. Lindsay's wedding gown still hung on the dressing room door. She sat in the same chair Katy had left her in, wearing that satiny red robe, staring glumly at herself in the makeup mirror. Candy hovered behind her, fumbling with her hair, attempting to style it into…

Well, Katy had no idea what. Princess Leia's cinnamon buns? A Bavarian barmaid's coiffure? With green streaks.

Jackie crept over to Katy. "Thank goodness you got the lights back on," she whispered. "But we have a new problem." She aimed a worried look at Lindsay. "She hasn't said a word. Just sits there, staring. Refereeing playground squabbles I can handle. This is *way* outside my skill set. Is there anything you can do?"

A shroud of guilt settled on Katy's shoulders. She'd been so preoccupied with all of the plans for today blowing up, and twice as preoccupied with thoughts of kissing Blaine, she hadn't given much attention to the poor bride.

Though doubtful she could do or say anything to coax Lindsay out of her funk, Katy lifted her chin and went over to try.

"Hi," she said softly, eyeing Lindsay's reflection in the mirror. The bride's tense and gloomy appearance matched Katy's inner turbulence. Even the lights on her ugly Christmas sweater seemed out of sorts. "Are you going to be okay?"

Lindsay shrugged.

Katy stepped closer and turned, leaning against the counter and facing her. "Is there anything I can do, anything at all, to help out?"

"Can you stop the snow?"

Katy's stomach tightened. No one but Mother Nature could solve that problem. She exchanged a concerned glance with Candy then tried again. "I'm sorry. I really wish I could. I *can* get you something to eat. Would you like that?"

Still staring at herself in the mirror, Lindsay shook her head.

"How about a hug from Todd? I can bring him up here." Katy regretted the words as soon as they escaped her mouth. Bad idea to add Todd to the stressful equation —one look at him and his many injuries and the gloom cloud over the bride's head would swallow her whole.

"No. We're not supposed to see each other before the ceremony. It's a tradition." Lindsay sighed a miserable sigh. "I planned and I planned, you know. This was going to be the best wedding ever. The best day ever." She dabbed at her eyes with a wad of tissues. "My mother loved Christmas. I inherited that from her. She loved the decorations, the presents, the carols. And she *adored* Santa Claus. Isn't that funny?" A wistful smile touched her lips. "I wanted a Christmas wedding for her, in memory of everything she loved. I wanted this day to be perfect, for her. And now it's ruined."

Katy's eyes misted over and a lump the size of a snowball lodged in her throat. She felt small and terribly self-centered to have been mooning over Blaine all afternoon when she should've been focused on what this important day meant to Lindsay.

"No, it's *not* ruined," Katy said. "You've done an amazing job. You've captured Christmas perfectly, everything your mother loved about it."

Lindsay met her eyes for the first time. "But the snow…"

"Snow on Christmas is a tradition." Lindsay looked skeptical so Katy rushed on. "You know, I lost my mother too. When I was young, like you. She loved Christmas, like yours did, *especially* when it snowed. Christmas and snow go together like milk and cookies, my mom would say." Emotion welled up and her voice trembled. "If your mother was anything like mine, I bet she thought the same thing. And I bet she wouldn't care about the snow today. I suspect the most important thing about this day would be *you*, and how proud she was. How happy she would be to know that you're happy."

Lindsay's eyes filled with tears, and the doom cloud around her lifted a smidge.

"Nothing can be done about the storm or people staying home," Katy went on. "But it's not your fault. You *can't* beat yourself up about something out of your control."

She paused to let that sink in. For both of them. Katy had repeated Blaine's words, his pep talk to her earlier when the electricity had gone out. Words she'd been too stressed to hear at the time but knew she should take to heart.

"I think the thing to keep in mind is, you're here, Lindsay. Todd's here. The people most important to you both are here. And you are all going to have *the* best time. I know everyone will love the food. Plus, there will be *plenty* of leftovers for second helpings."

A smile flickered on Lindsay's lips. The doom cloud dissipated some more.

"And don't forget the cake," Katy added quickly. "There's so much cake, everyone can have three pieces."

That reached her. She laughed. "Oh, right, my cake! I designed it you know. It took a lot of hunting, but I found this hole-in-the-wall bakery in town that could do *exactly* what I wanted. Isn't it beautiful?"

Not the word Katy would use to describe it, but beauty was in the eye of the beholder. Not to mention the one who'd paid for it. "It's the most, uh, stunning cake I've ever seen. Can't wait until you and Todd cut it and I can have a piece."

Lindsay dabbed at her eyes again, perking up even more, like a light bulb going from bleak to bright.

"Are you going to shove a piece of cake in Todd's face?" Angela asked, adjusting the candy cane headpiece atop her black hair.

"That would be mean. And messy," Lindsay scolded. Then she giggled. "But it *is* a tradition, so maybe I will."

"Do it!" Candy said and the other bridesmaids joined in. Chants of *Smash the cake! Smash the cake!* rounded the room until everyone howled with laughter and Lindsay's doom cloud had completely evaporated.

Grinning now, she snatched up a lipstick from the counter and painted her lips a brilliant Christmas red. "How's Todd doing," she asked, glancing at Katy. "Is he nervous?"

"Not really." He was making everyone else nervous, though, as they braced themselves for his next injury. But she wouldn't breathe a word of that to his bride-to-be, not with her back in a good mood again. "He's excited. Everyone is. Can't wait for the big event."

"Me too." Lindsay recapped the lipstick and caught Candy's eye in the mirror. "Hey you. Is my hair almost done? I want to put on my gown and get ready." She shifted back to Katy. "Tell Todd and Nick and everyone I'll be ready in about fifteen minutes." She grinned again. "And then we can get this party started."

Oh, crud. Nick. As in Nicholas Jolly, justice of the peace. Katy had completely forgotten about him. The last piece of this wedding day puzzle left to fit into place. He was still missing, perhaps not coming at all. Hearing that would crash Lindsay's mood for good.

The door burst open, and Daisy rushed in, her elf bells jingle-jangling a holiday tune. "Anyone ho-ho-hungry?" she called.

They were. They surrounded Daisy and plucked food from the trays like hungry birds dressed in red velvet. A bridesmaid named Clarice settled some treats on a napkin and brought it over to the bride, offering the appetizers like a supplicant. Lindsay nibbled on a veggie cup while Candy finished up her hair.

Katy breathed a sigh of relief. The Daisy distraction had bought her more time to try to locate Jolly Old Saint Nick. She excused herself and headed for the door.

"Any sign of the justice of the peace?" she asked Daisy hopefully as she passed.

"Nope. No one else has come in that I could see." She held out one of her trays. "Here, have a bite."

"Thanks." Katy picked up one of the veggie cups. "I forgot to have food sent up for the bridesmaids, but you didn't."

"Don't thank me, thank the chef," Daisy said. "He sent me up here. Thought the ladies might be ready for a snack."

Of course. Blaine had thought of everything. Took care of everything, too. Katy popped the pastry bite into her mouth. Not cold, not piping hot from the oven either, but still delicious. Because Blaine could also *do* everything. A man as skilled at cooking as he was at kissing.

She choked, thinking that, and swallowed wrong, launching into a coughing fit.

"Whoa!" Daisy pounded her on the back. "Something went down the wrong pipe."

Katy held up a hand and croaked out, "I'm okay. Just need a drink."

Daisy shifted her gaze to Lindsay. "You're not seriously going to let her walk down the aisle like that. That hairdo looks like the bride of Frankenstein."

Katy shrugged. "No stylist."

"No kidding. Let me have a crack at it. I've got sisters. I've wielded a styling wand or two in my day."

"Go ahead, but I have to warn you, Lindsay's stressed. She's simmering like a tea kettle about to boil over."

"That's different from my sisters, how? I've got this." Daisy shot Katy a sly look the matchmaking Mrs. Lathrop would envy. "Why don't you go downstairs and see if the chef needs any help?"

She jingled over to Lindsay and wrested the hairbrush away from Candy. Katy left the suite, determined to do two things, find Nick Jolly and, despite Daisy's recommendation, avoid the chef at all costs.

CHAPTER SIXTEEN

*K*aty hung up and put her phone away. She'd called Nick's number six times and still no answer. Dejected, she leaned against the banister at the bottom of the stairs, considering her next steps, when she saw something across the room that made her heart skip a beat. And not in a good, Blaine kind of way. Todd and his groomsmen swarmed toward the Christmas tree like a pack of curious canines and began pawing through the sack of gifts.

Katy's heels clacked madly on the floor as she dashed to the scene. "Excuse *me*," she said in an icy voice and snatched the sack from Todd's hands. "Did someone tell you to open this bag?"

She hoped for a *yes*, so she could finally discover the identity of the secret Santa. But the men shuffled their feet and wouldn't meet her eyes. They looked so much like six-year-olds caught with their hands in the cookie jar, Katy almost laughed. Maybe she would have, if she wasn't so frazzled and out of patience.

"I believe it's within my rights to open this," Todd said, holding up a rectangular-shaped package he'd managed to liberate from the bag. "It's got my name on it."

His *I-rest-my-case* self-confidence might've been more effective if he didn't look like he'd lost a boxing match, a wrestling match, and an MMA tournament all at the same time. Katy tallied up the damage—black eye, bruised face, torn tuxedo coat, stained shirt, injured arm in a makeshift sling, limping, a bump on his head, and was that a scrape on his chin?

The groomsmen weren't as battered but their tuxes were bedraggled, their hair mussed, and flaky pastry crumbs were sprinkled like snowflakes on their lapels. They joined Todd in a pleading chorus, begging her to let them open their gifts.

She sighed. If it would keep these guys occupied and out of trouble for a few minutes, why not give the boys their toys. No one had claimed the gifts anyway.

"Oh, all right," she said, completely devoid of Christmas cheer. "Only if you promise to sit down and be quiet."

They all solemnly swore not to make any more mayhem then crowded around her.

She dug into the bag and pulled out a package. She called out the recipient's name and the whole gang cheered like the guy had won the lottery. The *woohoos* repeated for every item she gave out. Generic grooms-men's gifts Katy had seen distributed at other weddings. A phone case for one guy, a deck of cards for another, shot glasses and pens for everyone else. The man's name and the date of the wedding were stenciled on each item.

Todd eagerly tore off his gift's wrapping paper. His expression morphed to disappointment when he saw what was inside. A whisk broom with stiff bristles. To clean up his many messes? The mysterious gift-giver sure had a weird sense of humor.

The men shambled off after she handed out the last of their packages. "Behave yourselves," she called after them, seriously doubting they would.

She went to get her much needed drink of water then slung the bag over her shoulder like Santa Claus himself and started around the room. Now that the gifts were out of the bag, so to speak, she might as well distribute the rest.

Todd's mother, looking as wilted as her Christmas corsage, opened her gift to find a small pillow with a design of a bride and groom waltzing across a winter scene. "Oh, it's lovely," she said. "I collect needlepoint pillows. I even stitch a few of my own. How did you know?"

Katy gave her the same answer she'd given to everyone else who'd asked, "It's not from me. It's from a secret Santa."

She took out the next present—a gift for someone named Cole. She looked around the room. Could he be one of bride's relatives seated at a table near the Christmas tree? Or the elderly man in the top hat and tail-coat chatting with Mr. Parker by the fireplace?

Her gaze landed on Blaine as he emerged from the kitchen, carrying a tray loaded with appetizers. She flushed hotter than a fireplace poker. Each breathless moment of their kiss came back, chasing Cole and the gifts and every other blessed thing from her mind. Every emotion and feeling flooded her, too. The amazing sensation of his lips on hers, the subtle pressure of his hand on her back as he brought her against him, the hungry way she'd responded.

Look away, don't make eye contact, she told herself. She was furious with him, the tantalizing jerk, for kissing her like that. For making her lose her head and forget about the wedding and her schedule and everything. Making her forget about Blaine's own problematic behavior. For making her feel giddy and restless and miserable and elated, all at the same time.

And worst of all, for making her think about how good his arms felt around her and how good they were together.

Don't look, don't look, don't...

Oh, crap, she couldn't help it. She looked.

He held the tray balanced on the tips of his fingers as he wended through the tables, moving with a panther-like grace that set her pulse racing. That got her winded and breathless and eager for him to take her out into the snow again and kiss her until her toes curled.

Two young women, the ones giggling at Ash's magic tricks earlier, sidled up to him. They weren't giggling now. They eyed Blaine as if they were ravenous and he was the only thing on the menu. The women pored over the appetizers. Blaine said something. They laughed. He dimpled, tossing in a sexy shrug for good measure.

Katy's eyes narrowed. What was so funny? Probably nothing. Just Blaine in standard flirt mode, like with the bridesmaids earlier.

Like him with her all day.

Put a leash on it, Katy. She'd flirted with him, too. Copiously and constantly. Since the moment he'd stolen that wine from her. And she'd enjoyed it. Enjoyed how loose and relaxed and thoroughly free he made her feel.

She resumed her Santa Claus duties and circled the room, avoiding Blaine as best she could. Avoiding eye contact with Ash, too. He repeatedly waved, frantic for her attention. She firmly turned away each time.

Unable to locate Cole, Katy gave up and took the next package out of the bag. A small box wrapped in different paper than the rest, a vintage design of reindeer playing in the snow. The tag read, *Buddy Lathrop*. She spotted Lindsay's dad pacing near the bar and approached him. Still on the phone, still nattering about the North Pole, he waved her off when she tried to hand him the box, so she moved on.

The gift bag grew considerably lighter, and the room quieted, with guests and groomsmen alike occupied with their food, drinks, and goodies. She pulled out a package addressed to the bartender next and headed over. The secret Santa had to be someone who knew everyone who'd be in attendance today. They had included a gift for all the guests, the bridesmaids, and even the functions staff like Natalia, Maggie, and Blaine.

Perhaps Cole was one of the staff who couldn't make it today, possibly the assistant Blaine had mentioned who'd gotten stuck in the snow. That would explain why she couldn't find him. She would have to check the names on her clipboard to find out for sure, if she could ever find where she'd put it.

Natalia's forehead crinkled in an unspoken question as Katy handed over a weighty rectangular box. Her confusion turned to delight as Katy explained the mystery of the gifts and their giver.

"I bet they're from the lady with the cane." Natalia held her present close to her ear and shook it, as if the sound would reveal the contents. "She seems to like doing over-the-top stuff like that. Not that I'm complaining." She put the package on the bar and turned a curious gaze on Katy. "So, what's your deal? Are you new? I haven't seen you on the functions circuit before. What happened to Maggie? Did she move on to brighter things?"

"Oh no, she loves this place. I doubt she'll ever leave." Katy gave her the *Cliff's Notes* version of why she'd stepped in for her sister today.

"Yay for sisters," Natalia said emphatically. "Biological or metaphorical, you can always count on them to help you out." She clenched her fist and came in for a bump and Katy obliged.

"Can I ask you something?" Katy said.

Natalia rested her elbows on the bar, her expression attentive. "Sure. Shoot."

How could she word this? Ask point-blank if Blaine was a womanizer? "Well, it's about Blaine," she began.

Natalia suddenly looked like she ate something bad. "Blaine? What about him?"

The man himself arrived before Katy could say another word, so she put her questions away. Blaine must've restocked his tray. It overflowed with appetizers. He caught her in his gaze, his scowl so scorching he melted every drop of snow for six miles around. And melted the ice wall she'd tried to build around her heart in a hot second.

Natalia watched them, her eyebrows hiking up to her hairline. "Hmm, interesting," she mused, but didn't get a chance to elaborate. A customer called to her and she moved away.

That left Katy and Blaine alone. With the kiss between them.

"Thanks for sending Daisy up with food," she said, scrambling for something to say. "The bridesmaids were beyond hungry."

"Good," he said, his eyes locked on hers.

"Daisy's still up there. She got drafted to do the bride's hair, since the stylist is a no-show."

"Good," he repeated.

"She should be down soon."

"Good," he said again, as if he'd forgotten every other word in the English language.

Katy seemed to have forgotten too. The only words she could remember were *kiss me* and *kiss me again*. Words she ached to say but couldn't dare.

"Snooky-poo?" a voice purred from behind her.

Katy stiffened. Ash had snuck up on them. The heat in Blaine's eyes flamed out. His posture went as rigid as a steel beam.

Ash plucked at Katy's sweater sleeve. "I know you're busy, but I can't wait. I *need* to talk to you."

"Yes, Ash," she said wearily. Was he going to take a trip down memory lane again? When he'd cornered her before she had gone out to help Blaine with the generator, he'd talked and talked about the good old days when they were together and barely gave Katy a chance for a rebuttal.

"Guess I'll be on my way," Blaine said, his voice glacial.

Katy watched him stalk away across the room like a lion looking for his next meal then she turned to Ash, her patience fully depleted.

"Well, what is it—?" She broke off as several groomsmen raced by. She aimed a Blaine-level scowl at them. They'd broken their promise to chill out and tossed around what looked like one of those stuffed elves that sat on a shelf. Thankfully, Todd had decided to sit this game out.

She drew Ash away from the bar toward the alcove and out of harm's way. The Christmas tree twinkled in the low light, spreading a cheery, holiday glow over the cake she and Blaine had placed there what seemed like days ago.

"Okay, Ash, talk. No, wait. You always do the talking. It's *my* turn. I want to say some things, what I should've said long ago, but didn't have the strength to." She took a breath, and it came out in a rush. "What you did hurt me. You disrespected me and were dishonest. You cheated on me. You were a total shit to me. I was furious with you for the longest time. But now I'm angrier with myself. For letting you get to me. For not speaking up, for not realizing sooner we would never work."

She knew that now. Knew it because in her year and a half together with Ash, she had *never* felt the connection she felt with Blaine mere hours after meeting him.

Ash sputtered and she held up her hand. "Face it. We weren't right for each other," she said. "With our jobs and everything, we spent so little time together we barely got to know each other. We have no common interests. You're into magic shows and partying and playing poker. I like old movies and running and playing with puppies."

She also loved laughing over puns and other terrible jokes. Ash didn't get puns and never told a joke he didn't steal. She had more in common with that impossible, but oh-so-kissable chef than she ever had with her ex.

"Come on, Katy. We had one thing in common. Each other."

"We did, for a while. It wasn't enough. You were restless and I was stubborn, determined to make our relationship work. When we met, I had this life plan. I thought you fit that plan perfectly, so I told myself I *had* to make us work. I tried to control something that couldn't be controlled. I've changed since then, Ash. I've finally figured it out. Life's not about sticking to some stupid plan. Or schedules or timelines. It's about doing what makes you happy."

Happy. An important word, a word she had neglected in her life and should learn to embrace. She could make a long list of things that made her happy. The part of her job where she got to meet people. The exhilaration she felt after a fast run. Chocolate. A book that made her laugh and cry on the same page. Hanging out with her friends. Spending time with Maggie. Dogs in general, playing with dogs in particular. And even Blaine. Especially Blaine.

The only thing missing from that list was Ash.

"You know it's true." Katy took his hand and softened her voice. "We were never happy together. The most important ingredient for a relationship to work, and it wasn't there. And that's what I need. Someone who'll make me happy. Who's happy to be with me, and *only* me. Someone I can trust. You're *not* that man, Ash, and you never were."

Neither was Blaine, she had to remind herself. Despite the explosive power of his kiss. And its promise.

She released his hand. "There, I'm done. I've said my piece." And it felt good. Letting it out and letting it go. "Now, what did you want to talk to me about?"

He gulped and tugged at the knot of his perfectly tied tie. "Well, after what you said, it's not that important. It can probably wait. In fact, let's forget about it altogether."

"Yes, let's. Though I have to tell you, my answer would've been no. There's no way we're getting back together."

He flinched. "How did you know that's what I wanted?"

"Wasn't tough, Ash. You paid more attention to me today than the entire time we were dating. And tell me, assuming my brain had gone on vacation, and I said yes, isn't there an obstacle to our reuniting? The woman you left me for?"

"Sasha?" He let out a nervous titter. "Yeah... She dumped me a couple of months ago. She said we were through and kicked me to the curb."

"Sorry to hear that," Katy said, without an ounce of sincerity. "So naturally, once you were single, you figured you'd go back to old faithful."

"No, it's not like that. You say you've changed. I have too. Sasha leaving me opened my eyes. I realized she wasn't what I wanted. *You* are. I was a selfish jerk to you. I treated you bad. Disrespected you, as you said. I was so busy chasing all the other shiny objects, I didn't see I had the real thing with you. I didn't figure that out until today. Seeing you got me thinking about us and what would've happened if things had been different. If I'd been smart. But..."

He paused and gazed at her. A thousand emotions flickered over his face. Remorse and regret. Resignation. Sadness, even.

"But you know me, Katy. I'm not that smart."

Katy's eyes widened in surprise. That was the most honest he'd ever been with her. The closest she'd ever felt to him. As they were saying goodbye. For good.

Impulsively, she hugged him. "Thank you for saying that Ash. It means a lot."

They broke apart and he flashed that perfect smile. "So, coffee? How about dinner?"

"Not a chance."

He laughed. "I know. Thought I'd give it a shot. But the truth is, the second I saw you with that guy, the chef, I knew I didn't have a prayer."

Katy's cheeks flamed. Was her interest in Blaine that obvious?

Ash straightened his suit jacket and smoothed his silky hair. "See ya around, snooky-poo." He turned and strode away. "And you *do* look amazing," he called back over his shoulder. "Even in that ugly sweater."

She watched him go with a mystified smile, feeling light and airy and thoroughly unburdened. Amazing what speaking your mind could do. Amazing what a bit of honesty could do, too.

"What did the chimney sweep want?" Blaine asked, suddenly by her side.

Katy jumped, and so did her pulse. As usual when Mr. Dimples invaded her personal space. "Just taking care of some unfinished business," she said. "Finished business, actually."

And on to new business, she thought, hope sparking in her heart. Ash had claimed to have changed. Could Blaine change too?

Suddenly, bleats of alarm rang out from the grooms-men. Katy and Blaine spun toward the commotion. Time seemed to slow down as the scene unfolded. Todd's friends had abandoned the stuffed elf and commandeered a table-cloth to play matador at the bullfight. Todd joined the fun and took on the role of the bull. Bent over, leading with his good arm, he charged at the makeshift bullfighter's cape. A groomsman named Joseph snapped the cloth away.

What happened next had been inevitable since the groom had first tumbled off the bus a few hours ago. Katy watched in open-mouthed horror as Todd rushed forward, unable to check his speed. He sailed past her and Blaine, arms flailing, and belly-flopped face down.

Into the cake.

The towering Christmas tree collapsed with an audible *splop.* Chunks of cake shot out, east, west, north, and south like pieces of a planet walloped by a meteor. A sizeable slice landed by Katy's feet. Frosting showered all around like green snow.

Aunts gasped and uncles moaned. Blaine swore. Katy swore too, but the groomsmen went as silent as the grave. They surrounded Todd, dug him out of the cake and carried him across the room as if they were his pallbearers. They deposited him in a chair, where he slumped, looking glum and somewhat comical now that he wore most of the cake. Crumbs and frosting smeared his napkin arm sling and the front of his tux, his face was painted green, and the white chocolate star that had once topped the tree now stuck to his lapel.

Blaine dashed to the scene of the cake crime. Katy dragged her feet behind him. She gaped at the flattened mess, the squished pancakes that were once colorful fondant gifts, and the chunks of chocolate cake and frosting that littered the floor.

"I. Give. Up," she muttered. Tears poked at her eyes. This was the disaster of disasters. Lindsay loved that cake. She would explode for real when she heard of its demise. A great big bridezilla supernova. Maggie would be furious. She'd never ask Katy to help her out of a jam ever again, not after the mess she'd made of today.

And Blaine. He stood next to her, his jaw working as he stared at the smushed mess. He probably wished he'd never heard of Newell-by-the-Sea. It was a sure bet he'd never, ever want to come back to Disaster Hall. Or ever want to see her again.

She choked on a sob.

"Hey." He turned to her and took her in his arms. Surprising, but what she needed at the moment. She sank against his chest, feeling his warmth and taking comfort.

"Remember what I said earlier? Don't panic. All's not lost. We can fix this."

"How?" She pulled away and gazed up at him. "Do you have a spare cake in your pocket you're not telling me about?"

"I have something better." He lifted his hand and brushed a tear from her cheek with his thumb. "I've got an idea. An idea that will fix everything. But I need your help. You in?"

Katy's anxiety began to fade. He *would* figure a way out of this disaster. No matter what else the man was, an incorrigible flirt, a bossy grouch, the best kisser in the world, and no matter how much her head spun and how confused she got just looking at him, Katy knew one thing for certain.

The man could fix *anything*.

"I'm in," she said, trying on a smile. "Let's get started."

CHAPTER SEVENTEEN

"*L*et's leave this mess where it is." Cole gestured to the deceased cake crumbled on the cart and the pieces splattered across the floor. "We can't move it, not without a trail of crumbs so wide Hansel and Gretel would have no trouble finding their way home."

Maggie laughed. A sound he was happy to hear. Cole had feared she'd lose it totally after Todd's swan dive into the cake, but her panic had downshifted. She'd backed away from the edge and her tears had dried. Those tears had nearly done him in. He'd wanted to kiss every single one of them away.

Yeah, not going to happen, not after what he'd seen before the cake disaster. Cole had been ready to lay it all out there and ask Maggie how she felt about Ash—and about him. His hopes had collapsed like an overcooked souffle when he'd seen her hugging the deejay. That was a real gut punch.

Maggie commandeered the tablecloth the groomsmen had used for the bullfight and together they spread it over the cake's remains. Then Cole took her by the arm and led her into the kitchen, closing the door behind them.

The two of them inside, the chaos outside.

"See if you can find some flour," he said, directing her to the pantry and heading for the refrigerator. He'd brought a lot of his own ingredients, including sugar for the blueberry vinaigrette and a small amount of flour, but he didn't have enough for what he had in mind.

"What are you doing?" she asked, looking perplexed. "Are you going to make a cake?"

"Not a cake. I don't have the tools for that, or the time. I'm making a sweet substitute that's quick and easy." He opened the fridge and took out the butter and the maple syrup he'd brought to glaze the lobster bites. Who knew maple syrup would save the day?

Maggie took one glance at the syrup and plunked her fists onto her hips. "You are *not* making pancakes."

He laughed. Couldn't help himself. She lit him up in every way. Even if she preferred someone else over him.

"I'm making cookies," he said. "Shortbread cookies, from my grandmother's recipe. The most delicious treat ever to emigrate from north of the border. Or...I *will* make them if we can find some flour. Now get moving."

While she hunted around in the pantry, he dug through the kitchen's cabinets and found two mixing bowls of the right size.

"See if there's any brown sugar in there," he called to her. If there wasn't, regular sugar would have to do, though the cookies wouldn't taste the same.

"Aye, aye, Captain Cook," she called back.

Grinning, he washed his hands then rinsed the bowls

and a couple of glass measuring cups he'd found. He dried them then attacked the drawers, searching for measuring spoons.

Maggie came back, arms loaded down. She plopped two bags of flour and a bag of brown sugar onto the counter. "This place has enough supplies to last until well into the new year," she said.

He checked the expiration dates on the flour bags before he opened one. "We could be here until then if this storm keeps up and we get snowed in."

"With the groom and his wild bunch? No thanks. I'll take my chances with the blizzard and walk home if that happens. Anything else I can do?"

Kiss me, he wanted to say, but he'd wanted to say that since he'd met her, so he settled for sending her on a hunt for some cookie sheets. Then he got to work, mixing the ingredients from memory. Not a strenuous task, with such a simple recipe—butter, sugar, flour, syrup.

"There's enough butter for a triple batch," he said. "That ought to be plenty of cookies for everyone. As long as that walking time bomb of a groom doesn't come in and wreck everything."

Maggie came back to the island carrying two long cookie sheets. "If Todd sets foot in here," she said. "I'll tackle him myself."

Cole poured flour into a measuring cup. "I didn't know tackling wedding guests is part of a wedding planner's job."

"Event manager, actually. And yes, page fifteen in the job description. Right after the instructions on helping the chef reboot the generator."

She leaned against the countertop and watched him work. Her nearness, her warmth, her sweet scent made it hard to focus, but he did his best, mashing the butter with a wooden spoon until it softened, then mixing it with the sugar.

"What, no mixer?" she said.

"Nope. My grandmother always uses a wooden spoon, not a mixer." Hard work, since this butter was chilled, but good for bicep definition. "The old-fashioned way is best, Mémé says. People can taste the difference." Next, he folded the flour into the creamed butter and sugar. "The syrup goes in last. That's the tricky part. Too much, and the cookies will come out soggy and super sweet. Too little and the dough cooks up dry and chalky."

"A classic Goldilocks dilemma, with the bears' porridge," she said. "Not too hot, not too cold. The ingredients have to be just right."

"Exactly. And Mémé gets it just right every time." He drizzled syrup into the batter, bringing the kitchen alive with the smell of family and home. "At least, every time as far as I know. Maybe she had hundreds of soggy or chalky batches to her credit before she achieved maple syrup perfection."

Maggie laughed softly. "Does your mother make these cookies too?"

"My mother is like you in the cooking department." Stirring, he tilted his gaze toward her and couldn't help a teasing smile. "The oven is her enemy, the stove her nemesis. My grandmother does it all, and she doesn't mind. She loves to have parties and feed people until they pop. She has this big Christmas Eve party every year. The whole family comes. It's like a command performance. I was supposed to be at the party tonight but..." Guilt poked his conscience and he shrugged it off. "Duty calls."

Her eyes clouded. Only a flash, but he caught it. What had he said to cause that?

"I had a party planned for tonight, too," she said. "Looks like we both changed our plans." She fidgeted a moment before looking at him again. "Can you tell me what happened with your fiancée? Unless it's too painful to talk about."

Cole scowled at the batter. Too painful? Yeah, once. At first it had hurt like an open wound. But now, after two years? He'd put that part of his life in the past. A wound healed over. He slid another glance at Maggie. He wanted to move on.

"Celia decided we didn't work together," he said, focusing on the cookie dough. "Would've been nice of her to tell me *before* I got the tux and showed up at the church, but she was right. I get it now. We hadn't been dating long, barely knew each other, and then we were engaged."

His fault. They were at a wedding for one of Celia's friends. He'd been feeling romantic. She'd felt left out of the matrimonial party. The bottle of cabernet they had polished off didn't help any. Cole had popped the question seconds after the *Lyft* had dropped them off at home. She said yes, and that had been it.

"Enough time's passed, now I can admit I had my doubts. I can admit *she* had doubts. But then?" He shrugged and poured a touch more syrup into the batter. "The wedding plans escalated, breaking the bank. More and more, it became about Celia and not about us. I catered to her, tried to make it work." He shifted and gazed at Maggie. "I couldn't, *wouldn't* admit to failure. I worked hard to smooth out every bump and fix every wrinkle."

"Taking charge, as always," she said.

"Yeah, the control freak in action. But ultimately, I couldn't fix anything. Couldn't fix *us*. The big day arrived, she got cold feet, and she left. She found a way to fix us, just not in the way I expected."

Cole looked into Maggie's soft brown eyes and felt a bittersweet sting. He'd never shared his thoughts about Celia with anyone. He'd shut down after the breakup and kept it all in. Now here he was, going on and on. Because of her. He felt connected to her, able to open up in a way he never had before.

"Okay, no more lounging," he said, with a cheerfulness he didn't feel. "There's still work to do. We need a cookie cutter. A maple leaf would be preferable, but since we're not quite in Canada, I don't have my hopes up. See what you can find."

"Will do."

While she searched through the drawers and cabinets, Cole got to work. He cleaned a space on the countertop to roll out the dough and sprinkled the area with flour. He shifted the beef onto one of the warming racks and readied to put the cookies in by adjusting the temperature. Twelve minutes at three-hundred degrees, slow and easy, until they were done.

"I couldn't find a maple leaf," Maggie said, coming out of the pantry. "Will this do?"

Her lips curved in a smoky smile as she held up a reindeer cookie cutter. Was she thinking of that deer that had horned in on their horizontal conversation in the snow? Cole's mind shot to something else that had happened out there, something he burned to recreate.

"Appropriate, don't you think?" he said, pulling back from those thoughts. "Have you noticed the Christmas theme today? Besides the obvious, the tree and the decorations. I mean the sleigh, the deer, Santa at the store and the *Grinning Reindeer* wine. Daisy's costume, your sweater. The bag of gifts. Mrs. Lathrop's first name, *Carol*."

"The bartender, Natalia. Even the bridesmaids' names are decidedly festive. Joy, Candy, Eve."

"And their outfits," he said. "That's like Christmas overkill."

Maggie's forehead crinkled and her smile melted away. She drifted to the sink to wash the cookie cutter. Cole threw a chunk of dough onto the countertop and attacked it with the rolling pin, wondering what he'd done to kill her Christmas spirit.

She came back a minute later and handed him the cookie cutter then leaned against the counter again. "You know, I met Ash two years ago tonight, on Christmas Eve," she said.

Cole sank the plastic reindeer into the dough then transferred the cutout to the cookie sheet. "So, he's the ghost of Christmas past *and* present?" He kept his focus on his task, and his voice cool, though he longed to let the sarcasm fly.

An enigmatic expression touched her face. "Yeah, he popped up today to show me the error of my ways."

"The ghost of Christmas future can't be far behind."

Another mysterious look, then, "Do you ever see Celia?"

Cole tensed. Where was she going with this? "I don't have the good fortune of running into my ex all over town, like you do." She cleared her throat, so he put the snark away. "I saw her once, after it was over. Haven't run into her since. I have no idea where she is now, but I wish her well. Always have."

Maggie traced two fingers through some flour on the countertop, like a skater gliding across a snowy lake, her gaze intent on the movement. "Ash says he's learned his lesson and that he's changed." She looked up, meeting Cole's eyes. "What do you think? Do you feel it's possible for a man like that to change?"

Cole stilled. How could he answer a question like that? People changed, it happened all the time, and maybe Ash could too. At least, it seemed that was what Maggie wanted to hear. She had her doubts about getting back together with him and needed validation. Something Cole wouldn't do.

He shrugged. "You know the old saying. A leopard can't change its spots. Habits are hard to kick. A man can say he's changed, but can he follow through?"

Her face paled and Cole's gut clenched as tight as a drum. He was a certified ass, but no way would he lie to her.

She shifted and looked down at the cookie sheet, now filled with a dozen maple-scented reindeer lined up in neat rows. "Those are perfect," she said, her voice strained. "How do you get them to come out like that? They'd be big, gushy blobs if I made them."

"Practice, persistence, and a whole lot of patience," he said. "Actually, it's not as difficult as you think." He threw out more flour and dropped a fresh glop of batter onto the counter. He stuck the rolling pin in her hand. "Give it a try."

"Seriously?" She gaped at the rolling pin as if it were a UFO that had just dropped out of the sky. "I already told you I can't cook. That goes double for baking."

"Go on, at least try. Don't press too hard and roll it out slow."

She did not. She leaned on the rolling pin and pushed it like she was operating a steamroller. The dough stuck to the wooden cylinder in a clump. Cole laughed. He could see he had his work cut out for him.

"I *told* you I wasn't good at this," she grumbled in frustration.

"You can be. Here, let me show you." Without thinking, he moved behind her and reached around, placing his hands over hers on the rolling pin's handles. "Now, nice and easy," he said, close to her ear. "A feather touch."

Together, they rolled the pin slowly forward, stretching their arms, then pulled back just as slow, flattening the dough. They moved as one in a rhythmic, sensual dance. The backs of her hands felt like silk under his palms. He smelled her hair, her neck, her scent. His blood raced through his veins. She might not be good at baking, but she sure knew the recipe for driving him wild.

"That's it," he said, hoping she couldn't hear the ache in his voice. "You're doing just fine."

She rolled the pin back and swiveled slightly, turning

her head to look at him. "I have a good teacher," she murmured, sounding breathless.

Their eyes met and a hushed quiet fell over the room, save for the wind blowing outside and the thunder of Cole's heart. He shifted his gaze to her lips. Rational thought shut down and instinct took over. He reached up and gently scooped her silky hair behind her ear, then traced her jaw line. He slid his thumb over her trembling bottom lip. The memory of her soft and velvety smooth lips against his burned through him and he longed to taste their sweetness again.

He cupped her chin and tipped her head back, leaning closer. She moved upward to meet him, parting her lips. A small, needy sound hummed in her throat, matched by his own low growl.

Their lips touched and fireworks exploded in Cole's brain.

"No," she moaned, suddenly pulling away. "We can't do this. It's wrong."

He slammed back down to earth. "What do you mean? We're good together. I feel like we have something real, something powerful. How can that be wrong?"

She shot him a look he'd never seen before. An expression that kicked him in the teeth, in the stomach, and in the groin all at the same time. A look filled with disappointment.

"How can you say that?" she cried. "You *know* it's wrong. There's an obstacle between us, well, several obstacles, and as far as I'm concerned, until that's fixed this—" She thrust out her hand and pointed at him, then at herself. "This thing…this *us* can never be."

He ground his teeth. She meant Ash. A big obstacle. An insurmountable obstacle, it seemed. A guy completely unworthy of Maggie, as Mrs. Lathrop had said. A cheater. A leopard Cole doubted would ever change his spots. A man who would hurt her over and over again. His shoulders sagged. A man she'd rather be with than him.

"*I* can't fix that," he growled, frustrated, hurt and full of jealous fire. "Only you can—"

The kitchen door slammed open, and they jumped apart. Daisy sailed into the room. Cole swore. How did he not hear her coming, with those damned jingle bells?

"I know all about the cake tragedy," Daisy said. She tossed two empty trays into one of the sinks and started to scrub them. "It's the only thing everyone down here is talking about. The crew upstairs hasn't heard yet, though it's only a matter of time."

Maggie eyed Cole with a comically pitiful expression. He would have laughed if the situation weren't so grim. Besides, he'd be laughing at himself. Because the joke was on him. He had finally decided to take a chance and move forward with someone new—and she didn't want him.

Daisy continued chattering, oblivious to the storm raging in Cole's heart.

"You'll be happy to know I fixed the bride's hair into a decent up-do." She glanced over her shoulder at Maggie. "You know, Lindsay ought to sue whoever's been doing her dye jobs. Her hair has got a *wicked* green tint to it."

CHAPTER EIGHTEEN

"You want these cookies in the oven?" Daisy asked from somewhere in the kitchen.

Or from Mars or wherever. Katy couldn't be sure. She'd gotten utterly lost in Blaine's eyes. So focused on him and his fiery gaze and the aching thoughts that crashed about in her mind, the world around them had faded away.

"Cookies?" Blaine snapped toward Daisy then stared down at the cookie sheet as if it had just appeared on the counter by magic.

Daisy laughed. "Yeah, the cookies. Want me to get them going?"

"No, I'll do it," he said, sounding grim. "You roll out the dough for the next batch." He seized the cookie pan and stomped across the kitchen to one of the ovens.

Katy watched him, her insides bubbling like hot lava as she flashed back to moments ago, when they'd rolled out the dough together, moving in unison, his hands on hers in a gentle but firm touch. She'd turned to him as naturally as water flowing down a stream and welcomed his kiss. Sensations flooded her as his lips touched hers, not just desire, something deeper, something exciting and terrifying that exploded into an awareness she had never known with any other man.

Could she be falling for him?

A terrible predicament, if so. Blaine was untrustworthy, a flirt. He may even have a girlfriend. And though that little fact didn't seem to bother him, it bothered Katy. She *couldn't* let herself fall for him. Despite her blossoming feelings, and the way she craved his kiss and wanted him with a longing that stole her breath, she'd gotten hold of herself and leapt away, stopping that kiss before it could really begin.

Mrs. Lathrop bustled in, providing a timely distraction. She carried the sack of gifts. Smaller than it had been an hour ago, but it still looked heavy. Katy abandoned her self-involved mental drama and rushed over, relieving her of the bag and leading her to a chair.

"Thank you, dear." Mrs. Lathrop sat down with a weary sigh. She nodded at the bag. "I thought I'd get that thing out of the dining room. The guests were picking through it like it was a sale bin on Black Friday." She scanned the kitchen, her gaze touching on Blaine and Daisy before settling back on Katy. "My, my, it smells delicious in here. Reminds me of a winter Sunday at the farm when I was a child."

"Our intrepid chef's found an alternative to the cake," Katy said, forcing a jolly tone. "His grandmother's maple cookies."

"How inventive," Mrs. Lathrop said with a delighted

smile. "I *must* have a cookie as soon as they're done. Or perhaps two." She patted the seat of the chair next to her. "Sit with me a bit, will you?"

"I don't think I can," Katy said. "I need to find a shield and some armor then go upstairs to tell Lindsay about the cake."

"Not before you have a cookie," Blaine said. "The first batch will be done in a minute. Stay. That's an order."

"I thought *I* was supposed to give the orders around here," Katy said.

"Maybe out there." He gestured toward the door. "Not in here. In here it's chef's rules. And I say sit down."

Nodding with a cool composure she didn't feel, she sank into a chair. She watched him move a huge pan filled with beef tenderloin from one oven to the other. His biceps flexed under his coat's sleeves. His hair looked as if it had been involved in a terrible accident. Katy touched her mouth, feeling the tempting brush of his lips on hers just moments ago, and earlier, that fuller, searing kiss outside in the snow. Heat drenched her like a summer downpour, and she had to look away.

What was going on with her? She'd heard stories of people falling for each other within hours of meeting. One of her friends had met a guy at a wine tasting and they were engaged within the month. *Love at first sight*, Micki had said. It was real, it did happen, but Katy never thought it could happen to her.

She sighed. And why did it have to happen with a man like Blaine?

"Any word from the justice of the peace?" Mrs. Lathrop asked, gazing at Katy with a puzzled expression.

"No," she said, focusing her thoughts on more important things. "We need another plan. Maybe there's someone here who's a notary public or certified to perform weddings. Daisy, how about you?"

Daisy had moved to the counter, working on cutting out the next batch of cookies. "I can slice tomatoes, chop carrots, and braise a lamb shank," she said. "But performing weddings is *not* in my skill set."

"Let's ask the guests," Mrs. Lathrop offered. "Perhaps one of them is a ship's captain and they can perform the ceremony."

"Don't you have to be at sea for that to be official?" Katy asked.

Blaine weighed in. "In my vast experience, all you need is a signature on the license and a couple of witnesses and you're hitched."

"That's not very romantic," Katy said.

"No, I guess not." He gave her a strange look, an almost melancholy expression she couldn't figure out.

"You know, we can still have one heck of a party without the justice of the peace," Mrs. Lathrop said. "A nice meal, some dancing, carols by the fire. Lindsay and Todd can skedaddle down to city hall to tie the knot when the snow's cleared after Christmas, and all will be well. As far as I'm concerned, it's not the event that makes the romance, it's the two people involved."

Her gaze darted between Katy and Blaine. Katy wished she'd stop that. She also wished she could brush off the JP's absence as easily as Mrs. Lathrop had. Lindsay surely wouldn't be as cheerful about it.

Blaine removed the first batch of cookies from the

oven and carried the cookie sheet to the side counter to cool.

"They look perfect," Daisy said, inhaling deeply. "Smell perfect too."

"Remember what I said about a man who can cook?" Mrs. Lathrop nudged Katy with her elbow. "That goes double for a man who can bake."

"Oh, I almost forgot," Katy said, changing the subject before this matchmaker could list the rest of Blaine's attributes that already took up too much space in her brain. She reached across the table for the bag of gifts, pulling it toward her. "There's a present in here for you."

"There is?" Mrs. Lathrop squealed in delight. "That's a relief. I was afraid Santa had never forgiven me for stealing that Frank Sinatra record from Woolworth's when I was nine." She grinned. "I was *such* a naughty little girl."

"I totally believe that," Katy teased and fished around in the bag until she found the gift addressed to Carol Lathrop. "Merry Christmas."

"Oh my!" She took the flat, rectangular package and inspected it with a wondering expression. "What in the world do you think it is?"

"Open it and find out," Katy coaxed.

Daisy came over. So did Blaine. They watched Mrs. Lathrop slowly unwrap the package, as if she wanted to make the suspense last. Finally, she spread the paper on the table, like opening a book, revealing a photograph in an ancient metal frame. She gasped and pressed her fingers to her mouth.

"Is something wrong?" Katy touched her slim shoulder. It trembled. She was crying.

Several moments passed before the old woman found her voice. "No, no, nothing's wrong." She cleared her throat. "This is a picture of me and my dear husband Wilfred on our wedding day." She lightly brushed her fingertips over the glass, her expression wistful. "That was almost seventy years ago."

Katy, along with Blaine and Daisy, leaned closer and gazed down at a five by seven-inch black-and-white photo of a young woman of eighteen or nineteen. She stood next to a skinny man of average height. He wore a white shirt, wide tie, and a pin-striped suit with a chrysanthemum blooming from his lapel. The bride's cream-colored skirt and jacket with long sleeves were tailored to perfection for her petite frame. A bowl hat trimmed with a lacy veil sat on thick waves of blonde hair that brushed her shoulders.

"You look beautiful," Katy murmured. "And see, the jacket has pockets."

"I knew it! Goodness I was young, and so was Wilfred." Her voice wavered, filled with emotion. "He was a rascal, that one. Look at us, smiling, ready to take on the world." She sighed. "We had our challenges, but, ah, how happy we were together."

Those words resonated in Katy's mind. *Happy. Together.* A team. Like Mrs. Lathrop and her Wilfred. Like the Parkers. Her sister Maggie and Jackson. And her own parents. She thought of their wedding picture she kept on her desk at home. How happy Mom and Dad looked, how happy they were, and how they faced the challenges of their lives together.

Could she find a love as perfect as that? A true love that would last a lifetime? She shivered, so very aware of Blaine next to her, his scent washing over her, his breath warm on her cheek. For two brief, glorious moments when they'd kissed, she thought she'd have the chance to find out. Then reality had set in.

"I thought I'd lost this picture." Mrs. Lathrop looked up at Katy with shining eyes. "I thought it was gone forever. Where in the world did you find it?"

Tears poked at Katy's eyes too. "I'd love to take credit, but none of the gifts are from me. I have no clue who sent them."

"Well, we must discover who this wonderful Santa Claus is. I want to thank them." She dabbed at her eyes with a handkerchief she'd slipped from her sleeve. "What a treat to get this today. The day my granddaughter gets married."

"*If* she gets married," Katy murmured.

Everyone went quiet. Katy glanced at the old-school wall clock hanging above the pantry door. Half past six. The ceremony should've started more than an hour ago and been over with by now. No matter what Mr. Bossy-pants had to say about her staying put, she couldn't procrastinate a second longer.

She gently squeezed Mrs. Lathrop's shoulders then looked at Blaine. "It's time for me to tell Lindsay the bad news. No more delays."

He nodded. "Bring backup. Bring Daisy. She's trained in the martial arts."

Daisy struck a karate pose. "I'm ready."

A shriek rang out in the dining room, so loud and so sudden, Katy jumped. Blaine reached out to steady her. Mrs. Lathrop clapped a hand to her breast.

Another shriek, followed by a long, wailing, "My *c-a-a-a-a-k-e!*"

"You don't have to tell her," Blaine said. "Sounds like she knows."

KATY FLEW to the door and out of the kitchen, with Blaine and Daisy hot on her heels. Mrs. Lathrop followed, moving more slowly, her cane tapping steadily.

In the dining room, the guests were on their feet, their gazes fixed on Lindsay at the top of the wide stairs. The Parkers came out the office, Ash cut off "Feliz Navidad" in the middle of the chorus, Natalia put down a bottle of wine mid-pour, and even the bride's father stopped his phone call to stare at his daughter.

Lindsay had yet to put on her wedding dress. She still wore her red dressing gown over her lacy white slip peeking out from under the robe's hem. Her veil had been pinned onto her swept-back hair, white netting with a crown of red roses and baby's breath that fluttered furiously as she dashed down the stairs. Her bridesmaids and Jackie raced after her like a gaggle of stressed-out baby geese.

"My cake! It's ruined!" Lindsay cried, rushing over to the squashed mess, red-faced and fuming. "*What* happened?"

All eyes turned to the party responsible for the cake's demise. He slunk down in his chair, trying to disappear under the table. Lindsay swung on him. She took in his wedding day wounds and her jaw dropped—torn tuxedo stained with cake and frosting, the left side of his face a startling shade of purple, and his arm dangling in its napkin sling.

"Todd!" She stamped her slipper-clad foot. "What have you done?"

"Oh, hey, hon," he said, hunching his shoulders protectively. "You know you're not supposed to see me before the ceremony. That's bad luck, right?"

Lindsay sputtered. "Bad luck? Really, Todd?" Her voice verged on hysteria. "*Really?*"

Todd struggled to stand. One of the groomsmen darted over and helped him up. Lindsay's expression grew more horrified by the second as he limped toward her. Globs of frosting and chunks of cake rolled down his lapel in a mini avalanche.

"Come on, Linds, I didn't mean to..." He grimaced. "It was an accident—"

"An accident?" she shrieked. "My groom has one eye and a broken arm! Maybe a broken leg! That's an accident? What have you been doing while I've been getting ready? Fooling around while *I've* been dealing with all the calls and texts. People are canceling left and right. No one's coming to our wedding. Not my stylist or photographer. Not my boss or Nancy from HR, or Doug and Kristy or..."

Lindsay ran through the roster of friends, family, and

coworkers who'd cancelled on her big day as if committing them to some kind of revenge memory book.

"...Bob and Belinda, and Herbie and everyone. And what about the justice of the peace! He was supposed to be here by now." Her exasperated gaze skimmed the room and landed on Katy. "Where is he? You're the wedding planner. You're supposed to know these things."

Katy squeaked in alarm and grabbed Blaine's arm for support.

"Lindsay, stop!" her father ordered. His voice was firm. And loud. "Stop it, this instant."

"No, Daddy, I won't!" Tears rolled down her cheeks, digging a trench through her makeup. "It's all ruined! Months of planning and it's *all* ruined. Look at my wedding cake! Look at Todd! It's the worst, most horrible mess in the world."

"Is she talking about Todd or the cake?" Blaine whispered and Katy shushed him.

"Lindsay, hon, listen to me." Todd held up both hands as if desperately trying to stop a speeding bus. "You need to calm down."

Lindsay's head snapped back, and she hit Todd with a knife-sharp glare. The room went silent. No one spoke. No one seemed to breathe. The whistling wind, the sleet tapping out a wintry tempo on the windowpanes, and Katy's own soft moan of dismay were the only sounds.

"Calm down?" Lindsay said between gritted teeth. "Why should I calm down? Everything's ruined! This day was supposed to be the best day of my life. Of *our* lives. The most *important* day. No one's coming and everything's a disaster and...and...and I can't believe it's freaking snowing!"

She shouted that last part, and she didn't say the word *freaking*. The profanity echoed around the room and ricocheted off the ceiling rafters. Pearls were clutched and cries of *Oh my!* made their way from table to table.

As if she'd run out of steam, Lindsay drew in a ragged breath and let it out in a long, dejected sigh. "I give up," she said with finality. "I'm done."

Katy squeezed Blaine's arm tighter than tight, her eyes on the bride. She feared what was coming next and knew she could do nothing to stop it.

"There's no point in trying anymore," Lindsay said wearily. She scraped her fingers through her hair and tugged off her veil. She let it drop and it fluttered to the floor like a sad dove gliding in for a slow landing. "Let's just call the whole thing off."

CHAPTER NINETEEN

That's a wrap, Cole thought, and mentally tossed the tenderloin and the rest of the menu into the trash bin. Who'd want to eat now? The bride had put a pin in it, called everything off. This farce had officially surpassed his own almost-wedding as the worst wedding ever.

Lindsay faced her groom, her posture rigid, her anger so palpable Cole could almost see the flames shooting out of her ears. Todd stammered and sputtered. Everyone else stared, shocked into silence.

Cole gazed at Maggie. She looked like she wanted to throw herself out into the snowstorm and give up for good. He was tempted to join her. She squeezed his left arm with both hands as if it were an anchor. In a strange way, her death grip gave him hope. If she still wanted to be with the deejay, how come she hung onto him?

Mrs. Lathrop caught his eye. She'd been standing next to Daisy, quietly watching the drama. "Don't worry, my dears," she said, as upbeat as her expression. "You've both done your part today. It's my turn. *I* can fix this."

She stepped toward her granddaughter, head high, a lot of confidence from a little lady, but Cole knew if anyone could take this bitter lemon of a wedding fiasco and make lemonade, Mrs. Lathrop could. All five-foot-nothing inches of her.

"Now, Lindsay," she said, nudging Todd out of the way with her cane. "What is all this ruckus?"

Lindsay refused to meet her grandmother's eyes. She crossed her arms and stuck out her bottom lip in a pout that would make Cole's four-year-old drama queen niece Jasmine jealous.

Mrs. Lathrop shifted and tried a different tack. "You love Todd, don't you? You want to be with him for always and forever, right?"

Again, no response. Lindsay stood as stiff and unyielding as a brick wall.

"Oh dear, I see I have my work cut out for me. I suppose I have to bring out the big guns, as your Grandpa Wilfred liked to say." Mrs. Lathrop cleared her throat. "Lindsay, darling, let me tell you a story."

"Grandmother, please, not now," Lindsay said with a groan.

"Now's as good a time as any, and you *will* listen." Her voice had dropped an octave, and she seemed somehow taller, the stern granny who would *not* be disobeyed.

That did the trick. Lindsay's pout stayed firmly in place, but she uncrossed her arms and looked her grand-mother in the eye.

"That's better." Mrs. Lathrop rested both hands on the

top of her cane and took a breath. "I think you may have forgotten what a day like this is about. I think we have *all* forgotten. It's not just a party, it's a commitment, to love and family and caring for each other. Being here, *fully*, for one another." Her gaze skimmed the guests, coming to rest on Lindsay's father, who shuffled his feet uncomfortably. "And we should *never* be too busy for that."

She moved closer and took her granddaughter's hand.

"You know, I married Grandpa Wilfred a long time ago, but I remember that day in every detail. It rained that morning. My goodness how it rained. Sopping, soaking rain that wet right through my shoes. All my plans ruined, I thought. My wedding day, ruined." A nostalgic smile touched her lips. "I threw myself on my bed and cried. I told my mother to cancel the whole thing. And then my grandma, a good, solid old Norwegian, came to me. She rubbed my back and calmed me down. Carol, stop your caterwauling, she said. They say bad weather on your wedding day is good luck, and here the good lord has sent you bucketsful."

Cole swallowed. Something seemed to be stuck in his throat. And stinging his eyes.

"I know I've been down on this wedding," she continued. "I've let myself be annoyed by all the bells and whistles and la-di-dah. I've complained about every little thing. Well, I'm sorry. I suppose since your grandpa passed, I've become cynical. I forgot what weddings are about. You've lost sight of it too, Lindsay. You've buried yourself in planning and worry about one thing or another. You've let the *reason* for getting married slip away. Two people who love each other decide they want to be together, no matter what. It's not about the cake or the gifts, though they're plenty fun to get."

Tearful laughter rippled across the room. Beside him, Maggie let out a soft gurgle. Cole closed a hand over hers, still holding onto his arm.

"Marriage is about being together, for better or worse. And of course, love." Mrs. Lathrop touched her granddaughter's cheek. A smile crinkled her eyes. "And today, my Lindsay, my angel, you have love. Bucketsful."

Lindsay started to bawl and so did everyone else. That lump in Cole's throat grew to the size of a boulder. Maggie's eyes glimmered. Sniffles filled the room. Natalia waved her hands in front of her face as if that would fan her tears away. Todd wiped teardrops—and green frosting —from his face. The guy in the chimney sweep's coat and top hat blew his nose on a handkerchief with a resounding *honk*.

"So, I'll ask my question again," Mrs. Lathrop said. "Do you love Todd?"

Lindsay nodded, and squeaked out an enthusiastic, "Yes!"

The old woman turned to the groom. "Do you love Lindsay?"

"With all my heart," he said, choking up.

Mrs. Lathrop beamed. "There, isn't that better?"

Lindsay gazed at her grandmother like a repentant child. "I'm sorry, Grammy. I truly am." She pulled the old woman into a hug that nearly lifted her off her feet. "It was all a misunderstanding. I love you so much."

"I love you too, sweetie-pie," she said when Lindsay released her.

The bride turned to Todd. "Can you ever forgive me for being such a brat?"

"Already done, my love." He moved to take her in his arms, stumbling on his untied shoelace. "Can you forgive me?"

"Always," she said, flashing a brilliant smile.

The couple hugged and kissed, and the guests applauded, letting out whooping cheers. Maggie gazed at Cole, smiling, her eyes shining with joyful tears that caused his stomach to flip and somersault and do all kinds of other happy gymnastics.

Mrs. Lathrop pounded her cane on the floor, demanding everyone's attention, and the room quieted.

"All right, you lovebirds," she said. "Save that mushy stuff for later. What do you say we get you married now?"

That set off a new round of cheers and applause, but Lindsay cut off in mid-*hooray*. Her shoulders slumped, and so did her expression.

"We can't, Grammy." Her pout returned. "We *can't* get married. We have no justice of the peace."

"Did someone call for a justice of the peace?" a voice boomed.

The front door burst open, bringing with it a gust of chill wind—and Santa Claus.

Cole blinked until the man who hustled into the dining room came into focus. Okay, not Santa Claus, but a reasonable facsimile. He had a snowy white beard, cheeks as red as cherries, an impish grin, red stocking cap, and a coat of the same color buttoned over his big belly.

Maggie pumped both fists in the air. "*Yes!* This wedding is on!"

She laughed. An unfettered sound of joy and relief at a volume so loud, people in the next county could've probably heard her. Cole felt like shouting too. After so many hours of stress and worry, Jolly Old St. Nick had arrived.

"Sorry I'm late," the man who would be Santa Claus said, grinning at the assembled guests. "The driving was treacherous. The roads are terrible."

"Maybe you should have travelled by sleigh," Maggie called out, laughing again, that adorable snort-giggle Cole had quickly come to love. She'd become downright giddy and that got him giddy too.

"What do you say we get this show on the road?" Nick said, unbuttoning his coat and shrugging it off. Cole expected to see him decked out in a Santa Claus outfit, so the perfectly correct gray double-breasted suit underneath was a disappointment.

Lindsay did a happy dance, spinning around as she had when she'd gotten off the bus what seemed like years ago, but had been only a few hours. She stopped, wobbling like a baby reindeer, and turned toward the maid of honor.

"Jackie, come on, help me get ready," she trilled, as giddy as Maggie. "Let me see. I've got something borrowed, the slip I'm wearing." She patted her leg. "I've got something blue, Todd's grandmother's wedding handkerchief." She yanked a piece of blue silk from her robe's pocket and waved it around. "My shoes are new, and— Wait, don't anybody move!"

Everyone obliged, freezing in place. Cole heard Maggie suck in her breath, bracing for the next disaster. He braced too.

"I forgot something old!" Lindsay cried, getting panicky again. "I *need* something old."

"Will I do?" Mrs. Lathrop said, breaking the tension. Laughter rippled across the room.

"I got this," Lindsay's dad said, stepping forward. He eyeballed Maggie. "Where's that bag of gifts I brought?"

"You, Mr. Lathrop?" Maggie said. "*You're* the mysterious gift-giver?"

"That I am," he said. "You seem astonished, young lady. Call me an old softie. I thought it would be fun to play Santa Claus today." He looked at his mother. "You look surprised too, Ma. I wasn't too busy to remember what's important about today. I just did it in my own way. For instance, you know those phone calls you've been nagging me about all day? It wasn't business. It's something special I've been working on for Lindsay and Todd. I told them their honeymoon would be on me. My gift to them. But I've been having trouble nailing down the final details. Had to go to the top, and down to the last minute, to make the deal."

He approached his daughter and Todd and rested a hand on each of their shoulders.

"And I succeeded." He broke into a wide grin. "I know how much you love Christmas, Lindsay, so I've arranged a trip for you both to the North Pole spa and resort in Minnesota, where it's Christmas *all* the time. Two weeks of sleigh rides and caroling, Santa's village, chestnuts by the fire, the whole holly jolly deal."

He tossed a raffish glance at his mother. She returned a *touché* salute. Todd *harrumphed* and Lindsay squealed in delight. She bounced up on her toes and squeezed her father in a hug.

"But wait, there's more," he said, his gaze on Maggie again. "Where's the bag of gifts?"

"It's in the kitchen. I'll get—" She cut off as a fast-moving blur ran up to Mr. Lathrop and shoved the bag into his hands.

"Doing my part to move this thing along," Daisy said, shooting Cole a wink.

Mr. Lathrop dug into the bag and came out with a small, square package. It had different wrapping paper from all the other gifts.

"The North Pole honeymoon is a gift from me," he said, handing the package to Lindsay. "This is a gift from your mother."

She stared at the package a long time before tearing off the paper, revealing a red velvet box. She snapped open the lid and took out a bracelet studded with Christmas-colored jewels, red rubies and green emeralds.

Cole didn't know much about women's jewelry beyond the hefty rock Celia had insisted he buy her when they got engaged, but even he knew the thing must be expensive. He also knew it wasn't the bracelet's value that got everyone sighing and teary-eyed as Lindsay slipped it over her hand to her wrist.

"This was Mother's," she said in an awestruck whisper. She twisted and turned her hand, making the bracelet sparkle in the light. "I remember her wearing it."

"I know she'd want you to have it." Mr. Lathrop's voice broke with emotion.

Lindsay's eyes glimmered and then everyone was

crying again, including Maggie. Tears spilled down her cheeks like a steady rain.

"Oh, Daddy." Lindsay sighed. "It's perfect. *The* perfect gift. Thank you." She gave her father a peck on the cheek then turned and ran upstairs. Her cupcake bridesmaids followed, their candy cane striped shoes tapping on the steps.

A gigantic sigh of relief spread over the room, morphing into a buzz of excitement as the guests realized the wedding was a go.

Wiping her drippy eyes, Maggie turned to Cole and threw her arms around his neck in an impulsive hug. She quickly pulled away before he could hug her back. Good thing. He'd never want to let her go.

"Well, I suppose I should go get things ready," she said, shifting into her event manager persona. She scanned the room with a calculating gleam. "This place is a mess and needs serious tidying."

"Anything I can do to help?" he asked, reluctant to leave her side.

"Sure," she said after a slight hesitation, and put him to work straightening up the tables.

He watched her walk away, heading toward the deejay. In a moment they were deep in conversation. Cole's heart stung like an entire hive of bees had taken up residence inside. Soon the ceremony would be done, dinner eaten, and the guests headed home. Maggie would leave and Cole would never see her again.

Come on, you can't give up this easily.

Maggie had warmed up to him as the day had gone on. The way she'd looked at him, teased him, and laughed with him, had grown fonder, more intimate. She'd said there were obstacles between them. They couldn't be together until that got fixed. Words full of regret, almost pleading. Did that mean Maggie wasn't as into Ash as Cole thought? That he might stand a ghost of a chance with her?

As Mrs. Lathrop had said, there was only one way to find out for sure—ask her. Get her somewhere alone and ask. He went to join Natalia in cleaning the place up. That bit of hope that had sparked earlier flared into a bright blaze.

Maybe he could fix this after all.

CHAPTER TWENTY

*K*aty gave Ash instructions for what music to play for the processional and the cere-mony. Next, she showed Nick Jolly where the wedding party should stand in front of the Christmas tree. Then she went to find Mrs. Parker to help her with the tough task of getting the groom into presentable shape.

She knew she should be thrilled the wedding was on. She should be pleased Mrs. Lathrop had fixed the Lindsay and Todd situation and Nick had made it here safely. Should be delighted Blaine had found a sweet alternative to the poor, doomed cake. And she should be happy to hear the rumble of the snowplow outside, clearing the parking lot so everyone could get home and not be trapped here for a week.

Everything had worked out. For everyone except her.

Soon the party would end, people would leave. And so would Blaine. He'd pack up his knives and skillets and walk his broad shoulders out the door and out of her life.

Katy's mind reeled. She'd started this day in a deep

funk. Now, everything had changed. She'd changed. She had squared things away with Ash, decided to start looking for a new job after the holidays, and also get moving on finding a new place to live, perhaps somewhere that allowed dogs.

Her future looked bright and pity party free. Except...

She looked toward Blaine, moving around the dining room, working with Natalia to right toppled centerpieces and upended chairs, and to straighten wrinkled tablecloths. The only thing missing from that future was *him*.

Heaving a dejected sigh, Katy found Mrs. Parker and they corralled Todd to get him cleaned up.

"Perhaps we should just hose you down, young fella," Mrs. Parker suggested, running a critical eye over his ruined tuxedo. Katy was almost certain she was kidding, but Todd squawked in alarm all the same.

In the end, that whisk broom Todd had received as a gift came in handy. While he held out his arms, Katy circled him and brushed with swift, hard strokes, dislodging the mess from his tuxedo jacket. He smelled like a candy shop and looked like a bedraggled puppy who'd been rolling in colorful crayons all day. Mrs. Parker followed Katy around with a dustpan, catching the crumbs as they fell. They cleared off most of the cake, but only dry cleaning could remove the frosting stains smeared into the jacket's fabric.

With the groom's grooming completed, Mrs. Parker took the whisk broom and dustpan away and Katy turned her mind to the final task, clearing away the pieces of cake strewn over the floor. She found a broom and swept crumbling chunks of all sizes into a corner of the alcove, then tried to push the cart out of the way. It wouldn't budge.

"I locked the casters earlier," Blaine said, coming up to her.

He kicked at the wheel locks to free them. Together they rolled the cart behind the tree, close to the windows and out of sight.

Katy smoothed the tablecloth they'd draped over the destroyed mess of a cake earlier. Her mind drifted back several hours, standing here in the alcove with him and wondering what it would be like to kiss him. Now she knew. And the desire to repeat that exquisite pleasure all but consumed her. Those kisses they had shared today hadn't been enough. She wanted more.

She wanted *him*.

Why not tell him? He'd said he felt something deep and powerful had sparked between them today. She'd felt it too. While there were obstacles in the way of fully following through on their growing attraction, she couldn't bear to leave without telling him how she felt. She'd regretted not speaking her mind to Ash, not speaking up for herself at work and so many other times in her life.

She knew she'd regret forever not speaking up now.

She turned to him. "I have something to say—"

"There's something I need to know—" he blurted at the same time as she spoke.

They fell into an awkward silence, their gazes locked on each other. His eyes sparkled from the Christmas lights and his own inner fire. The air between them crackled with heat and a tension that begged to be broken by a kiss. Butterflies attacked Katy's belly and she trembled all over. Her knees turned rubbery, threatening to go on strike.

"Oh, um…you go first," she managed. She'd forgotten what she was going to say anyway.

He scrubbed his fingers through his hair, tangling every strand beyond repair. "I have to know." He paused, swallowing nervously. "Before another second goes by, I *have* to know. Are you and the deejay getting back together?"

She gaped. "What? Ash and me?"

"Yes, Ash and you." He scowled, a challenging look. "The guy cheated on you, and you still want to be with him."

Katy huffed in confusion and indignation. "What *are* you talking about?"

"I saw you hugging him. All cozy and friendly. You think he's changed. You've forgiven him and you're getting back together with him. I figure that's why you ran, when we were outside, when I kissed you."

"I believe *I* kissed you," she said, with considerable heat. And annoyance. "And for your information, Ash and I are completely through. Have been through for a long time. You saw us hugging goodbye, you goofball."

"What?" he said, with surprise and something that sounded like glee. "You're done? The two of you are through? But when I kissed you outside—"

"You mean when I kissed you."

He shrugged. "If you say so. But I helped."

"Yes, you did. You helped a lot." Katy blushed, remembering how much he'd helped. "And your point is…?"

Blaine took a step closer, his own face flushed a manly shade of crimson. "If Ash isn't the reason, then why did you run away? Why did you pull away in the kitchen?"

Katy frowned. "Because...because of the others."

His eyebrows drew down. "What others?"

Was he playing dumb? "Are you serious right now? The *others*. All the women you've been running around with since your fiancée...um...broke it off."

"That's a polite way of saying I got dumped. I'm not going to apologize for going on a few dates since Celia left me."

"A few dates?" Katy said, incredulous. He called a revolving door of women a *few*? "That's not what I've heard. Everyone knows about your flirting and running around with tons of women. I've *seen* you flirting with the bridesmaids. You flirted with me, too, all day. And I fell for it. But I'll tell you, Mr. Flirty-flirt, I will *not* make myself vulnerable to another man like Ash, no matter how much you make me laugh or how happy you make me feel or how immensely good you can cook. Or kiss. No matter how much I want to be with you, I will *not* fall for you, only to be hurt again."

"Wait, wait. My flirting—?" He jerked back, looking stunned. Absolutely floored.

And then he laughed. A great big belly laugh that echoed across the room.

Katy crossed her arms and tapped her foot. "You think this is funny?"

He laughed again. "Yes." He held up a hand and shook his head. "I mean, no. Not at all. It's just..." He pinned her with a fiery look. "I have a question for you. What's my name?"

~

MAGGIE GAPED at him in confusion and disbelief, as if he'd just asked her to fly with him to the moon. Cole's spirits soared so high he felt he could fly there and way, way beyond. She'd said Ash was history. She'd fallen for *him*. She'd wanted to kiss *him*. Except, she thought the him she'd confessed that to was Blaine.

All damned day she'd thought Cole was Blaine.

The facts clicked into place. He knew why she'd been so offended every time Cole had opened his mouth earlier today. Why she'd been so skittish whenever they'd gotten close. Why she'd thought he was hitting on the brides-maids when he'd been trapped in that cupcake photo op against his will. Maggie had never seen Blaine, but she sure knew about his reputation.

Cole moved closer and gazed into her eyes. "What's my name?" he repeated.

She tilted her head, her expression mystified and annoyed. Adorably annoyed. "You've gone off your rocker, wine-stealer."

"Maybe I have. Or maybe you don't know who I really am." He inched even closer, almost touching, and asked one more time. "What's my name?"

Maggie's annoyance morphed to confusion, then astonishment. "Oh!" Her eyes widened. "You're kidding me! You're not Blaine?"

"*Hell* no. Blaine couldn't make it today. I took over for him. I'm Cole. Cole St. Onge."

"Oh, this is embarrassing." She pressed her fingers to her flaming cheeks. "Why didn't Maggie tell me? My sister said she'd call Blaine and tell him I was coming in her place. He should've filled her in on the situation with you, too. I've *got* to call Maggie!"

"I doubt Blaine answered his phone. I think he was otherwise occup—" Her words caught up to him. "Wait. You're not Maggie?"

Her turn to laugh. "No, I'm Katy. Katy Costa, Maggie's sister. This is the most ridiculous mix-up. I feel like I stepped into a TV sitcom."

"A sitcom with a happy ending, I hope." He took her hand, remembering the moment their hands had touched in the supermarket all those hours ago. How right it felt then, how right it felt now. "Hello, Katy Costa. It's nice to meet you."

Katy shook his hand, laughing again, her eyes bright, her cheeks flushed. "Likewise, Cole St. Onge."

"Now that we've gotten that straightened out, Katy, let's go back to the beginning. When I kissed you—"

"When I kissed you, you mean."

He sighed in mock impatience. "Okay, when *we* kissed, I felt something between us. Call it chemistry, Christmas magic, whatever. I've never felt anything like it before. And though we've just met, I hope you feel it too." He paused, gathering his thoughts. "Two years ago, I locked up my heart and vowed never to open it again. Then today, I met you. That Christmas magic hit me smack in the chest and there was no turning back."

He took her by the shoulders and looked deep into those liquid brown eyes.

"It's taken a while to get here, but I want to be part of a team again. With you, Katy. If you'll have me."

She didn't move and didn't speak. Just stared at him with a deer-in-the-headlights expression. *Way to crash and burn, Cole.* Even with Ash out of the picture, she wasn't ready. Damn it, how could he have misread her so badly?

He thought about checking her pulse for signs of life when she lifted her hand and placed her palm on his chest, right over his heart.

She broke into a smile that lit up the room. "You had me at Christmas magic, Cole St. Onge, you grumpy, impossible, extra-bossy, but *never* boring chef— Oh!" Her expression darkened and she snatched her hand away. "What about Lily?"

"Lily?"

"I heard you talking with Daisy about Lily earlier. You sounded totally enamored of her."

Cole's lips twitched. This day had been one long episode of mistaken identity and false assumptions.

"That's because I am," he said. "Lily's very special to me. She's loyal, and always there when I need her. But she drools sometimes, and I have to comb her hair several times a week." Katy's eyes went wide, and Cole finally relented. "But that's not unusual for a border collie."

"Lily's your dog?" Katy groaned. "I'm the world's biggest fool. I thought—"

He put a finger to her soft lips. "And I thought you were going to get back together with the chimney sweep, so we're even." He looked up and grinned. "Is that mistletoe up there?"

A sweet, almost shy, smile trembled on Katy's lips. "I do believe it is."

He reached for her and brought her into his embrace. She fit perfectly in his arms. Natural. As if they'd been made for each other. "As the wise old woman said, let's not let that go to waste."

There was only one thing left for them to do. He lowered his lips to hers.

Their first kiss outside in the snow had been rushed, almost desperate. The kiss in the kitchen had been interrupted before it had even begun. This kiss was a slow, soft blending of their lips. Tasting, getting to know one another. Getting to know Cole and Katy, their true selves. They explored each other as new lovers, lost in the moment, breathing in rhythm.

Kissing as the world fell away, until it was just the two of them, together as one.

The rap of a cane on the floor and a loud *Ahem!* tore them apart. Cole flushed. He'd forgotten about Mrs. Lathrop, forgotten about everyone. There was only Katy.

"If you two are quite through," Mrs. Lathrop said in a mock-scold. "My granddaughter would like to get married now."

Cole scanned the room. The whole crowd stared at them, even the deejay. The bridesmaids were lined up at the top of the stairs. He could make out a flash of white beyond them in the hallway. Lindsay, holding onto her father's arm, both of them no doubt impatient for the show to begin.

"What did I tell you?" Mrs. Lathrop said, gazing at them with a smile in her eyes. "You two make a great team. I'm so glad you finally figured that out. Now, let's get on with the nuptials, shall we?"

Katy laughed. A sweet, musical sound that touched Cole right down to his core. A sound he hoped he had the good fortune to hear tomorrow and the next day and the next and... He gave her another kiss, the appetizer to what he hoped would be a sumptuous meal to come.

Maybe he didn't hate weddings after all.

CHAPTER TWENTY-ONE

*K*aty nodded to Ash. He cued up the music and the bridesmaids and maid of honor did their bit. Daisy had been promoted to videographer. Using Jackie's phone, she recorded the bridesmaids' procession as they moved at a stately pace down the stairs, keeping exactly five feet apart.

At the bottom of the steps, they steered toward the alcove. Each woman carried an honest to goodness white fur muff instead of flowers, one hand tucked inside. Their puffy, tea-length red skirts swung like bells as they crossed the room, where they lined up opposite the groomsmen in front of the Christmas tree.

Nick Jolly and the spruced-up groom stood in the center of the group, lit by the glow of the tree's many shining lights. Todd looked up and a hush fell over the room. Show time for Lindsay. The bride's big moment. Katy signaled to Ash again, and the wedding march wafted from his speakers.

Everyone stood and turned their attention—and their

phone cameras—to the landing at the top of the stairs. The bride stood there beside her father, beaming at the assembled guests below. Light spilled down from overhead and bathed her in a serene glow.

She looked gorgeous, from top to bottom. From her veil with its roses and baby's breath crown, to her mother's bracelet sparkling on her wrist, to her white shoes with the six-inch heels peeking out from under her dress. *The* most beautiful wedding gown Katy had ever seen. The folds of the voluminous white skirt shimmered as Lindsay moved, the snug bodice glistened with crystal beads, and a red sash circled the bride's slim waist, tied in a bow in the back.

Lindsay floated down the steps, clutching her father's arm. Her gown's long train flowed over the steps like a satin waterfall. Mrs. Lathrop dabbed a handkerchief to her eyes as she watched her son guide her granddaughter past her to the groom. Todd took her hand in his own. Nick Jolly flashed a smile nearly swallowed up by his bushy white beard and the ceremony began.

Katy allowed herself a satisfied sigh. They had actually pulled it off. In spite of everything, with only minor casualties, and everyone was happy.

But she laid claim to being the happiest. She turned to look at Cole in the kitchen doorway. He leaned a shoulder against the doorjamb, holding something in his hand. He wasn't watching the bride, or the groom and his groomsmen, or any of the bridesmaids.

He gazed at *her*, with a smile that made her heart bubble.

All day, Katy had suspected something was off about

him and now she could kick herself for not figuring it out. The answer had been so obvious. He wasn't Blaine Dillard, the cranky chef who dated a string of women then broke their hearts. He was Cole St. Onge, sweet, sexy, smoldering Cole who'd had his heart broken. Who'd healed and moved forward, just as she had. Funny, caring, able to fix just about anything Cole. Plus, he could cook. And do dishes.

He gestured for her to come over and Katy didn't hesitate or wait for the ceremony to be over. She wanted to be with him. The guy she'd run away from earlier today, she ran toward now. Well, not exactly. She walked toward him at a sedate pace. She didn't want to disturb the happy couple exchanging their vows.

She remembered there was a present for Cole in the gift bag, so she snatched the bag off the table where Daisy had left it as she moved past.

"Hi, Katy," he said in a soft voice when she reached him. She didn't think she'd ever tire of hearing him say her name. Especially in that gruff, sexy voice that turned her knees to jelly.

"Hello yourself, Cole." She leaned against the wall next to him. "Well, here we are."

"Yup."

"Do you still hate weddings?" she asked in a quiet voice.

"I could get used to them."

That made her glow, inside and out. "What are you doing for New Year's Eve?" she asked.

He shifted and turned to face her. "Spending it with you, I hope." He held out a paper napkin holding a maple-scented reindeer cookie. "For you, fresh from the oven. Try it."

She took the cookie with her free hand and bit into it. It was soft and syrupy and so delectable it tickled the back of her throat.

Cole watched her intently. "Well?"

"It's...good," she said, with an impish smile.

He matched that with a devilish grin of his own. He tucked the napkin into his pocket and put his arms around her. His gaze dipped to the bag in her hand. "What have you got there?"

"Looks like Santa Claus didn't forget you," she said, but made no move to open the bag and find his gift. She leaned against him, content to be with him, reveling in his closeness, his body's warmth, and the feel of him holding her.

She hadn't planned to end the day in Cole's arms. She hadn't planned for any of this. Could that be why it felt so right? Why he felt so right for her. Why *they* were right, together.

"What about you?" He ran his thumb along her jaw in a slow, soft stroke, making her tremble. "Did Santa bring you a present?"

"I don't need a gift." Katy let the bag fall to the floor and looped her arms around his neck. She gazed deep into his eyes, sparkling with life and laughter, and her heart lifted right up to the sky. "I already got what I wanted. I got Cole for Christmas."

*K*aty tied a big red bow to Lily's green collar and clipped on her leash. The border collie hopped out of the car and in a moment, they were hurrying through the falling snow down Portland's High Street. Lily was in such a hurry her paws barely sank into the inch of snow that covered the sidewalk. Katy knew what sparked her excitement and she felt equally eager.

They were going to see Cole.

Downtown, just past dusk on Christmas Eve. Wreaths dangled from streetlights and shop windows sparkled with festive light displays. People bustled past, on their way home or to gatherings with family. Fat snowflakes swirled in the somewhat tame sea breeze and fell lightly on the ground like a blanket. A picturesque scene from a holiday movie. A far cry from the raging nor'easter of last Christmas Eve.

It had been one year since the fateful events of the wedding at Newell-by-the-Sea, when Katy had met Cole.

He'd changed her life. She'd changed her life. They'd both changed, and for the better. Last year, she'd been caught up in her plans and worries and disappointments. This year, she was happy simply to *be*.

Not that she wasn't hard at work. She was, with Cole by her side. They'd moved in together in April. Katy had left her job in September to work with him full-time, putting her planning skills and love of schedules to good use in opening their restaurant.

She'd discovered she loved the new Katy, and she loved Cole. Not at all what she had expected last Christmas Eve when he'd stolen that wine from her. She'd fallen in love with him, and she knew without a shadow of a doubt he loved her.

She bent down and brushed snowflakes from the silky fur along Lily's back. Almost as much as they both loved this energetic girl.

Lily danced from paw to paw in anticipation when they reached the restaurant, the newest gem on High Street's restaurant row. Katy pressed close to the window and peered through the glass. A shimmer of delight raced down her spine to see Cole, puttering around inside, wearing a Santa Claus hat.

Thanks to Mrs. Lathrop's investment, *Carol's on High*, named in her honor, had opened on Black Friday with a big splashy event, a fundraiser to benefit the Gray Street Food Pantry. A good deal of Portland's foodies and wine fans had turned out. So had Maggie and her husband Jackson, Daisy and Mrs. Lathrop, Jackson's parents, and the entire mob of Cole's extended family—now Katy's family—including his grandmother. She'd offered a toast, delighted to discover her maple cookies were on the dessert menu.

Business had been great since the opening, strong and steady the whole month of December and *Carol's on High* looked to be a success. Hopefully, that would tide them through the January lull and business would stay strong through the coming year. The first year was the toughest for a new restaurant, but Katy had faith it would work out. As long as she and Cole worked together, as a team.

She knocked on the window. Cole waved, grabbed his jacket from a coat hook and a moment later he came out, locking the door behind him. He pulled her into his arms and gave her a kiss that scorched her right down to her toes.

Lily nudged Cole's leg, demanding equal time. Cole obliged, releasing Katy to squat down and scratch the dog behind her ears. Lily practically grinned in delight.

"Love Lily's new bow," Cole said, standing up and smiling at Katy.

She flicked the pom-pom on the end of his Santa hat. "Love the hat. If I didn't know you were a grumpy old Scrooge, I might think you were really into Christmas."

"How could I not be into Christmas," he said. "When Christmas means you?"

He kissed her again, so deep and so hot she thought the snow might melt around them. A passing car honked its horn. Lily barked.

"That'll do for now," Katy said, reluctantly breaking away. "We're supposed to stop at Mrs. Lathrop's before going to your grandmother's, so we should get a move on."

"Wait. I have something for you." He reached into his coat and pulled out a sprig of mistletoe tied with a red velvet bow. He held it over his head.

"Cole, you goof." Katy laughed, remembering the mistletoe always overhead at the wedding last year. "I love you. Don't you know I'll kiss you anytime, anywhere, and I don't need mistletoe as an incentive?"

"This isn't just any mistletoe." He looked up, his expression turning mischievous.

That's when she saw the diamond ring nestled in the green leaves, between the white berries. The gem glimmered, reflecting the Christmas lights in the restaurant window.

"Cole…" she murmured, her mind racing in a thousand directions.

He dropped to one knee. In the snow. He gazed up at her, his eyes twinkling in the light.

"Katy Costa," he began, a catch in his voice. "When I met you, I stole some wine from you. You got your revenge by stealing my heart. I've loved you from that first moment and each day, I love you more. I love you, Katy, and I want to spend the rest of my life with you." He slipped the ring off the mistletoe and held it in his palm. "Will you marry me?"

She touched her fingers to her mouth, barely able to breathe. "Oh, Cole," she said.

"Is that an answer?"

He smiled a smile that lit his whole being. Katy saw love, laughter, and the future, their future, in his sparkling eyes. She saw happiness.

"Yes. Yes," she said, tears clogging her voice. "Yes, I will marry you, Cole St. Onge, you impossible, adorable man."

He jumped to his feet. Taking her hand, he slid the ring onto her finger. "Now, about that Christmas kiss."

He drew her into his arms. Katy's pulse raced with joy as he lowered his lips to hers. A zillion champagne corks seemed to pop inside her, flooding her whole body with delight. She floated on that champagne tide, filled with love and the promise of tomorrow.

She had not only gotten Cole for Christmas, she would have him for New Year's and the Fourth of July and Thanksgiving and every single day in between, happily ever after.

Katy and Cole. Together forever.

* THE END *

Dear Reader,

I hope you had a holly-jolly time reading Cole for Christmas! If you did, please help others find Cole and Katy's merry mistletoe adventure by leaving a review.

And please take a moment to stop by my website to check out my other stories, sign up for my newsletter (plus a free book!), and for all the news of what I'm up to.

Just click to join the fun!

www.janetrayestevens.com

All the best,

Janet Raye Stevens

OTHER BOOKS BY JANET RAYE STEVENS

Beryl Blue, Time Cop

Join feisty librarian Beryl Blue as she journeys to the past, the future, and everywhere in between to save the man she loves, in this first adventure in the Beryl Blue, Time Cop series.

A Moment After Dark – a WWII paranormal mystery

Addie sees the future with a simple touch. A valuable gift in a time of war. Will a determined federal agent get to her before the enemy does?

ABOUT THE AUTHOR

Meet award-winning author Janet Raye Stevens – mom, reader, tea-drinker (okay, tea guzzler), and teller of hilarious and sometimes totally true tales. Winner of RWA's 2018 Golden Heart® award for her holiday rom-com, *Cole for Christmas*, Janet writes contemporary romance and paranormal and time travel with humor, heart, and a dash of mystery. She lives in New England with her husband, who's practically perfect in every way, and their two sons, both geniuses and good-looking to boot.

www.janetrayestevens.com